My Butterfly

A NOVEL BY
LAURA MILLER

Butterfly Weeds SERIES

This book is a work of fiction. Names, characters, businesses, places and incidents are the product of the author's imagination or are used fictitiously. Any resemblance to actual events, locals or persons, living or dead, is coincidental.

Copyright © 2013 by Laura Miller.

LauraMillerBooks.com

All rights reserved. Except as permitted under the U.S. Copyright Act of 1976, no part of this publication may be reproduced, distributed or transmitted in any form or by any means or stored in a database or retrieval system.

ISBN-13: 978-1481089852
ISBN-10: 1481089854

Printed in the United States of America.

Cover design by Laura Miller.
Cover photo © aleshin/Fotolia.
Title page photo © aleshin/Fotolia.
Author photo © Marc Mayes.

To the Keeper of the stars,

For first loves

And for last loves

And for every love in between.

CONTENTS

Prologue 1

Chapter One: Eleven Years Earlier 3
Chapter Two: The Volleyball 11
Chapter Three: Caught 22
Chapter Four: The Bonfire 27
Chapter Five: Donna's 36
Chapter Six: The Stars 43
Chapter Seven: Fireworks 61
Chapter Eight: Senior Year 73
Chapter Nine: College.. 78
Chapter Ten: False Alarm 88
Chapter Eleven: A Movie 99
Chapter Twelve: Anniversary 104
Chapter Thirteen: Cold 116
Chapter Fourteen: Schemes 122
Chapter Fifteen: The Girl 127
Chapter Sixteen: New Year 132
Chapter Seventeen: Gone 148
Chapter Eighteen: The Call 154
Chapter Nineteen: The Band 160
Chapter Twenty: The Gig.................................. 173
Chapter Twenty-One: The Card 178
Chapter Twenty-Two: Angel 185
Chapter Twenty-Three: Fall 194
Chapter Twenty-Four: Breakfast 198
Chapter Twenty-Five: The Note 206
Chapter-Twenty-Six: Haunting 211
Chapter Twenty-Seven: Promise 217
Chapter Twenty-Eight: Deal 227

Chapter Twenty-Nine: Wedding 233
Chapter Thirty: One Step 241
Chapter Thirty-One: District 9 245
Chapter Thirty-Two: Reunion 249
Chapter Thirty-Three: New York 260
Chapter Thirty-Four: Jessica 263
Chapter Thirty-Five: Even.......................................273
Chapter Thirty-Six: Ticket.......................................284
Chapter Thirty-Seven: The Song 290
Chapter Thirty-Eight: A Favor 294
Chapter Thirty-Nine: The Find 301
Chapter Forty: The Concert....................................307
Chapter Forty-One: The Chase 316
Chapter Forty-Two: Radio 329
Chapter Forty-Three: One Knee 334
Chapter Forty-Four: I Do 340

Epilogue 345

It's been said that you never forget your first love.

Prologue

I've only got one story to tell, and it's about a girl, and it starts with you. But first I've got to do this one thing because I worry if I wait a second longer, I'll lose even more of what I've already lost. I promise, though, there is a method behind my madness. And if everything goes to plan, you'll see why very soon.

But like I said, I've got this story to tell, though I don't yet know the ending. All I know is that it can end only one of two ways—with or without you. But despite which way fate will have it, the way I see it, I'm left the same—still in love with the one that got away.

My Butterfly

You've given me hell, Julia Lang, just by being you. But then what's love if it ain't worth the fight? And I've got some fight still left in me.

"Are you ready, Will?" a young man with shaggy hair asks from the other side of the glass.

I anxiously readjust the big microphone hovering above me.

"Yeah," I eventually say.

A restless sigh is attached.

"Okay," I hear the man say, "I'm going to start the track."

I look through the glass and slowly nod my head.

My palms are sweaty; my heart is pounding. But it isn't the young man on the other side of the glass or the taller man sitting next to him who is making me sweat. It isn't even that I am about to sing in front of them or that I am here at all. In fact, now, right now, I only have one thought cycling over and over in my mind. The only reason I am standing here, gripping an old, metal pin as if it were my lifeline, continuously praying my silent prayers in my head and replaying all the memories that have led me to this place is for a chance that she will hear this song.

I suspect that she doesn't know it's coming. But I also pray that she hasn't forgotten her promise. I pray silently that this song will make her stop, will make her remember—a different time, years ago, lifetimes ago.

A soft melody starts playing in my headset. I press the metal pin tighter against my palm. I am waiting for my cue, my lips almost touching the mesh in front of the mic. Then, suddenly, as if by instinct, my mouth opens, and my first words fill the tiny, soundproof room. And my only thought is: *Here goes everything.*

Chapter One

Eleven Years Earlier

"Jeff, is that Julia Lang?" I asked, as I leaned up against my locker.

"Who?" Jeff asked.

Jeff was busy digging up remnants of pens from the bottom of his backpack and scribbling faded lines onto the front cover of his notebook. I, on the other hand, knew full well who the girl was, but he didn't have to know that.

"Her, trying to stuff that bag into her locker," I said, directing his attention to the girl.

Jeff stopped scribbling and looked up.

"I don't know," he said, shrugging his shoulders. "She must be from that little, country school."

He turned back around, as if not interested, grabbed a book from his locker's shelf and then slammed the metal door shut.

"But I know who I'm asking to the homecoming dance," he said, setting out in the girl's direction.

Without hesitation, I grabbed the collar of his shirt.

"Whoa there, son," I said, pulling him back. "First of all, homecoming's months away. Second, you're not taking her anywhere."

"Geez, buddy, watch the threads," Jeff said in a higher than usual pitch as he paused to readjust the shirt's collar around his neck. "And why can't I ask her? If I don't, someone else will."

I kept my eyes on the girl across the hall. She had just gotten the oversized duffle bag into the tiny locker. Impressive, except now I watched as a book slipped from underneath her arm and fell to her bare toes, causing her nose to scrunch up and her eyes to wince in pain.

"You got a point there, buddy," I said, patting him on the shoulder.

I handed Jeff a working pen and then quickly pushed past him.

"I got it," I said, bending down to pick up the book from the floor at the girl's feet. "Are you all right?"

The girl looked up at me, still cringing a little.

"I'm fine," she said, softly smiling.

She took the heavy text book from my hand and shoved it into a row of books already on the locker's shelf.

"Thanks," she said.

"It's Will," I said, extending my hand.

She stopped, and her stare found my hand. She looked suspicious.

"I know," she said, cautiously placing her hand in mine. "Will, it's Julia."

"Julia Lang," I said, smiling and acting as if I had just now put her face with her name.

"Yes," she replied, slowly nodding her head.

I watched as a coy smile fought its way to her face.

"You remember me?" I asked, hesitantly.

I was really hoping she only remembered the good parts—if there were any of those for her.

I noticed her eyes fall on my hand, still holding hers, but she was smiling, so I kept a tight grip on her hand. It was soft and girl-like.

"Yes," she said. "How could I forget?"

"The hardware store?" I asked.

She nodded her head.

"We used to play on those toy tractors outside, and all the old people would give us candy as they walked in," she said.

The corners of my mouth started to lift as I watched the green in her eyes light up.

"That's right," I said, starting to laugh.

But just then, her smile faded slightly.

"You would never let me ride the big tractor," she said, sharply pulling her hand back from mine.

My laughter stopped. And then what was left of her smile turned into a smirk.

Ugh. She remembered.

"If I remember right, you said that it was a boy's tractor and that girls weren't supposed to drive tractors anyway," she said. "And then, when we were nine, you..."

"Okay, okay," I said, stopping her. "That's probably enough memories for one day. The good news is that the big tractor is still up at my grandpa's store, and you can

My Butterfly

ride it anytime you want. Oh, and best of all, I have finally come to the ultimate conclusion that girls really don't have cooties."

"Really?" she asked, giving me a sarcastic look.

"Really," I said, leaning against the row of lockers. "It was all a myth. Turns out, it was just some scorned second-grader who didn't get a Valentine from his secret crush one year."

She glared at me with narrowed eyes.

"And then after that," I continued, without missing a beat, "the kid decided to ruin love for all kids from then on, declaring every girl was stricken with the cootie disease."

She laughed once and then went back to fidgeting with something inside her locker.

I smiled, silently hoping that getting her to laugh was enough to erase the memories I had accidentally resurrected.

She turned back toward me a second later and gave me a soft side-smile.

"I have to get to class," she said, pulling a book from her locker and then slamming the door.

The door didn't close on the first try, so I watched her put her weight into her next try.

"Can I walk you there?" I asked, once she had successfully shut the locker door. "What's your first one?"

She shot me a suspicious look again and then pulled out from the back pocket of her tight-fitting jeans a small piece of paper with a set of classes and times printed on it.

"Umm, history," she said, stuffing the piece of paper back into her jeans. "It's just down the hall. I think I can make it."

"*I think* doesn't sound very confident," I said. "I should walk you, just to make sure you're not late for your first high school class. This isn't kindergarten-through-ninth-grade anymore."

I smiled a confident smile. She, on the other hand, stared at me with two impatient eyes, then turned and started walking in the opposite direction.

I shuffled to catch up to her.

"So, I really did recognize you," I said.

She looked a little irritated, but she smiled anyway.

"You do look a little different from the last time I saw you, though," I said.

She looked me up and down once.

"So do you," she said.

"It's the muscles, isn't it?" I asked.

I watched her eyes follow a path from my shoes to my eyes again.

"What muscles?" she asked.

I grabbed my heart and pretended to shrink in pain.

"Ouch," I said.

She smiled a satisfied grin.

"Don't you have to be getting to your own class?" she asked. "What's your first one anyway?"

"Oh, I'm not worried about that," I said. "The teacher's my neighbor. Plus, I already know my way around a kitchen."

She stopped in the history classroom's doorway and faced me.

"Kitchen?" she repeated.

I cringed on the inside, and my smile faded.

"Did I say kitchen?" I asked. "I meant woodshop."

"No, you didn't," she said, accusingly.

"Okay, look, I promise you I can build a coffee table, but home economics is a guaranteed *A*," I said. "I couldn't pass it up."

She rolled her eyes.

"Quite the scholar," she said, while shaking her head and stepping into the classroom.

"We'll see who's laughing when you're eating my lasagna for dinner one night," I said.

She glanced up at me and smiled that sideways smile that I was already starting to crave.

"You know, I just can't see that happening," she said.

"Me cooking lasagna?" I asked.

"No," she said.

I could only see the side of her face now, but I could see that her lips were slowly turning up. I was thinking about how I could trick her into letting me hold her hand again some time.

"I don't see me eating it," she continued, taking a seat in a desk near the front of the small room.

"But there's still hope for the dinner—well, minus the eating part?" I asked, hopeful.

She gave me an impatient look again. And suddenly, a loud ring made me jump, and my eyes darted to a clanging bell right above my head.

Julia giggled, and at the same time, opened a notebook to its first page. I stood there watching her for a second longer. She did look different, as if she had grown up overnight or something, but then she looked exactly the same too. Her hair was down, and it was wavy or curly or whatever girls call it—that about her hadn't changed. Even at eight years old, she had had that same pretty, long, blond hair, that same perfect nose and those same pretty, green eyes.

A thought suddenly came to me then, and I quickly tore off a piece of my own notebook paper and scribbled a sentence onto its tiny surface.

"Jules," I said, getting her attention one, last time.

She looked up at me, kind of startled, as if I had called her by a secret alias or something. She looked cute the way she always tried to act impatient with me.

"Hey," I said, tapping a kid I had known since kindergarten on the shoulder. "Pass this to Julia, that girl in the black shirt, would ya?"

The boy dutifully followed my request and reached across a row to hand Julia the piece of scrap paper. I watched her open the folded note, and then, I watched her eyes follow over the words. But before she had a chance to look up again, I disappeared back into the hallway.

I figured I would give her some time to think about her answer. The last thing I wanted was a rash decision based on a somewhat rocky childhood. God, if I knew then what I know now, I probably still would have thrown rocks at her. It was fun hearing her scream. But I also would have kissed her—knowing that I probably could have gotten away with it then. I could have easily blamed it on being a stupid kid.

And come to think of it, there is actually a quote by George Bernard Shaw that has hung in my grandpa's store for God only knows how long. I never really paid attention to it. It hung on a plaque in the corner, probably had a couple of layers of dust on it. I thought about it now, as I made my short journey to the home economics room. And I thought of all of the years I had wasted not chasing after Julia Lang—well, at least not chasing after her in a more productive manner. *Youth is wasted on the young*, the old quote said. I didn't know much of anything

My Butterfly

about this Shaw guy, but he did get at least one thing right—I should have kissed her when I had the chance. God only knows how long I've got to chase this girl.

Chapter Two

The Volleyball

"Are you looking for something, Jules?" I asked as I watched her push aside the heavy stage curtain.

Her face turned back toward me and then quickly went back to the stage. She didn't look startled this time, and I wondered for a second if she had already gotten used to me calling her *Jules*.

"My volleyball," she said, annoyed. "I left it here after P.E., and now it's gone, and I promised Jeff I'd meet him after class and help him with algebra…"

"Jeff?" I blurted out, as I twisted the features of my face into a puzzled expression.

She stopped and glanced back at me again before returning her attention to a box of rubber balls.

My Butterfly

"Yeah, he's having a hard time, and we've got a test coming up," she casually said. "He asked me to help him figure it out, and I'm supposed to meet him in ten minutes, and I can't find…"

"Figure out algebra?" I interrupted again.

She caught my stare, furrowed her eyebrows and then went back to doing whatever it was she was doing.

"Yeah," she said.

I shook my head.

"Jeff doesn't need help with algebra," I exclaimed. "He was the smar…"

I stopped myself, having just added up the math mid-sentence, and allowed my eyes to rest on her.

She was searching on the stage now, probably not even paying attention to me. I smiled as I watched her turn over sweaty, hockey jerseys just before scrunching up her nose and flinging them back down.

"I'm not leaving here until I find that ball," she said.

I took a second to think, and after a quick moment, I had a plan.

"I'll help you find it," I blurted out.

I anxiously looked around the gym. I knew I had to find that ball before she did or my plan would be foiled, and she would be out the door to help Jeff, who, by the way, has had an A in math since the first grade. In fact, he was the reason I had passed algebra in junior high. *That little weasel.*

Suddenly, my eye caught a white, round object out of its corner. I looked closer and spotted a ball tucked away behind a set of bleachers on the other side of the gym. I glanced back at Julia. She was rooting through the ball closet near the stage. I slowly started to mosey my way over toward the ball, trying not to bring any attention to my find.

"We'll find it," I reassured her.

I eventually planted my feet in front of the ball and acted as if I hadn't seen it.

"Hey, why don't you go look out in the hallway, in case it bounced out there or something," I said. "I'll look for it under these bleachers."

She looked my way with a disheveled face, almost as if she had just noticed that I was still there. But then, without a word, she sauntered off into the hallway. I watched her disappear behind the glass-paned doors, and then I quickly reached for the volleyball and scooped it up. I turned it over. It was her ball all right. Her name was etched in its stretched material in black, permanent marker, right above her volleyball number. I spun it around in my hands as my eyes darted toward the glass-paned doors again. Then, my mind in auto pilot, I scanned the room, thinking. I saw bleachers, some exercise machines and a couple of wooden blocks—none of which would work. I let my head fall back in desperation. And then I saw it—the rafters high above me. There was already a ball stuck up there, and this one would give it some company. I took the volleyball in one hand and arched it behind my head. Then, I lobbed it up into the air. It hit a beam in the rafters and came colliding back to the hardwood floor. The ball bounced only once before I scurried over to it, scooped it up and glanced again toward the doors. There was still no sign of her. I retook my place and tried it once more. This time, the ball hit the inside of one of the beams, slightly knocked the other ball and then wedged itself in between the ball already there and the beam. *Success.*

"Will," a voice suddenly called out from behind me, causing my body to stiffen.

My Butterfly

I turned quickly on my heels to Rachel standing there, staring at me. She had a questioning look plastered across her face, and I couldn't tell what she was questioning exactly—why I was throwing a ball into the rafters or why I was standing there alone staring at the rafters. What had she seen?

"Hi, Rach," I stuttered.

She squinted her eyes, as if she were shaking off a thought.

"Have you seen Julia?" she eventually asked.

I thought about her question for a second. If Rachel were to find Julia, she might tell Jules what I had just done—if she had, in fact, seen what I had just done—and then I'd be busted. Or she could end up chauffeuring Jules off somewhere to look at shoes or a furry caterpillar or something until Julia forgot about her ball and had to go see Jeff. And then I would have thrown that dumb ball up in the rafters for nothing.

"Uh-uh, nope, haven't seen her," I said, being careful not to look her in the eyes until after I was done lying.

She stared at me with a suspicious glare.

"O-kay," she said, her eyes burning a hole straight through my forehead. "Well, if you do, tell her I'm looking for her."

"Will do," I said.

Then, I smiled at her and casually strolled back toward the stage.

When I reached the base of the stage, I turned and glanced back at the doorway that Rachel had just been standing in, staring at me with her cat eyes. She was gone. I let out a sigh of relief.

"It's not out there either," I heard Julia say.

I quickly turned my attention to the other side of the gym.

"Here," I said, holding out my phone. "Call Jeff. Tell him that you can't help him tonight, and we'll search the whole school for your ball. The first forty-eight hours are the most critical."

She gave me a wary look. Then, she glanced at the phone and then back up at me. She was clearly agitated. But I couldn't tell if it was because of me or because of the fact that she couldn't find her ball. She had better not be upset that she couldn't help Jeff. *That little...*

She snatched the phone out of my hand.

"Number four," I said.

"What?" she asked.

"He's number four on speed dial," I said.

She pressed a key and then brought the phone to her ear. After a couple of rings, I heard Jeff pick up. He loudly called her a *toolbag*, and I cringed.

Julia glanced up at me and rolled her eyes.

"Jeff," she said. "This is Julia."

I heard Jeff verbally recoil and apologetically take back his greeting.

"It's fine," she said, smiling. "Jeff, I'm calling because I can't make it tonight. The test isn't for a couple of weeks. Can we maybe get together sometime later this week?"

I heard his voice through the phone's speakers when she finished talking, but I couldn't quite make out what he was saying.

"No, I'm up at school," she said. "I borrowed Will's phone."

Her explanation made me smile. I quickly cleared my throat and wiped the smirk off my face.

She ended the call a moment later and handed the phone back to me.

"Thanks," she said. "You'll help me look for it?"

My Butterfly

Ugh, her eyes were doing this soft pleading thing, and it was taking everything in me not to pull her close.

"Of course," I managed to say without sounding too eager. "It would be my pleasure."

※

"It's not back here," I heard her say.

I could hear the frustration in her voice.

"No one would take it, right?" she asked.

"No, no one would take it," I said. "It's here somewhere. Let's go look down the hall. Maybe it rolled down there or something."

I watched her take a deep breath and then sigh.

"Okay," she eventually agreed.

I smiled and waited until she was by my side to start toward the hallway and to ask her my question.

She eventually caught up, and I couldn't take it anymore. I had to ask.

"So, what's your answer?" I blurted out.

My words had come out kind of sheepish. I cleared my throat and concentrated on producing something in a lower octave and a little less Bo Peep.

"What answer?" she quipped back.

"The note I gave you before history class," I said, hoping it would jog her memory.

"Aah," she said, smiling. "That answer."

I watched her peek under a table near the office and then keep walking.

"Well?" I asked again.

She stopped and squared up to me. She looked as if she were really thinking hard about it.

"No," she finally said and then started walking again.

I hesitated for a second but then caught back up to her.

"Now, have you really thought this through?" I asked her. "You can take some time if you need it. Tell me tomorrow or the next day or the next day or any day when the answer is *yes*."

"I don't need time," she said.

I stopped and smiled.

"You do realize it's only a date?" I asked. "If you said *yes*, you wouldn't be locked into anything."

She turned her face up at me and smiled.

"It's not so easy hearing *no*, is it?" she asked.

I paused and tried to hold back my grin.

"Julia, Jules," I said, as if I were a used-car salesman. "Jules, look, no rocks this time," I said, showing her my open palms and then the inside of my jeans pockets. "No big, rubber balls. I'll even let you drive my truck."

I held out my keys.

She looked at me sideways and sympathetically smiled, as if I were the weird kid who was completely oblivious to his social status.

My own smile grew, and I took her silent cue, as I watched her sympathetic grin fade into her new smile—the one that I already loved. I remembered it being that cute, girly kind of smile—that smile that made you wonder why you despised girls so much just the year before. But now, it was sexy too. It was girly and sexy, all at the same time. Damn it, she was too darn cute not to smile back at her, even when she was saying *no*. And maybe it wouldn't be now, but I would eventually wear her down. Everyone has a breaking point. *Retreat. Replenish. Conquer.* I smiled wider.

"So, Ben's having a bonfire next weekend," I said.

"So I've heard," she said.

She smiled politely this time.

"You going?" I asked.

"If Rachel has anything to do with it, we'll be there early," she replied.

"Good," I said, nodding my head.

Suddenly, she stopped and peeked her head into a classroom.

"Coach Hill, you didn't see any volleyballs lying around after P.E., did you?" she asked him.

My eyes instinctively fell to the floor at my feet.

"Okay, thanks," she said and then continued her hike down the narrow hallway.

"No luck?" I asked her.

"He didn't see any," she replied.

"Don't worry, we'll find it," I said.

We made our way down the rest of the hall and then outside toward the school's only other hallway. I held the door for her as she walked in.

"So, you and Rachel are friends?" I asked her.

I watched her as she peered into the band room, littered with instrument cases, chairs and stands.

"Yeah," she said, without looking up. "She's pretty cool."

"Yeah, she's all right," I said. "She talks a lot, but she's all right."

"You've known her for awhile?" she asked.

Her thin frame was still preoccupied with the search, and every once in a while I would act as if I were looking under or around something.

"Yeah," I said. "All of us *townies* pretty much grew up together. Rachel was my neighbor when we were kids, until she moved to a house right outside of town. I'm sure it was kind of the same for you guys, right?"

I picked up a chair and looked under it.

"Us country folk, you mean?" she asked, pausing to look up at me.

She sounded as if she were trying to act offended, but I could tell it really didn't bother her.

"Julia, my dear, I know that toy tractor in front of my grandpa's store wasn't the last tractor you've driven," I said, with a boyish smirk smeared across my face.

She stopped what she was doing and looked me square in the eyes. She was wearing a half-smile, but I didn't so much see the smile, and the other half scared me.

"Don't call me *dear*," she said. "And you're right, turns out I found some much bigger tractors to play with. I didn't need yours after all."

She smiled, and then her dagger eyes fell from mine. I let out a happy sigh and followed her back into the gym again.

"I just don't understand where it could have gone," she said, dramatically throwing her hands into the air.

I silently prayed that she wouldn't look up.

"Hey," I said, stopping in front of her.

I took a chance that she wouldn't punch me, and I grabbed her small hips and hoisted her up onto the stage.

"Look, it's late," I said, looking at the imaginary watch on my wrist and positioning my body so that it was square with hers and touching her legs.

She looked a little thrown off, but she didn't protest.

"We'll look for it again tomorrow and the next day and the day after that, if we have to," I said. "And we'll keep looking for it, until it turns up."

Her eyes fell to her lap. She looked defeated. And I wasn't sure if she even noticed that I was touching her.

I dramatically sucked in a big breath of air. Then, I brought the back of my hand to her chin and gently lifted it until her eyes were in mine.

"We'll find it," I said.

She smiled a pouty smile.

Damn it. I loved that smile too.

"It's just my favorite," she said. "I bought it with my babysitting money. I've had it for a long time."

Ugh. For the first time, I started to feel bad about hiding it from her. I paused, while the words, *Let's look for it in the rafters,* fumbled around on my tongue.

But quickly, there was a second thought. That precious ball of hers could buy me some precious time with her. Time, I quickly and easily decided; I wanted time.

"I'm sure it's in a safe place," I reassured her.

She half-heartedly smiled.

"Thanks for helping me look for it," she said, meeting my gaze.

My eyes immediately turned guilty, and I quickly tossed them to the floor before she could read them.

She sighed, and then I looked up again.

"In the meantime, are you hungry?" I asked.

Her green, suspicious eyes were on me fast.

"I was thinking maybe we should grab some dinner at Donna's," I continued.

"Will Stephens," she scolded and pushed past me, jumping off of the stage and landing with both feet onto the wooden gym floor.

"Nice try, but I've got to get home," she said, grabbing her duffle bag.

"Maybe tomorrow then?" I called out after her as she made her way toward the glowing exit sign.

"Bye, Will," she said, glancing back one, last time and sending a confident smile my way.

I smiled, then shoved my hands into my pockets and watched her walk away until her thin frame disappeared into the hallway. When she was gone, I sighed, shut my eyelids over my eyes and allowed my head to fall back. A second later, I forced my eyes open, and then gradually, I felt a grin returning to my face because high up in the ceiling was her little, white volleyball.

"Yeah, I'm pretty sure it's in a safe place," I mumbled, chuckling to myself.

Then, I lowered my head and started my own journey toward the glowing, red exit sign.

Chapter Three

Caught

"I don't know, Jules," I said, tossing a tennis ball into the air and catching it. "We might be searching for this volleyball for the rest of our days."

She turned her face toward mine. Her blond hair was in a ponytail and was spread every which way over a straw bale left over from archery class. I had constructed us a pretty nice lounging bench using the bales, and now we were each lying against a home-made straw pillow. She was squinting. The sun was in her eyes, and her big eyelashes looked as if they were trying to shoo away its rays.

"I'm sure it's somewhere safe," she said and then turned her head again so that it was out of the direct path of the sun's rays.

I lifted my head off the straw bale.

"You don't seem that worried about it anymore," I said.

"Hmm?" she asked, as she turned her face back toward mine and used her hand to shield her eyes from the sun.

"It's your favorite ball, right?" I asked. "You still want to find it, right?"

"Oh, yeah, it's not that big of a deal," she said.

I hesitated before I continued.

"Well, I mean, it's got to be around here somewhere," I said, fearing my time with her might be coming to an end. "Maybe it'll just take a couple more days."

"Uh," she said, shrugging off my comment and turning her head again. "We don't have to look for it anymore. It's okay."

"No," I almost shouted, sitting up.

I paused then and took a second to regain my composure and to clear my throat.

"Actually, you know where we haven't checked?" I asked.

"Hmm?" she replied, not bothering to turn her head this time.

"The shop," I said. "We haven't checked the shop."

I watched her shrug her shoulders again.

"I don't think it's in the shop," she said.

She was facing away from me, and her eyes were closed, so I took the opportunity to stare at her without her knowing it. And why was she acting so strange all of sudden? A few days ago, all she wanted was that dumb ball. Now, it seemed as if she could care less about it. She was a strange creature, but she sure was pretty. She was about an hour removed from volleyball practice—little, spandex shorts, cut-off tee shirt and all. Pretty.

"You know where we haven't looked?" she asked, opening her eyes and turning her face toward mine again.

I sat back against the straw bail, startled, hoping she hadn't noticed me staring at her.

"Where?" I asked.

"The rafters…in the gym," she said.

My heart stumbled and then came to a complete halt for a second. Then, I watched the corners of her lips slowly start to turn up, and I couldn't help but smile too.

"The rafters?" I managed to get out, through my grin.

"Mm hmm," she said, nodding her head.

We were both silent for a moment, each searching the other's eyes.

"Yeah, we could look there," I eventually said.

Just then, she shoved my shoulder. She shoved it hard, but it didn't do much to move me, in the end.

"Will Stephens," she said, raising her voice and now standing over me.

She was pouting, but she was smiling too—sort of.

"I know you put it there," she said.

My jaw dropped open. *Caught red-handed.*

"I…," I stuttered. "How, how do you know?"

She rested her hands on her hips.

"Rachel told me," she said. "She saw you do it."

Damn it, Rachel.

The corners of my mouth started to turn up again. I knew they weren't supposed to, but I couldn't help it. She looked so darn cute. And besides, it had been worth it. That ball had given me her undivided attention for a week. As it turned out, I had grown to love that dumb ball after all.

"Jules, I promise it wasn't on purpose."

I sighed and then lowered my head. That was a lie. I couldn't lie to her.

"Okay," I said. "It was on purpose, but I had to."

My gaze traveled back up to her face again, while she dropped her shoulders and dug her dagger eyes deeper into my forehead.

"You knew I was looking for it," she said. "I just don't get why…"

"Wait," I interrupted her, as a smile slowly started creeping its way back to my face again. "When did Rachel tell you?"

Rachel couldn't keep a secret to save her life.

"The day I lost it," she said. "I ran into her later. You were also supposed to tell me that she was looking for me."

"Wait," I said again. "You knew where it was and that I had put it there this whole time, but you still pretended to look for it with me."

Had she liked hanging out with me too?

She narrowed her eyes at me, and I knew she had read my mind. A new, obnoxious smile beamed across my face now over the obnoxious one that was already there.

Then, I watched as she grabbed her duffle bag from the ground and slung it over her shoulder.

"Will, the point here is that you threw my ball into the rafters," she said. "Nothing ever comes down from there."

I really tried hard, but I couldn't stop smiling.

"You're such a child," she said, letting out a deep sigh and then turning and walking away.

My Butterfly

I sat there frozen—and speechless.

"You owe me a ball, Will Stephens," she called out over her shoulder once she had gotten several yards away.

I watched her strut into the sun as I leaned my back against the straw bale in our makeshift bench again. There was a permanent smile now tattooed to my face, and on that smile in big, bold letters, I was pretty sure it read: *Today was the best day of my life. Today, I learned that Julia Lang actually liked hanging out with me.*

Chapter Four

The Bonfire

I bent down and concealed my face behind his before I brought my hand to my mouth.

"Hey, uh, I didn't want to say anything in front of the girl, but I'm pretty sure you left the dome light in your truck on, and there's a copy of that *Cosmo* your sister left in there on the seat," I whispered.

Jeff's eyes grew wide, but he kept his stare straight ahead. I was pretty sure he was calculating the cool points he'd lose if anyone were to see the magazine in his truck. I was waiting for him to question why I hadn't just turned off the light myself and hid the magazine, but he never did. He just sat there for a second, then stood up, dusted off his blue jeans and squared up to Julia.

My Butterfly

"I'll be right back," he said to her then.

And just like that, he hopped over the log he had been sitting on and disappeared into the night behind the fire.

When my eyes fell from watching Jeff trot away, they stumbled onto Julia. Her bright green stare was already on mine, and there was a soft, questioning smile planted on her face. It was cute.

"Will Stephens, what did you say to him?" she asked.

She was trying her best to scold me, but I could tell she wasn't that upset by whatever it was I had just said to make the lanky boy dance away.

A smile edged across my face, as I took Jeff's now vacant seat next to her on the log.

"I told him his truck lights were on," I said.

Her eyes lingered on me, and she didn't say anything for a good second.

"Are they?" she asked.

I knew she already knew the answer.

"No," I said, grinning into the flames.

I watched the flames pop and dance among the logs being consumed by the fire. I watched them for long seconds before I felt her stare still on me. Then, I turned my attention back toward those pretty eyes of hers.

Her face was angled just enough into the light the flames gave off that it made her features glow with warm colors. Her lips were soft-looking but sexy, as if she could give one, out-of-this-world kiss. And her eyes, even without the fire's light, were that shade of green that made you stop and want to stay in them for awhile. My own eyes were drawn to them like a moth to light. I loved those eyes of hers. I had always loved those eyes.

"When are you going to say *yes*?" I asked.

She kept her smile, but her eyes broke from mine and returned to the fire.

"Depends on what the question is," she said, gradually returning her gaze to me.

"Same question," I said.

I traced the path her eyes made. They seemed to be searching every feature on my face.

"Then, same answer," she softly said.

She was smiling with that temptress smile of hers. It was beautiful, but, God, what did it mean? Did she want me to pull her against my body right now and finally touch those lips of hers I had been dying to kiss? Was I supposed to just sit here? Woman, what do you want from me?

"Come on, Jules," I protested instead. "I know you like me. And you're gonna love me, someday," I added for effect, while throwing a piece of bark into the flames.

"Love?" she questioned.

She had this surprise in her voice. I expected it.

"Jules, just let me take you to Donna's," I pleaded.

She laughed, and I watched her long curls fall from her shoulders to her chest as she shook her head.

"That sounds like a date, Will," she said.

I paused for a second and pushed my lips together.

"Yeah, it kind of does," I admitted, smiling and nodding my head.

I glanced at the fire for a moment and then returned my eyes to her, but her gaze was already planted on me. She wasn't smiling anymore, and her face had grown sincere.

"You're serious, aren't you?" she asked.

I was speechless, while I thought about her question.

This girl must be completely and utterly out of her mind. Of course, I was serious. Why wouldn't I be serious? She was gorgeous; she was smart; she thought Jeff was an idiot; and she was the sexiest woman I had ever met. Done. Done. Done. And done.

"Jules, I was always serious," I finally said.

"Will, you threw rocks at me in third grade."

I couldn't help my smile turning up a little more. I tried to hide it by sending my eyes to the ground at my feet.

"It was out of love, I promise," I assured her, as I met her eyes again. "You could think of it like Cupid's arrows, only they were rocks."

She pursed her lips, and her pout refused to waver. Could I kiss her now?

"No?" I asked. "Not Cupid's arrows?"

And the pout disappeared.

"I guess I just had a funny way of showing it back then," I said.

"Will, you purposely got my favorite volleyball stuck up in the gym's rafters," she went on.

I laughed once and shook my head.

"You still remember that?" I asked.

She glared at me through her sexy, green eyes.

"It was last week, Will," she said.

I took a deep breath and then slowly let it out, allowing my eyes to come to rest in hers.

"Can I just take you to Donna's—to make up for all my past wrong-doings?" I asked again.

She hesitated as silent seconds drew on.

"You know, you kind of owe me," she said, as a soft smile found her face.

My heart fluttered, and I couldn't help but smile too, but before I could get another word out, a group of girls appeared on the other side of the fire from out of nowhere. They were giggling and seemed to have no clue as to what epic moment they were interrupting.

"Will, sing us a song," a girl's voice commanded.

My eyes reluctantly followed Julia's gaze to Rachel, standing directly across from us. I found a piece of bark on the log I was sitting on then and pulled it free.

"Rach, I can't sing," I said, throwing the bark into the fire.

"What?" Rachel asked. "Then why was THIS in your car?"

She pulled out an object from the dark shadows behind her and passed it around the edge of the fire. I knew immediately what it was.

"My car?" I asked.

"Yep, that little SUV next to all those other cars in the field back there," Rachel said, pointing into the darkness behind her.

She was wearing a proud smile. I kept my stare on her.

"It's a truck, Rachel," I said.

"What?" I heard Rachel ask. "Does it have a bed? No. It's definitely an SUV, Will. But don't worry; SUVs can be just as manly, even if they do have girly names."

She playfully rolled her eyes, and I sent her a sideways smirk and returned my attention to Julia.

Julia was giving me a strange look too now, but I brushed it, along with Rachel's comment, off.

"Jules, remind me to lock up next time," I said under my breath.

The object finally reached me, and I extended my arm and took a hold of its neck. And with my other hand, I grabbed its body.

I smiled then and shook my head.

"Play us something," Rachel demanded again.

I let a steady breath pass through my lips as my eyes fell back onto Julia. She was smiling up at me with that beautiful, sexy smile of hers.

"The girls want a song," she said.

I let my eyes linger in hers, forgetting for a second the audience that had just joined us, before I glanced back down at the strings on the guitar and felt my grin widen.

"Okay," I softly conceded, shaking my head.

I tickled the strings for a moment and then found a melody. It was the same one that poured through Julia's jeep's stereo every time she turned it on. I might have learned it a little while back. I figured there would come a time when Jules wanted to hear it and she didn't have her CD. Plus, it reminded me of her, and it felt good to sing it. And now, it was the first song that came to my mind.

Eventually, I started in on the words as well, and after a few moments, I heard the girls on the other side of the fire chime in. They didn't seem to know all the words, but they tried anyway. I caught Julia's stare and smiled. She returned an almost-bashful grin.

I tickled the guitar's strings until the melody ended. Then, there was a strange, awkward silence before Rachel said something first.

"Wow, Will," Rachel exclaimed. "I'm not going to lie. I was really expecting a voice from the boy who starts a band in his garage only to still be in his garage forty years later with a beer belly and a mullet. I wasn't expecting a rock star."

My eyes instinctively darted toward Julia but then hit the ground just as quickly as they had found her.

"Well, I can see that maybe you two have something new to talk about, so...we're just going to get some more hot chocolate," Rachel said before motioning for the other girls to follow her away from the fire.

It was only moments before Julia and I were alone with the fire's flames again. Then, I listened for seconds to the fire's soft popping before Jules spoke.

"Will, that was really good."

My face turned up toward hers.

"Really?" I asked.

"Yeah, really," she said, starting to laugh. "Will, all these years...How didn't I know that you could play the guitar–or sing? And that good?"

I returned my eyes to the flames, as a slight grin found my face.

"Not many people do know, I guess," I confessed. "I'm pretty good at keeping secrets around here."

I winked at her then and propped the guitar against the log beside me.

"So, I see," she said, smiling wider.

"Do you write songs too?" she asked.

My gaze stopped in her eyes. I wasn't quite expecting her question.

"I try, when I get a chance," I said. "Writing's the best part really. It's the words that change people's lives in the end, right?"

She paused, as if she wasn't expecting my answer.

"Hmm, I guess that makes sense," she said, eventually. "I've never really thought about it."

I laughed once.

"I'll have to write a song for you sometime," I said.

I wanted my words to have come out gentle and honest, but I was pretty sure they just came out cheesy.

I watched her smile and then try to hide it.

"Do you write a song for every girl you have a crush on?" she sarcastically asked, returning her attention to the fire.

"Well, I will once I write one for you," I said.

My Butterfly

She let go of her smile and then looked back at me, locking her stare in my eyes before she spoke again.

"I'm pretty sure it's brown-eyed girl, by the way," she said.

Her voice was playful again.

"What?" I asked.

"In the song, you said green-eyed girl," she said, looking away again.

I hesitated but kept my eyes on her.

"Let me see," I said, as I gently touched her chin and turned her face back toward mine.

"Nope, pretty sure it's green-eyed girl," I said.

I watched as a slight smile lingered on her lips.

"Will Stephens, what am I going to do with you?" she softly asked.

I grinned wider and took a deep breath. I could think of plenty.

"Jules, I'm sorry about the rocks, your ball and every other stupid thing I've ever done," I said, lowering my hand from her chin.

Her eyes fell toward the ground, and she laughed.

"It's okay," she said. "You get the ball down for me someday, and we'll call it even."

I slowly nodded my head.

"Okay," I said. "But I'm not gonna stop askin', you know?"

Her eyes quickly found mine again.

"I considered that," she said. "And what if I never say *yes*?"

I sucked in a deep breath.

"Well, then I suppose I would have spent my life doin' something worthwhile," I said. "My parents can't be disappointed in that."

"Will," she protested.

I watched her toss her head back and laugh again, then lift her eyes toward mine, catching my stare. My heart was racing. My breaths were short. I wanted to kiss her. I was going to. I memorized the short path to her lips, and I closed my eyes and tried to remember the path I had just memorized.

"Will," a voice suddenly called out from the darkness behind us.

The voice was already annoying and unwanted. And before I could even acknowledge it, a skinny figure was squeezing himself into the small space on the log between Julia and me.

Damn it, Jeff.

"Will, those were Ben's lights, not mine," he quickly informed me.

He didn't even bother looking at me as he spoke.

"Here, Julia, here's some hot chocolate," the lanky boy announced, facing Julia and presenting her with a steaming, Styrofoam cup.

My eyes shot back toward the orange flames as I scooted over and ran my hands against my thighs, trying to recover from my thwarted *move*.

"Thanks, Jeff," I heard Jules say.

Her voice resurrected my attention, and I turned my face back toward hers. Jeff had already resorted to poking a stick into the fire's ashes and had, by now, all but faded into my background again. I watched Jules's eyes follow the flames for a couple of silent moments. Then, suddenly, her eyes found mine, and I caught her soft lips slowly turning up at their sides. Her smile was different this time. In fact, this might be her best—forgiving and curious and sexy—though I loved them all. I kept my eyes locked on hers, and I smiled too. If I didn't get my *yes* tonight, I'd happily settle for this.

Chapter Five

Donna's

We turned the corner, and I saw her. And instantly, I wondered if I jumped off the wagon, would anyone notice me gone? She smiled and waved. I waved back. I couldn't take my eyes off of her. Her hair was down and in those blond curls she always wore. Her green eyes matched the jacket she was wearing—the jacket everyone was wearing. I seriously gauged the distance from the wagon bed to the street and then tried to guess at what rate of speed the tractor trailer was going. But by the time I looked back up to find her, she had disappeared into the sea of green. I sighed, but a smile quickly returned. It couldn't take that long to loop around town.

The tractor and wagon pulled catawampus into the school's parking lot, and fourteen guys and a couple of coaches jumped off. My feet hit the ground, and my eyes hit the crowd. Where was she?

"One state championship and one championship parade down," I heard a voice call out from behind me.

I turned and felt the corners of my mouth start to rise.

"Julia, I wasn't sure you'd come," I said.

She laughed and glanced at the big crowd behind us.

"I didn't want to be the only one who missed it," she said, still smiling.

My eyes turned down to the ground at my feet. There was something about this girl that made me nervous every time I was around her.

"You hungry?" I asked her, as I kicked a rock back and forth on the asphalt.

I didn't hear anything, so I looked up. She was still smiling at me, but her smile looked less soft and more suspicious. I stared at her staring at me. If this were some kind of staring competition and the winner got his way, I was determined to win.

Just then, her smile widened, and she nodded her head.

I stood there dumbfounded. I was pretty sure that that meant *yes*—even in girl talk, but I couldn't be certain.

Her eyes faltered for a moment but then returned to mine, and as if she had been reading my mind, her next word was all the confirmation I needed.

"Okay," she softly said.

"Really?" I asked.

There was a part of me that felt as if she were pulling my leg.

She nodded her head again.

My Butterfly

I stared at her for another, full second. Then, I quickly scooped her up into my arms.

"Will, what on earth are you doing?" she squealed.

She was laughing, so I figured I was okay.

I hurried over to my truck, pulled open the passenger's door and gently set her down onto the seat. Then, I closed the door and ran over to my side and threw myself behind the wheel.

"What are you doing, crazy person?" she asked, as I jammed the keys into the ignition.

"We've got to hurry, before you change your mind," I said, only semi-joking.

I saw her out of the corner of my eye toss her head back and laugh. And within seconds, I was peeling out of the parking lot and heading toward the little diner at the edge of town.

<hr>

Donna's was filling up, no doubt because of all of the people in town for the parade. Julia and I quickly found a corner booth and slid in. A few seconds later, I watched as a shorter boy with shaggy hair and a Donna's Café polo noticed us and shuffled toward our booth.

"Hey, man, congrats on your guys' win," the boy said after he had planted his feet at the end of our table.

I looked up at him. He had a cheesy grin on his face, and he was wearing a pin with our mascot on it.

"Thanks," I said, through a smile.

"Hey, Adam," Julia warmly said.

"Hi, Julia," the boy replied, cowering a little.

He looked at her a little too long with that cheesy grin of his. Julia had already returned her eyes to the menu, so she didn't even notice. I cleared my throat, which seemed to do the trick. It broke the boy's stare, and he started instinctively scribbling something onto his little notepad. It couldn't be words.

His pen eventually stopped, and he looked up and caught my stare. I was pretty sure I had a puzzled, though now slightly intrigued, look on my face. It was interesting how he had been so drawn to her to the point that I might as well have been invisible. But I couldn't be mad at him. He probably only saw what I had always seen in her.

"Uh, I'll just give you guys some time to decide then," the boy said, smiling awkwardly.

I watched him jam the little pad of paper back into his pocket and scurry off.

My eyes fell back onto Julia then. She was still looking at the menu. I had a smile on my face that I couldn't imagine wiping off.

"Cheeseburger or chicken strips?" she asked me, without looking up.

I heard her, but her words sounded more like a song than a question, so I failed to answer her.

Her eyes eventually turned up toward mine, and soon, her lips broke out into a smile.

"Cheeseburger it is," she said.

She glanced at the paper menu one more time and then slid it behind a ketchup bottle against the window.

"So, how does it feel to be a state champion?" she asked.

My eyes faltered, and a laugh followed.

"Pretty good," I admitted. "But I'm not so sure it's better than this."

She stared at me for a second and then laughed.

"You're ridiculous," she said. "I know that every one of you guys have been dreaming of a basketball state championship ever since the day you picked up a ball."

My Butterfly

I lowered my eyes and chuckled to myself.

"Julia Lang," I said, pausing and then returning my eyes to hers.

"If you only knew how many cheesy Valentine's cards I wrote you that never reached you," I said.

She stopped and sent me a slightly puzzled look.

"Yeah, I know it might seem like I'm head over heels for a girl I barely know, but I know more about you than you think," I said.

"Really?" she asked.

She sat back in the booth and smiled, in a challenging kind of way.

"Really," I said.

Her suspicious eyes locked onto mine.

"You guys ready to order?" asked the boy, in a high-pitched, cracking voice.

He had reappeared from out of nowhere.

Julia looked up at him and smiled. He smiled back, held his stare a second too long, then quickly hurled his gaze in my direction.

I knew I must have given him a puzzled look again because he quickly forced his eyes back to his notepad and started scribbling nonsense again.

Eventually, my puzzled stare left the boy and caught Julia's bright green eyes, and I smiled.

"I'll have the cheeseburger with fries," she said, her eyes still locked in mine.

I'll have the same," I said, only taking my eyes off of her long enough to make sure the shaggy-haired boy had gotten our order.

He finished scribbling onto his pad and then quickly disappeared.

"So, we played on tractors together when we were kids," she said, resting her elbows on the table, her hands under her chin. "That hardly counts as 'knowing me.'"

I chuckled and sat back in the booth.

"Okay," I said. "Fair enough. What about the basketball game in junior high when you broke your arm?"

I watched her brows dart together and her eyes squint a little.

"You were there?" she asked.

"I was," I said. "I had my mom drop me off. We almost got lost finding the place. Turns out, those little, rural schools are pretty well-hidden."

She slowly sat back in the booth again. She seemed to be thinking—back, maybe.

"You didn't cry," I said.

Her lips started to part into a half-smile.

"I was the one who held the door for you when you left the gym to go to the emergency room," I said. "You said 'thank you,' and I remember thinking, *Why isn't she crying?*"

Her expression looked soft and thoughtful, as if she was playing back each moment in her mind.

"And when we were nine," I continued, "I was at the park, and I fell trying to skateboard and tore my knee to pieces. You stayed with me until my dad came and got me."

"That was you?" she asked.

There was surprise—almost disbelief—in her voice.

"And there was another time," I went on, "when you were at the movies with your friends and Jeff was being Jeff, and he strolled right up to you and hit on you—like you would expect a seventh-grader to hit on a girl. I couldn't hear what you said to him, and he never told me,

My Butterfly

but you whispered something into his ear. But as you were whispering, you were smiling at me."

I watched her cock her head a little. Her stare was now off somewhere in the distance.

"I said, 'I have a boyfriend,'" she eventually said, returning her eyes to mine. "But I didn't have a boyfriend."

She shook her head, and a wide smile danced to life on her face.

"I remember looking at him—you," she said and then paused. "I remember looking at you and then coming up with that excuse."

Her stare faded away again before returning to me.

"Wow, now I see it was you all along, but it's like it wasn't you—like..."

"It was like you didn't notice me," I said.

Her smile softened and then slowly, she shook her head.

"It was like I didn't notice you," she confessed.

"Well, as long as you notice me now," I said, smiling what I was sure was a goofy grin and sliding deeper into the booth.

Her lips broke open into a wide smile, and she softly laughed.

"I notice you now," she said.

She was piercing my eyes with those beautiful, green weapons of hers. And I loved the hell out of it.

"I notice you now," she said again.

Chapter Six

The Stars

"Julia," I whispered as loud as I could. "Julia."

I took out the few small rocks I had gathered from her driveway and had stuffed into my pocket and thrust one up into the half-open window. Then, I waited.

Nothing happened.

"Julia," I called out a little louder.

I took a second rock and tossed it up at the glass, then a third. Then, suddenly, I saw a figure in the window. The shadowed outline pushed back the curtains and pressed a forehead against the screen.

"Will?" I heard a soft voice say. "What are you doing?"

"Julia," I said, trying to keep my voice down.

Her head disappeared from the window for a second and then returned.

"It's two in the morning," she said into the screen.

"I know," I said. "I want to show you something."

She was quiet for a second.

"Will, it's two in the morning," she said again, but this time, she said it with a little more emphasis on the *two* part.

"Just this once," I pleaded.

There was a long pause.

"Okay," she conceded. "I'll be down there in a minute."

Her head started to disappear from the screen again.

"No," I quickly said.

"What?" she asked, returning to the window.

"You're kidding me?" I asked. "You'll wake your parents, and they'll never let me see you again. Just climb out the window."

There was a long pause again, and I was imagining her giving me a sarcastic look, as if climbing out the window was a better way to her parents' hearts.

She disappeared again from the window and then returned within a few moments. Then, I heard her fidgeting with the screen, and I smiled.

After a handful of seconds, the screen was out and one of her legs was swung over the windowsill.

"Now, be careful," I said up to her, still trying to keep my voice down as much as possible.

She rested one foot on the porch roof and then swung the other leg over the sill as well. It was only then that I could fully see her with the help of the rays from the dusk-to-dawn light in the background. She was wearing those tiny boxer shorts that girls wear and a tank top that had the high school's mascot plastered on the front of it. And there were little flip flop shoes on her feet.

"You don't do this much, do you?" I asked.

Her eyes met mine with a blank stare.

"Your shoes," I said, eyeing her feet. "Just be careful. Those don't tend to be the best shoes for roof-climbin'."

She tossed a sarcastic, but playful glare my way. Now, I didn't have to imagine it.

"Now, what do I do?" she asked, perched near the windowsill.

"Just inch your way down," I said. "I'll catch you."

She hesitated for a second, then raised her chin and eyed the ground where I was standing.

"It's not far, I promise," I assured her.

She found my eyes again and then hesitantly left the windowsill and used her arms to balance as she slowly shuffled down the tin roof. It took a minute, but she eventually reached the edge and then stopped.

"Come on," I said, holding out my arms.

Her eyes were planted on the ground, and she looked as if she were frozen.

I threw my hands on my hips.

"If you sit there and stare at it too long, you'll never jump," I said.

Her gaze slowly found its way back to me.

"William Stephens," she softly said, kneeling down closer to the tin, "you better catch me."

There was a serious demand not only in her words but also in her eyes that now pierced mine. I felt a sly smile start to crawl its way across my face.

"Oh, I will," I said, holding out my arms again.

She gave me a reprimanding smirk, while I tried to tame my wide grin. Then, she closed her eyes.

"One. Two. Three," she slowly whispered.

My Butterfly

Then, she opened her eyes, took a deep breath and stepped off the roof. I caught her inches before her feet hit the ground and wrapped my arms tightly around her little waist. And the next thing I knew, her lips were inches away from mine. But her eyes were closed, and she was laughing. She made me laugh too, and eventually, she opened her eyes and found mine. Then, her laughter faded into a sweet smile. I wanted to kiss her pretty lips right then. But I didn't. Instead, I gently set her feet onto the ground and took her hand.

"Come on," I said.

"Where are we going?" she asked.

I could hear her giggling behind me as I pulled her along.

"You'll see," I said.

I led her down the long, gravel driveway. It was dark, but the big light above us made it easier to see our steps.

"How did you get here?" she asked.

"Lou," I said, stealing a glance at her. "How did you think I got here?"

"Lou?" she asked, scrunching the features of her face together.

"My truck," I said and then paused. "Or…SUV or main form of transportation—whatever you fancy calling her," I said, with a sideways grin.

"The girly name," she exclaimed, as her expression brightened and she nodded her head in slow, exaggerated nods.

I was guessing she was remembering the night of the bonfire and Rachel's big mouth.

"You named your truck?" she asked, with a wide grin.

I just smiled and shrugged my shoulders.

"Okay, but why Lou?" she asked.

"Why not Lou?" I asked.

"Come on," she said. "I know you named it…"

She stopped and then started again.

"I mean, I know you named HER after someone."

I felt my smile start to edge a path up my face.

"Come on," she said again, lightly shoving my arm. "Who was it—a girl you had a crush on in first grade, on TV?"

I threw my head back and laughed. If that were the case, I would have named the truck *Jules*. And believe me, I had thought about it, but in the end, decided against it. I had already been stalking her since we were kids; I didn't need to make it any more obvious.

"No," I said, shaking my head. "You're way off."

She flashed me a baffled look. Her puzzled face was cute, so I drew out the moment studying the perfect way she pushed her lips to one side and peeked through her big eyelashes from squinted eyes. And only after I had memorized her expression, I spoke.

"It was my grandmother's name," I said.

I continued to watch her as she paused in thought, maybe, for a moment.

"But isn't her name Willamina?" she asked.

"No, the other one," I said. "She passed away before I was born."

"Oh, right," she somberly said, while tossing her eyes to the ground.

"Her name was Louisa," I said, trying to lighten the mood again. "Lou for short."

Jules looked back up at me and smiled.

"Well, where is Lou, the truck?" she asked.

"On the county road," I said.

"It's on the road?" she exclaimed.

Her question fit somewhere in between scolding and surprise.

"I pulled it off to the side, in the field; it's okay," I said.

I watched as a smile slowly returned to her parted lips. God, I couldn't wait to show her my surprise.

We reached my truck a minute later. I made my way over to the passenger's side door first and pulled it open. She playfully eyed me up and then jumped inside. I closed the door behind her and wondered how many more playful smiles I could take from those lips without kissing them.

Then, I jumped in behind the wheel and made a u-turn back onto the dusty, gravel road.

"Will, seriously, where are we going?" she asked.

I looked over at her. Her eyes were big and bright, and a wide grin hung on her lips. I smiled and returned my focus to the road.

"It's a surprise," I said.

I noticed out of the corner of my eye her head fall back against the headrest.

"I hate surprises," she groaned.

I glanced back over at her.

"No, you don't," I said.

I watched then as her head quickly snapped back up and her eyes caught mine.

"When did you become the expert of me?" she asked.

"An expert?" I asked, making sure she caught my teasing stare before I returned my eyes to the gravel road.

"Oh, that was just recently," I said.

A wide, devious smile danced its way to my face.

"They give that title to ya after ten years of study," I said.

She tossed her head back and made a sound that resembled either surprise or sarcasm—I wasn't sure.

"Ten years of study, huh?" she asked.

I found her stare again and gently smiled.

"And they wonder why I'm not so good at math," I said, shrugging my shoulders.

Her laughter filled the cab. I loved her laugh. I wished sometimes that I could secretly record it and play it back when I needed it the most—like when the school counselor was asking me what I wanted to do with the rest of my life or in the middle of a set of walls during basketball practice or something. Hell, I'd play it back when Mrs. Ritter was on her second piece of chalk in English class too. I was trying to force back a wide smile fighting its way to my lips at the thought when I felt her eyes on me.

"What's that?" she asked.

"What's what?"

I glanced over at her. Her eyes were already fixated on a spot behind the wheel.

"That photo in your dashboard," she said.

I took a quick glance at the dash and then noticed the photo propped up to the right of the speedometer.

"Oh that?" I asked, first eyeing the photo and then her.

She sent me a cocked, sideways smile and then slowly nodded her head.

"That would be Julia Austin Lang—the object of my studies," I proudly said.

Her crooked smile instantly straightened.

"I've made your dashboard," she said.

I glanced over at her again and caught her happy expression. I couldn't help but chuckle a little.

"Jules, dear, the center of my dashboard's nothin'," I said, sending her a wide grin. "You made the center of my life years ago."

I could tell she was trying her damnedest to muster up a sarcastic glare, even as her eyes grew softer by the second.

"Get over here, pretty girl," I said, pushing up the center console and gesturing her to my side.

I returned my eyes to the road and then, seconds later, felt her body collide gently into mine. Then, I wrapped my arm around her shoulders and squeezed her as close as I could to me.

"We're almost there," I said, as I felt her head fall against my chest.

I could get used to this.

It was another minute before we crossed over an old creek slab and landed at the edge of civilization. The gravel road pretty much ended there. I pulled to the side so that Lou pointed toward a big, clover field, and I turned off the ignition.

Then, I looked down and found Jules already eyeing me up with those green jewels of hers. And I just knew her smile was asking me what the hell I was doing taking her to a dark, clover field in the middle of the night.

"I swear my intentions are pure," I said to her, with a soft side-smile.

She laughed into my chest.

"Come on," I said, leaning into the door. "It's outside."

She hesitated but then followed my lead and scooted back over to her door and pulled on the handle. Then, I switched off the lights, and suddenly, the world around us was pitch-black, and I had to stop for a second to let my eyes readjust.

"Will," she squealed, laughing. "I can't see a thing."

"Good," I said. "Close your eyes and just wait there."

I rushed to the front of Lou and slid my hand against the grille to feel my way over to the passenger's side.

When I reached Jules, I took her hand and led her back to the front of the truck. Then, I put a hand on each side of her hips and squared up to her. I couldn't really see her face—just its outline—but it didn't stop me from trying. I held her like that for a second, soaking up the way her little hips felt in my hands and how it felt to have her body so near to mine. Then, before it could get awkward, I hoisted her up onto the hood in one, swift motion.

She squealed again.

"Will, what are you doing?" she asked. "Can I open my eyes yet?"

"Not yet," I said. "Now, don't move."

I stepped to the side and hoisted myself onto the hood next to her. Then, I slid back and brought her hips back with me, until we were both resting our backs against the windshield, side by side.

"Okay," I whispered into her ear. "You can open them."

My eyes had readjusted, so I could see her face go from blank to wide-eyed in the seconds that it took her to soak up the scene in front of us—all around us. I watched as her lips turned up and her green eyes sparkled the way they did when she was excited about something.

"Wow," she exclaimed. "It's beautiful."

Above and all around us, dashes of light danced against a black background littered with thousands of tiny stars and a sea of fireflies. It was like our own, little light show. And the crickets and tree frogs were our little, country symphony. I took in a deep breath of fresh air and then rested my head back against the windshield.

"You like it?" I asked.

Her eyes left the lights and found my stare.

"I love it," she said, resting her head on my shoulder.

She was quiet then. I guessed she was watching the fireflies dance in the distance. I, on the other hand, was watching her and the way her fingers played with the edge of my tee shirt at my side and the way her long hair fell in pieces across her shoulders, which had already been tanned by the pre-summer sun.

"So, you really never thought about singing?" she asked, while resting her head back against the windshield again.

Her voice surprised me a little and helped to snap me out of my trance.

"Singing?" I asked.

I turned my face toward hers.

"You know, as a career," she said.

I chuckled to myself and lowered my head.

"Nah, it's not for me," I said.

"Then, what would you like to be if you could be anything?" she asked.

I sat there for a second and thought about it.

"You know, I really don't know," I said. "I figure it'll come to me someday, though."

She smiled.

"It will," she said, reassuring me.

"What about you?" I asked. "I'm sure you've got plans to take over the world."

I noticed her smile. It seemed bashful.

"I want to be a lawyer," she said.

"A lawyer?" I asked.

I know I must have sounded a little surprised.

"Yeah," she said, smiling. "I've wanted to be the same thing since I was eight."

"That's pretty young," I said.

"Yeah," she said. "I guess so."

She paused before she continued.

"There was just this guy who helped my dad a long time ago, and I guess I just decided right then and there that I wanted to be whatever he was and help someone else too."

Her eyes traveled off into the heavens somewhere. She seemed to be lost in another time.

"You think it would have been the doctor, but I guess I never saw the doctor then," she continued. "It was the lawyer that was there by the time I had gotten there."

My eyebrows instinctively furrowed.

"What happened to your dad?" I asked.

My words seemed to have snapped her back to the present because her eyes darted back to mine, and a soft smile returned to her face.

"Why did you never ask me out when we were younger?" she asked.

I paused but then smiled.

"I did," I said, "in my head, a thousand times."

"What?" she asked, starting to laugh.

"It's true," I said.

She lifted her head slightly from the windshield and caught my eye. Her lips were parted, but a smile lingered on them.

"Let's play a game," she said.

"Okay," I said, smiling.

"What's your favorite sport?" she asked.

I paused for a second.

"Uh, basketball, I guess," I said.

"Okay. What's your favorite food?" she continued, without missing a beat.

"Umm, I don't know. Uh…," I stuttered.

"Will," she scolded through her laughter. "The game doesn't work if you don't answer the first thing that comes to your head. It's supposed to be the truth, but you have to do it fast."

I met her pouty eyes. They seemed to be fighting back a smile.

"Okay, pizza," I said, flashing her a grin.

"Who are you named after?" she asked.

"My grandmother," I said.

She stopped, and her eyes slowly traveled to mine.

"You're named after your grandmother?" she asked, not even bothering to try and hide the teasing grin now slithering its way to her face.

"Well, sort of," I said.

Her perfect eyebrows darted together.

"Willamina?" she asked.

I nodded my head.

Her eyebrows relented a little, but the grin stayed. I didn't want to have to tell her the whole story, but it didn't look as if I had much of a choice. Though, the truth was, I'd do anything she asked me to do—even if it was explain to her how I had come to be named after a woman.

I exaggeratedly sighed through a wide smile.

"It means protection—Willamina," I said. "My mom said that my grandmother protected my mom and her family and that she protected me and my family, and that someday, I would protect someone special too."

I watched her lips turn into a warm smile and the features on her face grow soft again.

"That might be the sweetest thing I've ever heard," she said.

"Yeah, yeah, yeah," I said. "At least they didn't name me Willamina."

"No, I'm serious," she said, gently sliding her shoulder into mine.

"So, you don't think I'm less of a man now that you know I'm named after a woman?" I asked.

She laughed a sweet and gentle laugh.

"No, that makes you stronger," she said, sending me a wink. "And after that story, you couldn't possibly be less of a man in my eyes."

I smiled, as my cheeks grew warm.

"Well, what about you?" I asked. "Who are you named after?"

"No one," she said, laughing. "My mom just liked the name. It means youthful, I think."

"That fits," I said.

I so wanted to kiss her.

"The game," she suddenly exclaimed. "We're not finished."

My eyes faltered from hers, and I leaned my head back against the windshield again.

"Okay," I said, still smiling.

"Okay, what's your favorite summer job?" she asked.

"Easy. Umpiring," I quickly replied.

"What do you want to be when you grow up?" she asked.

"Okay, Jules, that one I really don't know. You know that. Skip," I pleaded.

"Okay, fine," she said. "I thought I'd try. But I'll answer for you—a famous musician."

One corner of my mouth slid up my face.

My Butterfly

"What's a hobby not many people know you have?" she continued.

"Uh…playing guitar, I guess," I said.

Who are you going to marry?" she asked.

"You," I said.

She stopped suddenly. She looked surprised.

"Really?" she asked.

I cocked my head toward her again.

"That surprises you?" I asked.

"I guess I just never really thought that far ahead," she said, bringing her legs to a bent position.

"You really want to marry me?" she asked.

"Of course I do. Well, if that's okay with you?" I asked.

My voice had turned shy.

She smiled a happy smile and pressed her head against my shoulder again.

"You want to grow old and wrinkly with me?" she asked, twisting the corner of my shirt tighter around her finger.

I hesitated for a second, which attracted her stare.

"Maybe old, but not wrinkly," I finally said.

She was wearing a half-smirk by the time I had finished.

"Oh, that's right," she said, pinching my side. "I was blessed with the good genes, so that means you'll have to grow wrinkly on your own."

I shifted my weight on the hood, then wrapped my arms around her little body and held her as moments flew by like they were speeding trains.

"Look, a shooting star," she suddenly exclaimed, pointing to the sky above us. "Make a wish."

I watched her eyes fall shut, causing her nose to rumple. And I kept my stare on her for a second, until her eyelids started to slide open. Then, I quickly shut mine.

I had never wished on a star before, and I wasn't exactly sure what I was supposed to do, so I just kept my eyes closed and prayed that I would have the courage to finally kiss this girl tonight.

Within a couple of seconds, I felt her tugging at my arm, and I lifted my eyelids to her smiling face.

"What did you wish for?" she asked.

I felt my lips start to turn up at their corners, as my eyes traveled from her eyes down to her lips and then back up to her eyes again. Then, I took a piece of her long hair that had come to rest on the side of her face and tucked it behind her tan shoulder. Something crazy strong was drawing me to her, and I didn't even try to fight it. My heart pounded. I searched her pretty, green eyes. They seemed to be searching mine too. She was motionless, but on her face was this beautiful smile that I could never do justice by simply describing. It was happy and comfortable and sexy, and it was as if it were daring me to do exactly what I craved to do. I brought my face closer to hers, until my lips were hovering over her lips and I could feel her soft, steady breaths. I stayed there for several seconds, taking all of her in—her fiery eyes; the way her lips parted ever so slightly, giving way to her sexy, little smile; and the subtle, familiar scent of the perfume she always wore. Then, I closed my eyes and pressed my lips against hers. Her lips were soft and full and warm to the touch. They were perfect, and they made my heart race, but they also made me feel so at home. How could something I had never done feel so natural?

I brought my hand to the side of her face and gently rested it there. Then, I slipped my tongue into her mouth, and I kissed her as if my life depended on it. I think I was kissing her for all those years I hadn't kissed her. And if I hadn't known better, I would have thought she were kissing me for all the years I hadn't kissed her too because she kissed me like she wanted me—like I was the only guy she desired. It made my heart race faster, and I couldn't get enough of it. In fact, my heart was still pounding against the walls of my chest when my lips finally broke from hers—and only because I needed a second to catch my breath. I would have kissed her forever.

"You gonna be my butterfly?" I whispered, resting my lips against her ear.

"Your butterfly?" she whispered back.

I met her pretty eyes again. They seemed to be smiling—just like her pretty lips.

"Yeah, you're as beautiful as a butterfly, and you know you want to be," I playfully coaxed her.

She softly laughed, forcing her tan shoulders slightly forward.

"Well, you've never asked it that way," she said.

"Does that officially mean *yes*?" I asked her, not even bothering to hide my wide grin.

She paused for a moment, as if to drag out my torment. I was learning that she was pretty good at that and also that I didn't so much mind it.

A quick glance down revealed a glimpse of her hand, and the next thing I knew I was intertwining my fingers in hers.

"That means *yes*," she softly confessed, allowing her gaze to fall to our hands.

My grin grew wider, and I lowered my eyes again too before meeting her stare.

"That's what I've waited my whole life to hear," I said.

She smiled her sweet smile. Then, I kissed her pretty forehead, and we both fell back onto the windshield again, her hand still intertwined in mine.

"You never told me what you wished for," she whispered into my ear moments later.

I turned on my side and faced her.

"Well, since it came true, I guess I can tell you. That is how it goes, right?" I asked.

"Of course," she said, confidently nodding her head.

"Well then, I wished for my first kiss—but only if it could be with you," I said.

I watched her lips break into a smile again. Then, she brought our locked hands close to her mouth and kissed the back of my hand before returning her attention to the heavens.

I couldn't help but smile as I followed with my eyes a firefly making its path across the front of the truck. The firefly eventually disappeared behind a tree, leaving me to my thoughts and to my ultimate conclusion, which was that someone could surely try, but I was pretty sure that he couldn't convince me that life could get any better than it was right now.

"What did you wish for?" I asked, eventually breaking the silence.

Her eyes brightened.

"I can't tell you," she said. "Mine hasn't come true yet."

I held my stare on her for a second longer. Then, I chuckled and kissed her soft lips again. They were still perfect.

"Will you tell me what it is when it does?" I whispered near her ear, after I had withdrawn my lips from hers.

I watched her as she seemed to toss the idea around in her head for a moment.

"Yes," she eventually said.

"You promise?" I asked.

"I promise," she said.

I nodded in satisfaction, smiled and then returned my head to the windshield.

"Jules," I said then.

She turned her face toward mine, and I locked my eyes in hers.

"I'm glad you said *yes*," I said.

She was quiet for a moment.

"Me too," she said.

Chapter Seven

Fireworks

Jules tugged at my hand and pulled me forward. I hesitated for a moment to let a little kid with a stick of ice cream in his hand run in between us. There were people all around us and little booths lined the narrow street, selling everything from balloon animals to bratwursts.

"Look, Will," Jules exclaimed, scooping up a cat from a big pile of stuffed animals.

"I want him," she said, sending me her best pleading face—batting eyelashes, pouty lips and all.

"You want that?" I asked, eyeing the stuffed cat.

It looked pretty ugly to me.

"Aren't its eyes a little big for its head?" I asked.

Her own eyes turned down toward the cat clutched within her small hands, and I watched as her fingers carefully traced over the cat's big, glass eyes.

"They're perfect," she said, looking back up at me. "They remind me of this cat, Furballs, I had when I was little."

I couldn't help but cringe a little at the thought of a real cat looking that ugly. Then, I looked back at Jules's unwavering eyes and felt a smile breaking across my face.

"We'll take Furballs," I said into the booth.

The old man in the booth gave me a bewildered look.

"The cat," I said, pointing to the stuffed animal.

"Aah," he said, nodding his head. "Good choice."

I held a suspicious stare on the man in the booth, until I felt Julia's arms around my neck.

"Thank you," she said, into my chest. "I loved Furballs."

I laughed. I loved her—and that's the only reason why ugly Furballs had a home now.

I handed the man in the booth a bill.

"Thanks," I said and then turned back toward Jules.

"Now, come on," I said, squeezing her body tightly against mine before reaching for her hand. "You ready for our hike?"

I watched her turn and set her sights on the towering bluff above us. Then, she took a big, exaggerated breath and then slowly let it out.

"Come on," I said. "I'll give you a piggyback ride."

Her eyes immediately grew wide.

"All the way up?" she asked.

"Sure," I said.

She was grinning and shaking her head by the time I met her eyes again.

"You would never make it all the way up that bluff with me on your back," she said.

"Is that a bet, Miss Lang?" I asked her.

She smiled wide.

"That's definitely a bet," she said.

"Okay," I said. "You and Mr. Furballs, hop on."

I clutched the quilt I had been carrying since the car in one arm and hunched over. Then, I felt her weight on my back seconds later.

"Is Mr. Furballs on too?" I asked, cocking my head to the side and trying my best to look behind me.

All of sudden, an unattractive cat came flying into my line of vision.

"All right," I said. "We've got Mr. Furballs. Let's go."

I made my first hundred feet up the path without much trouble, even though every once in a while I had to maneuver over a fallen tree limb or carve my on trail through some overgrown weeds.

"You still okay?" I heard her ask after I had just successfully scaled a pile of brush.

"Oh," I said, stopping for a second. "You're still there?"

She laughed and tightened her arms around my neck. I felt Furballs press up against my ear as I started up the path again. The truth was my feet were starting to feel heavy and my quads burned like hell, but this was a bet I wasn't going to lose.

Finally, I could see the clearing at the top of the bluff. And there were only about a hundred feet to go, but each step was beginning to take everything in me.

I heard Julia's soft laughter behind me again.

"Will," she said. "I'll just walk. It's okay."

"No," I said. "I'm fine. We do hills like this all the time in basketball conditioning."

She laughed again.

"You run up bluffs, Will," she sarcastically said, "with people on your back?"

I stopped for a second.

"Well, we might as well," I said, trying my best to laugh through the pain.

I took another labored step. I was only about ten feet away now and feeling every foot. But just then, my shoe caught a root or something, and I tried to catch myself but didn't have the energy. I stumbled and realized I was heading right for the ground. Seconds later, I heard her scream or laugh or something, and the next thing I knew, we were in a pile in the dirt.

"Aah," I sighed, exhaustedly thrusting my head back against the ground. "I almost made it."

"What are you talking about?" she asked. "You did make it."

I could barely move, but I forced my head out of the dirt and grass and looked up. We were in a clearing, and I could see downtown below us and all its people walking every which way. I must have fallen the rest of the way.

I met her eyes, and she kissed my lips.

"Thanks, sweetie," she said, giving me the most perfect smile.

I squeezed my arms around her with the little strength I had left, and then I kissed her forehead.

"Told ya I'd make it," I proudly said.

She smiled and playfully rolled her eyes.

"Did Furballs make it?" I asked.

I watched as her eyes made a circle around us. Then, eventually, they stopped. And within the next second, she was out of my arms and moving toward the edge of the bluff.

I slowly pushed myself up from the ground and watched her secure her ugly cat again. She had dirt on the side of her little jean shorts, and I think there was a twig in her hair, but she still looked beautiful. I sat there for another second watching her dust off Furballs. Then, I got up and grabbed the quilt from the ground and made my way back from the edge a little.

I tossed some twigs and some little rocks out of the way. Then, I stretched the blanket out over the grass and dirt, sat down and caught Jules peering out over the edge.

This bluff was probably the highest point in town. Down by the river and on this side of the levee, people danced around little, brick buildings and short, narrow streets. The Fourth of July had always brought people downtown. Otherwise, this part of town was pretty quiet, except for maybe when there was a state game playing at the little theater or when the river was extra high and people couldn't stand not to come out and stare at it.

And now, even though we were pretty high up and the evening was quickly turning to night, I guessed Jules was still finding things to look at because she had been lost in the scene below us for a good while now. Then again, I guessed she was good at that too—good at always getting lost in little things. Her head seemed as if it were always churning out little thoughts.

I smiled at the thought and then lowered my eyes and noticed the edge of the quilt sticking up. I leaned over and pulled it back. There was a twig underneath, so I tossed it to the side.

"You need some help with that?"

I looked up and found her eyes on me. I smiled and shook my head.

"Now you ask, after all the work's done, as usual, my dear," I answered her.

A playful side-smile hung on my lips.

She gave me her best pouting face and threw her hands on her hips.

I, on the other hand, made a quick decision to take full advantage of the moment and get a good look at her. Her hair was down and fell in waves against the sides of her face. And she was wearing a tight tank top and jean shorts, and at the bottom of her long, tan legs, were her favorite, little boat shoes. She called them something else, but I was pretty sure, in the end, they were just plain old boat shoes. Though, somehow, she still managed to look as cute as hell in them.

"Get over here, pretty girl," I demanded then.

I watched her saunter over to me, her playful smile growing. And when she got close enough, I reached up, scooped her into my arms and fell back against the quilt and the soft earth.

"How much longer do we have?" she asked, nuzzling her head into my chest.

"Oh, probably about a couple more minutes," I said, squeezing her closer still.

"Sing to me then," she said.

She pulled her head back and found my stare just as a smile was forcing its way to my lips.

"What do you want me to sing?" I asked.

"A song about us," she said, tracing with her delicate fingertips the places around my eyes and nose and then lips.

"Okay then," I eventually said, slowly nodding my head.

Satisfied, I guessed, she rested her head back onto my chest, and I watched pieces of her hair fall over her sun-kissed shoulder as she made herself comfortable. Then, my mind went to stringing together some words for her song. And when I had them, I brought my lips closer to her ears and whispered her a melody:

> *"Though you'd rather watch a sappy ending*
> *Than a football game*
> *And you're not very good at fleeing the scene*
> *Without a sprain,*
> *I wouldn't want it any other way*
> *I'm yours forever, My Butterfly*
> *So, looks like you're stuck with me*
> *'Til the end of time."*

When I finished singing, she was laughing.

"How romantic," she exclaimed.

There was sarcasm in her voice.

"I wrote it myself—just for you," I proudly said.

"Thanks. I'll just do some creative interpreting, I guess," she said, meeting my eyes before returning to her place on my chest.

"But seriously, though, minus those passionate words, you can really get a girl's attention," she said. "You should sing, you know, for people, as a career. You've got a gift. You can't hide it forever."

I raised my head off the ground again.

"Why can't I?" I asked.

She met my gaze. Her long eyelashes batted impatiently.

I saw an opportunity to kiss her pretty forehead, so I did. She smiled but seemed to stay focused on her mission.

"Because someday, somewhere, somebody's gonna find out. Then what are you going to do?" she asked.

"Easy," I said. "Tell them I've got everything I need right here."

I squeezed my arms tighter around her little body.

"Wouldn't it be a dream come true though?" she asked. "Plus, you would be doing the world a severe injustice if you didn't."

I quietly chuckled to myself.

"Mine is a far simpler dream, my sweet Jules," I whispered into her ear.

"See what I mean with that voice; I almost believed you," she said, softly laughing.

"Jules, trust me," I said. "My life's a dream already. I don't need to go chasin' somethin' somewhere else."

She paused before she spoke again.

"You haven't even thought about it just once?" she asked.

I smiled and shrugged my shoulders.

"Not once," I said.

"But you like singing, right?" she asked.

I traced the little lines in the green part of her eyes for a few seconds. Then, I kissed her lips to slow down her thoughts.

She was smiling when I pulled away from her.

"All right, my little Hollywood agent," I said. "I've got you, and that's all the fan I ever wanted."

She tried to put on another one of those pouting faces she keeps in that little expressions box of hers, but she wasn't quite successful at it. Her smile never really went away.

I intertwined my fingers in hers. Then, suddenly, I felt something wrapped around her finger, and I brought her hand closer to my face to get a better look at it.

She must have noticed me examining her hand because I felt her eyes on me again.

"Funny story about that little, grass ring," she said.

I started to smile.

"Oh, really?" I asked. "Let's hear it."

"Okay," she said.

I noticed her eyes travel back to the ring on her finger.

"See, one night, this boy and his buddies decided to take this girl and her best friend—practically as hostages—to this old windmill at the edge of town."

"Hostages?" I asked.

Her smile grew as she nodded her head and continued.

"Evidentially, the boy had a plan to dress up like Spider-Man and to climb said windmill to fool all the townspeople into thinking that Spider-Man was alive and well in their own town."

"Hey, I bet some people still believe it," I said.

She stopped and playfully rolled her eyes.

"Anyway, that same night, in the shuffle of almost getting caught, I sprained my ankle and wound up hiding from Officer Brian on the other side of a mound of dirt and grass next to, who other than, Spider-Man himself."

I angled my head back and laughed.

"Baby, I still don't know how you managed to sprain your ankle," I said.

I heard her giggle.

"I don't know either," she said, shaking her head. "But anyway, this boy or Spider-Man made me this grass ring," she said, eyeing the ring again. "And right there in the grass and the dirt, he asked me to marry him someday."

I was quiet and busy trying to fight back a wide smile after she had finished her story.

"That sounds made up," I eventually said.

My Butterfly

She lifted her head and met my gaze.

"But I have the ring to prove it," she said, positioning her hand so that the ring was clearly in my view.

"So, you do," I said, bringing her hand to my lips.

I kissed the ring and the finger it was on.

Then, suddenly, a loud thud forced both of our eyes to the river where a stream of reds, whites and blues were already sprinkling the night sky and lighting up the bluffs opposite us in the distance.

Julia giggled and pressed her hips against mine. I pulled her closer and watched the next firework race to the sky and then explode into tiny, little pieces of light. Jules squealed, and I felt her arm squeeze tighter around my side as she nestled her head deeper into the muscles in my chest. My eyes fell onto her face, and I smiled and noticed a piece of her long hair resting on her cheek. I picked up the strand and then gently laid it back down onto her bare shoulder. It was hard to just simply watch the fireworks because I couldn't stop thinking about what I wanted to tell her—what I had wanted to tell her for a long time now. Suddenly, there was another loud shriek, followed by a big thud and a colorful burst of light in the sky again. Jules looked up at me with wide eyes and a happy smile, and I just couldn't hold it in anymore.

"I love you, Jules," I said, in almost a whisper.

She was quiet, and her smile was starting to fade, but her eyes were still on me, still locked in mine.

My heart sped up. *Say something, anything.* I watched her eyes trace a path in mine. I wondered if she had even heard me. But then, I saw her lips fall slightly open.

"I love you too," she whispered.

Her eyes smiled before her lips did. Then, she returned her head to my chest and her attention to the lights still dancing in the night's sky.

My heart was pounding. I bet she could feel its thuds. I wanted to shout something, but I didn't want to scare her or cause her to move from the exact place she was resting on my chest. So this was what *I love you* felt like. I started to replay all the days and all the moments and all the memories I had of Julia Lang. My grin widened as I realized that each moment involved me being in complete awe of her and her not even knowing it. God, I loved this girl, and I bet she still didn't even know how much.

"Will," I heard her soft voice say then.

"Hmm?" I asked.

"Will you sing me another song?"

"What about?" I asked.

"About us," she said.

I could hear the smile in her voice.

"Okay," I said, taking a second to think.

I gathered the words and then whispered into her ear another melody, but this time, it was soft and low:

"Little girl, little boy
If love has a way
Fill their fields with laughter
And scatter the sun on their day
And if it should happen to rain
Make their raindrops kisses
Straight from heaven above
That touch their hands and faces
And that fill them with love
And make the moon reflect their smiles
And their stars plenty

And, above all, keep them together
And hold them as you may
Forever and ever
Until their last days."

She squeezed her arms tighter around my side when my lips stopped singing her song.

"It's perfect," she said.

I watched for a second as her eyelashes followed the path the fireworks made from the barge in the river to the heavens. Then, I kissed the top of her head, pulled her hips closer to mine and smiled.

Chapter Eight

Senior Year

I heard a knock at the door just as I was signing my name to the last page of paperwork.

"Come on in," I said.

I heard the door push open, and I took a quick glance back.

"Hey, babe," I said, setting down the pen and flipping through the healthy stack of pages.

"Hey," I heard her say, making her way over to me.

And within seconds, I felt her arms wrap around my neck and her weight press down onto my shoulders.

"Whatcha' workin' on?" she asked.

My hands left the pages and found a spot to rest on her arms, and I reached up and kissed her.

"Oh, just filling out forms for the fire department," I said. "Even if you're a volunteer, it requires an autobiography, evidently."

I heard her take a deep breath as she pushed off of my shoulders.

"Can I have some water?" she asked.

I turned in my chair and watched her make her way into the kitchen and pull out a glass from the cabinet. She filled the glass with water from the faucet and took a drink. I smiled at her when her eyes finally met mine again, but her lips only slightly turned up.

"What's wrong, Jules?" I asked.

She took another deep breath, then set the glass down onto the counter and walked back over to me. My eyes followed her as she fell into the chair next to mine and began to study my face.

"You really want to be a firefighter?" she asked.

Her question made me pause. Yesterday, when I had told her that I had driven by the fire station and the thought had just sort of overtaken me, she seemed happy for me.

"Yeah," I said. "I mean, I can't believe I hadn't thought about it before. At least, then I could have gotten Counselor Old Fart off my back a lot sooner."

She seemed to be tracing the lines in my eyes, until she eventually nodded her head.

"It's just so…," she started.

I furrowed my brows and tilted my head.

"So?" I asked.

I watched as she took another deep breath.

"So what, Jules?" I asked again. "You seemed fine with it yesterday."

"I know," she said. "It's just so dangerous, you know?"

My eyes settled on hers, and I started to smile.

"Jules, it's not that dangerous," I said. "And, you know, it's me. Jules, you know I'm not the type of guy who can sit in an office all day. Hell, I can hardly sit through a class."

A soft, guarded laugh fell from her lips, but then her smile went limp again.

"It's just...," she started and then stopped.

My eyes stayed on her expression, even though I couldn't read even the slightest part of it. Her eyes, on the other hand, were turned down toward the floor. Then, it finally dawned on me. I sat back in my chair and took a deep breath.

"It's just that future lawyers who are future presidents don't date future firefighters," I said, crossing my arms.

I felt my expression turning cold, as her eyes quickly shot up at me, and her sad stare seemed to grow annoyed.

"That's what it really is, isn't it?" I asked in a firm tone.

She was quiet.

I knew it. I should have known. If I could be a lawyer or a doctor, maybe I would, maybe I wouldn't. But I knew how the world worked even so, and I should have known that girls with ambitions like Julia Lang didn't stick around long with guys like me.

I watched as her eyes narrowed into little, cat-like slits.

"What are you talking about?" she asked.

"Just say it, Jules," I said. "You want a doctor or a lawyer or some senator or someone who's smart enough to cure cancer and who makes six figures and who can take you to fancy parties and buy you everything you want."

I paused for a second and swallowed hard before continuing.

"Well, that's just not gonna happen with me, Jules," I said. "That's not in my stars. I'm just a small-town, country boy, and that's all I'll ever be."

Then, I pushed up fast from my chair. Its wooden legs scooted across the floor hard and made a loud, unpleasant sound. Her eyes were still narrowed on me and were now piercing my thick skin. I kept my own eyes on her for a second longer, and then I darted toward the back door and pushed hard through it.

My feet hit the wooden porch boards, and I stopped and ran my fingers through my messy hair as I took a deep breath. The air was cold and merciless. It stung my throat and lungs, but after a second, I forced the breath back out and watched its fog leave a trail from my lips and eventually disappear. Then, I walked over to the railing, doubled over it and cupped my face in my hands.

I couldn't even remember a time that I didn't want this girl. How could I, in all that time, never have thought that I wasn't the one who she would want?

I brought my fingers to my lips and took another deep, cool breath, and suddenly, I felt a hand on my shoulder.

I stood up fast, turned and squared up to Julia.

"It's not that," she whispered.

I searched her expression—her eyes and her lips. Nothing I found on her was angry. It all seemed sad, and suddenly, I felt like a jerk.

"I'm so sorry, Jules," I said.

I nudged her arms, willing her closer to me. She hesitated but then gave in and fell into my chest.

"Say that you forgive me," I whispered low and near her ear.

She felt so small in my arms.

"Forgive me, Jules," I said.

I squeezed her tighter, then pulled away and lowered my face to hers and rested a hand gently against each side of her face.

"Say that you forgive me," I said to her again, bringing my forehead to rest on hers.

I watched as her mouth tried to turn up a little.

"I forgive you," she whispered.

Her words made me smile, and instantly, I pressed my lips passionately against hers. The first thought of losing her was the most terrifying thought I had ever had. And her words had saved me from it.

When our kiss broke, I caught her gaze in mine.

"It's not that, Will," she said in a soft voice.

I nodded and brought her head to my chest again.

"I know," I softly said. "I know."

I pulled her closer to me and caressed the strands of her long hair.

Honestly, I didn't know if I fully believed her, but I also didn't know if I blamed her either. She deserved those things I would never be able to give her. She deserved those things, but there was also a little part of me that believed that maybe, just maybe, what I couldn't give her in riches, I could make up for in love.

Chapter Nine

College

"What about this one?"

I twisted the features on my face and shook my head.

Jeff gave the flower a sideways glare and then tossed it back into its bin.

"Well, what do they look like again?" he asked.

"You know, they're those flowers on the side of the road," I said. "My grandma always called them butterfly weeds."

He stared at me blankly.

"The ones the butterflies are always hovering around in my grandma's backyard," I said.

His stupid face didn't change.

"They're orange, little flowers," I said. "Just look for orange flowers."

The corners of his mouth turned down and his eyebrows made a crease in the center of his forehead.

"Orange. Got it," he said and scurried off.

I shook my head and went back to rummaging through the bins of flowers. Who knew that there were so many different kinds? I browsed over blues and yellows and reds before I finally found the section that was mostly orange. My eyes traveled over each flower, looking for the perfect match, until finally, there it was.

"Found it," I called out to Jeff.

Jeff didn't answer. I snatched up the flower and examined it some more. It was a perfect match. I moseyed out of the aisle lined with every flower you could imagine and eventually found myself in the front of the dime store again. I glanced around for Jeff and quickly spotted him leaning against a tall display full of those big, birthday balloons. His elbows were propped up on the counter, and it looked as if he was talking to someone behind it. I wondered for a second why I had even brought him. Then, I quickly remembered that places like this scared the hell out of me.

"Jeff, could use some help," I said, coming up behind him.

It took him a second, but he eventually half-turned toward me, revealing a young girl behind the counter. The girl's eyes caught mine, and she smiled.

"Nice flowers," she said.

My eyes darted down toward my hand that was tightly gripping the orange bouquet. I felt my cheeks grow hot. I really just wanted to get out of the store.

"What do you need now?" Jeff asked in a way that sounded as if I were inconveniencing him.

My Butterfly

"Uh, could you tell me where I would find some string?" I asked the girl.

The girl giggled.

"You probably want ribbon," she said, smiling wide.

The corners of my mouth nervously turned up.

"Here, I'll show you where it is," she said.

The girl stepped down from behind the counter and made her way to the other side of the store. I felt a jab at my bicep and looked up to see Jeff's dumb, smiling face.

"She's cute, huh?" he asked, under his breath.

I impatiently glared at him and then followed after the girl.

"Okay," she said, stopping in an aisle full of string in all different colors "What kind do you need?"

My eyes fell back on the flowers still gripped tightly in my hand, and suddenly, I felt her fingers on my forearm.

"Do you need it for these flowers?" she asked.

Her voice wasn't sarcastic anymore. Now, it was more soft and almost teacher-like.

I nodded my head.

"Yeah," I said.

I noticed Jeff out of the corner of my eye. He was scowling at my forearm.

"They're for his girlfriend," Jeff blurted out.

Both the girl's and my attention turned to Jeff, propped up against a display of string.

"Well, I'll help find you something pretty then," she said, warmly smiling at me again.

She left me then and hurried over to a row of white string.

"I saw her first," Jeff whispered, charging toward me.

"What?" I asked.

"I saw the way she was looking at you," he said.

I squinted my eyes and cocked my head.

"This should be perfect," the girl said, returning with a spool of white string.

She reached in between Jeff and me and took the flowers.

"What do you think?" she asked, holding the two up together.

"Looks great," I said.

"Your girlfriend will love it," the girl said, placing her hand on my arm again.

My stare found Jeff. He was rolling his eyes.

"Unbelievable," he huffed, turning away.

I smiled and returned my attention to the girl.

"Thanks," I said.

"Don't mention it," she said, sending me a wink.

I stopped Lou at the top of the county road. My chest was tight. It had been tight all day, which made it kind of hard to breathe at times. I took in a deep breath, and it came right back out. My eyes fell on the butterfly weed in the passenger's seat. Its plastic stem looked exactly like it had the day I had bought it. The girl in the dime store said the orange flowers were made of "real silk." I hoped Jules liked them. But more so, I hoped she understood why I had chosen them.

I picked up the flowers and examined them again. The note I had written was attached to the flowers' stem by the little, white string or ribbon. It was a ribbon—not a string, evidently. I had promised the girl in the dime store that I wouldn't call it a string anymore.

I peeked at the note one more time. It still said the same thing it had said the last twenty times I had looked at it: *I'll love you until the last petal falls, Jules.*

I took a deep breath again, and this time, I let it out slowly. My grandmother was the reason I had thought to do this for Jules. She had always had these flowers planted all over her garden. I remembered asking her one day why she had planted them everywhere, and she had told me that these were the flowers that brought the butterflies back every spring. I remembered watching out her window one warm, April afternoon, just to make sure she hadn't been pulling my leg. But sure enough, I saw the butterflies. And I went back last weekend to see the butterflies. They were one thing certain, when everything else wasn't.

I tugged at a petal on one of the flowers. It didn't move much. It seemed to be on there pretty tight. I smiled a satisfied grin and turned my eyes to the gravel road again. It was time to face the music. I laid the flowers back down onto the passenger seat and stepped on the gas.

Moments later, I pulled into her parents' driveway. The thought of her leaving made my stomach sink. I edged down the white gravel and eventually brought Lou to a stop at the base of the drive. Jules's jeep was there too and already stuffed full of the life she wanted to take with her to college. I sighed when I noticed that there wasn't any room for me.

Jules was on the passenger's side. I watched her for a moment try to stuff one, last piece of her life into the jeep. It reminded me of that first day of school when I had watched her try to squeeze her big duffle bag into her locker, and it made me smile. And for a moment, I almost couldn't believe that I had had the chance to call her mine for these last, perfect years.

Eventually, it looked as if she had finally gotten whatever it was that she was trying to fit into the front seat secured, and she met my stare. I smiled at her. Her hair was up in a ball on the top of her head. Pieces of it, though, had come loose and now invaded the sides of her face. After a few more seconds of taking her in, I lifted the door handle and stepped out of my truck.

"You all packed?" I asked.

She peeked inside the passenger's window and then looked back at me.

"I think so," she said.

I watched her take two tries to close the door, each time putting the little weight she had into persuading the door shut.

"I told you you'd get in," I said.

She paused and looked up.

"And I was right about the scholarship to run track too," I added.

I could see her lips starting to give way to a smile.

"Well, we can't all make it into the fire academy," she said, finally getting the door closed.

I chuckled once as my eyes turned down toward the ground at my feet.

"I brought you something so you remember to remember me," I said.

I tried to swallow, but there was a lump in my throat. Instead, I looked up to see her taking steps toward me. She was wearing those little jean shorts that she always wore and a tank top with her favorite band stretched across its front. And she was tan—that summer sun kind of tan that made her blond hair blonder and every part of her that much more irresistible. I tried to smile, but in the end, I knew that I couldn't hide how I really felt.

Eventually, she got close enough to touch me. Then, she threw her arms around my neck and pulled my face close to hers.

"How could I forget about you?" she asked. "If I forget about you, I've lost the happiest years of my life."

I tried so hard to force a smile, but the more I got lost in her eyes, the more I wanted this all to be a dream—a dream where I wake up and she's telling me that she'll stay in our little town forever.

"Jules," I said.

"Hmm?" she asked.

"Sometimes I love you so much it hurts," I said. "Is that normal?"

Her smile faltered and turned sad before it grew happy again.

"Mm hmm," she said, nodding her head.

"How do you know?" I asked.

"Because I'm normal, and it hurts me too sometimes," she said.

I felt the corners of my lips naturally edging up my face. Then, I let my eyes rest in hers for a little while. It was always comfortable and happy in her eyes. Then, suddenly, I remembered the flowers again, and I broke our stare to retrieve them. After snatching them from the passenger's seat, I brought them to rest at a place in between us. Then, I watched her eyes lock onto flowers.

"It's a butterfly weed," I said, in almost a whisper.

She took the flowers into her hands.

"It's pretty for a weed," she said. "I've seen it before?"

I smiled.

"Yeah, along roads and in fields, pretty much everywhere around here," I said. "They keep cuttin' 'em down, but they always grow back. They never give up," I added, softly.

I watched her smile brighten as she stared into the flowers. And eventually, she came to the note attached to the stem by the little white ribbon and stopped to follow over its words.

"Do you know why they never give up?" I whispered near her ear.

She slowly shook her head back and forth.

"No," she whispered.

I met her eyes.

"Because they want the butterflies to come back to them," I whispered. "They need each other to survive."

Her gaze slowly fell to the flowers clasped within her slender fingers.

"Julia," I said again.

"Hmm?" she replied.

"You'll be my butterfly, right? You'll come back to me?" I asked.

She looked up at me again, and I could see her eyes filling with water. I didn't mean for her to cry. I didn't mean to make her sad.

"I love you, Will Stephens, and I'll never forget you," she said in a soft, broken voice. "I'll be your butterfly. I'll always come back home."

I wrapped my arms around her then and held her as tightly as I could. I imagined never letting her go.

"You're brave," I said, "doing this all alone."

I felt her body press harder against mine.

"Don't leave," I whispered into her ear.

She held me a little longer, then slowly pulled away when her parents came out to meet her.

Her lips seemed as if they were trying to force a smile when her eyes met mine again. I knew she wouldn't stay, and I didn't expect her to, and I knew she knew that.

I watched her turn and felt her hand squeeze mine for an instant and then let go as she made her way to her parents.

"Mr. and Mrs. Lang," I said, tipping my cap.

"Hi, Will," her mom said to me with a warm smile.

I could tell she had been crying too.

I watched as Jules hugged her mom and then her dad and then made her way back to me.

"You ready?" I asked her.

"No," she softly said, shaking her head.

"Sure you are," I said, doing the best I could to muster up a smile.

I walked her to the driver's side of her jeep. Then, she pulled me close and pressed her lips against mine. The feel of her kiss sent a shiver down my spine. It was almost as if her lips were sealing her promise—the promise that she'd come back.

But eventually, she pulled away and locked her green eyes in my blues.

"I'm not brave," she said, shaking her head. "I'm just determined, and if I don't leave here alone, I just might change my mind about all of this."

My smile brightened, and my eyes faltered and fell to the ground at our feet before returning to hers.

"Go get your dream, Butterfly," I said.

I watched as a wide, perfect smile eventually found its way to her face. Then, slowly, she climbed behind the wheel.

"Drive carefully, Jules, and call me when you get there," I said, leaning into the driver's side window to meet her lips one, last time before she pulled away.

"I love you," I added, when our kiss broke.

"A million times a million?" she asked.

She was forcing a smile now, so I did too.

"A million times a million and to the moon and back," I said.

"I love you too," she whispered, through her drying tears.

Her eyes lingered in mine for a second or two longer. Then, I took a step back from her door. It seemed as if she tried to smile again, but the corners of her lips just never quite succeeded at fully turning up, in the end. Then, she planted her eyes straight ahead and stepped on the gas.

I watched as her jeep ambled over the rocks in the driveway, leaving me behind. I pretended that she was just going to get a pizza from the next town over or a movie from Wally's.

Then, at the top of the driveway, she stopped. I stood up straighter and looked for her. And through the passenger's window, I caught her kissing the palm of her hand and then blowing it my way. I threw my fist into the air and acted like I was catching it. Then, I waved goodbye.

Chapter Ten

False Alarm

"Damn it," I said, under my breath, as I turned the knob that quieted the tones.

My eyes found hers. She was disappointed; I could tell. But she put on a soft smile anyway.

"I'll get it to go," she said.

I felt a heavy sigh escape past my lips.

"Thanks, babe," I said, pushing out my chair and stepping toward her. "Do you mind hangin' out with Jeff for awhile."

Still smiling, she shook her head.

I kissed her lips and gestured over to Jeff. Jeff scurried over and planted his feet in front of me.

"Are you getting off soon?" I asked him.

"Yeah, in about ten minutes," he said, glancing at his watch.

"Good," I said. "Can you take Julia to wherever she wants to go?"

"Sure," Jeff said, smiling a wide, toothy grin in Julia's direction.

"Thanks, buddy," I said, patting him on the shoulder.

"I'm sorry, baby," I said to Jules. "I'll call you when we're finished."

"Okay," she said. "Be careful."

"I will," I replied, before turning and hurrying out the door.

Moments later, I was jumping into my truck and reaching into the backseat for my light. It took me a second, but I eventually found it, stuck it to the roof and flipped it on.

The first week she was back in town from school, and I had a call. I let go of another big sigh and then threw the truck into reverse and then first.

The fire station wasn't even a mile down the road from the tiny bar, and about a minute later, I was already pulling into the little parking lot. It looked as though I was the first one there, except for the captain, who always seemed to be there. I quickly turned off the ignition and jumped out, slamming the door behind me.

Within seconds, I was inside the station and thrusting my hand against the button on the wall that sent the bay doors flying open.

By the time I reached my gear, someone was already behind me. It was Mike. He usually drove the tanker truck if we needed it, but we wouldn't be needing it today.

I stepped into my pants and boots and threw the suspenders over my shoulders. My jacket was hanging on a hook on the wall. I grabbed it and forced my arms into its holes. Then, I grabbed my hat.

"Nothin' like gettin' a call in the middle of an argument with your wife," Mike said, with a wide grin.

I paused and smiled back at him. He was still wiggling into his pants.

"You kissed her though, right?" I asked.

"Yeah," he said, chuckling. "But I'll still hear about it later, I'm sure."

I laughed once and flung open the driver's side door and climbed behind the wheel. Then, I started the engine and flipped a switch, and immediately, red lights bounced off of the walls of the station and back into the cab. My eyes scanned the gauges in the dash. Everything looked okay. My attention then turned to the captain's door when I saw it fly open. I watched as the captain climbed into the seat next to mine, and seconds later, Mike followed, jumping into the back.

As soon as the doors slammed shut, I let off the brake and stepped on the gas. And when the front tires hit the street, I reached up and flipped another switch. Instantly, loud sirens poured from the top of the truck.

We arrived at the address on the scanner within minutes, almost beating the chief, who had just pulled up in his own vehicle. There was a woman standing outside with two, small children. I recognized the woman's face. She was new in town—just moved into old-man McConnell's house. I had met her at the hardware store just last week.

"You got this one, Will?" the captain asked.

"Yes, sir," I said.

"Okay, we're just going to go on inside then and check things out," he said.

"All right," I replied, as I pulled the truck near the curb on the street.

As soon as the engine stopped, the two guys in the cab with me slid out, and I followed after them.

"Ms. Evans," I said, greeting the woman with a head nod.

She smiled. I wasn't sure if she recognized me or not. She looked a little shaken. The two kids in her arms looked as if they couldn't be any older than seven. One looked scared, maybe on the verge of tears. The other, however, was bright-eyed and seemed to be more fascinated by the fire engine's lights and the strange men wearing space suits on his lawn than any threat of danger. I smiled at the kids and then looked back up at their mother.

"Did you smell any smoke, ma'am?" I asked her.

I watched as the captain, Mike and the chief opened the door to the house and slipped in. Then, I saw the woman shake her head.

"No," she said, softly, squeezing her children closer. "The smoke detector went off in my daughter's room. I couldn't smell anything, but I just wanted to be sure. It's an old house, you know. Maybe I shouldn't have called, but I just wanted to be sure..."

I stopped her.

"I'm glad you called," I said, gently smiling. "We'll take a look. We'll make sure there's nothing unusual."

A soft smile started to grow on the woman's face. Then, she took a deep breath and then forced it out.

"Thank you," she said.

"You're welcome, ma'am," I said and then made my way toward her front door.

Just inside the heavy storm door, I could already tell the house was in a world better shape than when old-man

My Butterfly

McConnell had the place. There were curtains now, and the blinds were open. And there weren't stacks of newspapers sitting in dark corners anymore. I scanned the first level one more time. Then, I headed up the stairs to the second floor and saw the captain and the chief when I reached the top of the steps.

"Anything?" I asked.

They shook their heads.

"She said the smoke detector in the daughter's room went off," I said.

"Yeah, there's no smoke, no smell, nothing burning," the captain said. "The smoke detector in one of the rooms needed its batteries changed. Was that a girl's room, Mike?"

"With the detector?" Mike called out from down the hallway.

"Yeah," the captain hollered back.

"Yeah, I think so," Mike bellowed. "It looked like it, unless the boy has some obsession with *The Powerpuff Girls*."

The chief shot me a puzzled look.

"What the hell is he talking about?" he asked. "How does he know that?"

I laughed and shook my head.

"I don't know," I said. "It's Mike."

"Anyway," the captain said. "We put new batteries in the girl's room. Otherwise, it looks fine. I think we're clear."

"All right," I said, turning back down the stairs.

The chief followed after me, and the captain and Mike followed after him.

"This place looks a lot different from when old-man McConnell lived here," Mike said, legging behind us.

"You miss the dust and the cobwebs, Mike?" I asked him.

"Yeah, that and the cigar smell," he said, laughing.

I laughed once and then made my way to the front door and pushed through it.

"Ms. Evans," I said, nearing her. "Everything looks fine. We changed the batteries in your daughter's smoke detector. But if it goes off again or if you think anything's unusual, don't hesitate to call us again."

The woman bashfully smiled.

"The hardware store," she said.

I paused for a moment.

"Yes, ma'am," I said, smiling.

"Will," she said.

I nodded my head.

"Yes, ma'am," I said.

I watched her lips rise at their corners.

"Thank you," she said.

I smiled again, then tipped my hat and made my way back to the engine.

◈

"Hey, baby," I said, hopping back into my truck. "Where are you?"

She giggled and said something to someone in the background.

"Is that Jeff?" I asked.

"Yeah," she said.

I could tell that she was smiling on the other end of the phone.

"He misses you," she said.

Jeff rambled off something else, but I couldn't understand it.

"I don't care if he does," I said.

"Well, I miss you too," she said.

I smiled into the phone.

"Where are you guys?" I asked.

"Jeff's," she said.

"Just you two?" I asked.

"Yeah," she said, laughing at something Jeff had said again.

I paused and waited for Jeff's mouth to quit running in the background.

"Okay, I'll be there in five minutes," I said.

I threw down the phone and forced the truck into gear.

A handful of minutes later I was parked on the street in front of Jeff's house. His porch light was on, but from the way it looked, every other light in the house was off. I furrowed my brows for a second as I stared into a dark window but then brushed off the foolish thought. Then, I got out, walked to his front door and pushed it open. The darkness on the other side of the door blinded me, until I reached for the switch on the wall and flipped it on.

"Julia," I called out. "Jeff."

I listened for a second but didn't hear anything. Then, I shuffled through the living room and then the kitchen, until I saw the back porch light on and then heard their voices.

"Hey," I said, stepping out onto the deck.

Julia jumped.

"Will," she exclaimed, forcing her hand to her heart, "you scared me."

My eyes went to her first. She was lounging back in a chair. Her feet were propped up on the porch's railing. Jeff, on the other hand, was on the opposite side of the porch, sitting in a chair with his feet propped up on a cooler.

I took a second. My mind was definitely playing tricks on me. It was either that or it was the thought of all those college guys looking at Jules the way I knew they were looking at her that was making me paranoid. Jeff was my best friend. He might well be an idiot sometimes, but he'd never purposefully hit on Jules—not anymore anyway.

"I called for you guys at the door," I said, pulling out a chair from the table and scooting it next to Julia's.

"Sorry about dinner, Jules," I said, kissing her on the lips.

"Me and your girlfriend were just talking about you," Jeff interjected.

I turned my attention to Jeff and then forced it back to Julia.

"Oh, yeah?" I asked.

Jeff tossed me a can from the cooler under his feet. I caught it, and little pieces of ice flew every which way.

Julia squealed.

"Jeff, a piece of ice flew into my eye," she exclaimed, now shielding her face and rubbing her eyes with the back of her hand.

"Sorry, J," Jeff said, his eyes planted on Julia.

"You all right?" I asked her.

"She's all right, but we both think you need a job that's not so demanding," Jeff announced. "You know, one that won't cut into our weekends."

"Jeff," Julia scolded.

She was smiling but still rubbing her eye, as she turned toward me.

"Sweetie, I didn't say that," she said, at the same time sending Jeff a playful, sarcastic glare. "I used the word *dangerous*, I think, instead."

"Dangerous?" I asked.

A playful smile was edging its way across my face.

"You wanna hear how dangerous my job was tonight?" I asked her.

She was trying not to smile but wasn't being very successful at it.

"How dangerous?" she asked, playfully rolling her eyes.

"Well, tonight, I almost hit a squirrel with the truck—a big, fat one," I said. "It probably wouldn't have caused too much physical harm—to the squirrel maybe, but not to us anyway. I mean, it could have busted out a piece of the grille maybe. But the real harm would have been emotional. I'm pretty sure it would have been a real kick in the morale."

I smiled wider as I went on.

"And then, when I got inside the house, I went to step over a stack of old-man McConnell's hunting magazines from the 1970s, and I almost tripped because, much to my surprise, they weren't there," I said. "Oh, and Mike threw a battery at me when we got back to the station. He hadn't meant to, of course. He had asked me to throw it away, but I wasn't paying attention, and it hit my head. Can you see the mark? I think it left a mark on my forehead?"

I pointed at a spot on my head.

She shoved my arm, then tossed her head back and laughed.

"Will, what am I going to do with you?" she asked, through her laughter.

I looked at her with what I liked to call my sex-appeal eyes.

"I can think of several things," I said to her.

She laughed again and shoved me harder. I dramatically fell back into my chair as I heard Jeff start to cough up a hairball in the background.

"Get a room," he groaned.

He made another disgusted face and then cleared his throat.

"Anyway, Julia, like I said before, this guy's job is about as dangerous as mine," he said.

I cocked my head to the side and sent Jeff a puzzled look.

"Yeah, I burned myself last week," Jeff said, nodding his head. "It was like a third-degree burn. Those hamburger grills are hot."

I laughed.

"So, back to MY point," Jeff continued. "Your job is a real buzzkill for our weekends, not that I mind hangin' out with your beautiful girlfriend all night—every night."

He smiled and winked in Julia's direction. Julia rolled her eyes and smiled back at him.

"I get it," I said. "Julia, baby, can you forgive me for leaving you with this sorry example of a man? You know I never want to leave you."

She looked into my eyes. It was dark all around us, but there was a ray from the little porch light that hit her eyes just right and made them sparkle.

"I know," she said, softly smiling. "I know."

She took my hand with both of her hands, kissed it and brought it to her lap.

"And Jeff," I said, "how 'bout we go fishin' next week?"

He rolled his eyes.

"All right," he said, starting to crack a smile. "But you can't buy me off forever."

My Butterfly

My eyes returned to Julia then, and she sent me a sweet, comforting smile, which instantly melted my heart. She looked so pretty, so perfect. I couldn't imagine not having her in my life.

I smiled back and then brought my lips to her ear.

"I love you, babe," I whispered.

Chapter Eleven

A Movie

I opened the door, and she rushed in and threw her arms around me. I caught her and squeezed her close. Then, she pulled away and pressed her lips against mine.

"Let's go out," she said, pulling on the end of my tee shirt.

"Out?" I asked, laughing.

"Yeah," she said. "We can go to Max's or I heard that there's this new place in Chester."

"Or," I said, taking a long, dramatic pause. "Or we could order pizza and watch a movie. What's that one you wanted to see?"

I watched as, first, her smile and then her face turned down toward the floor.

"But we watched a movie the last time I was here," she said, sounding discouraged.

"I know, babe, but I had a call this morning, and I didn't get to bed until four," I said. "Why don't we do that next time?"

Her face turned up toward mine again.

"You said that last time," she said. "And I thought you were coming to see me next time."

"Oh," I said, taking a moment to think back. "Oh, I'm so sorry, babe. I'm on-call the next two weekends. They kind of don't bother me during the week so much because of the paramedic classes. You know, they said I need that certification if I ever want a full-time firefighter gig."

I watched as she slowly nodded her head.

"But that means they really count on me for the weekends sometimes, and they needed me those weekends," I said.

Her stare fell to the hard floor again, and I used the back of my hand to gently lift her chin up so that I could see her pretty eyes.

"Babe, I love you a million times a million," I said. "It won't always be like this. We won't always be far apart."

Her lips stayed planted where they were in the straight position on her face, but I could tell that she was making an effort to smile.

"Come here," I said, drawing her body close to mine again.

I squeezed her tightly and took in the smell of her hair. It always smelled like some kind of garden or fruit or something. Whatever it was, it always made me smile.

"And to the moon and back?" she asked.

I smiled wider.

"And to the moon and back," I confirmed, gently kissing the top of her head.

We held each other for a moment then without saying a word. It was her whisper that finally broke the silence.

"*Gone With the Wind*," she softly said into my ear.

I slowly pulled away from her and met her eyes.

"The movie I wanted to see was *Gone With the Wind*," she said.

Her voice was still soft.

I tried to hold back a suspicious grin. I knew that wasn't the one. The one she had mentioned before was at least a couple of hours shorter.

"Are you sure?" I asked her.

She nodded her head. There was a new, mischievous smile planted on her face.

"That was the one," she said, with more conviction this time.

One of my eyes narrowed slightly, but I didn't say anything. I knew enough to know when to keep my mouth shut.

"Okay," I said, as I felt the corners of my mouth slowly start to turn up again.

"And we're getting pepperoni pizza—with extra cheese," she added.

A wide smile finally won the battle and shot across my face.

"Pepperoni pizza with extra cheese it is," I said, as I watched her push past me with her little, pleased self.

"And we're going out for our anniversary," she said.

Her words trailed behind her as she made her way into the kitchen.

I swallowed hard. I wondered if she had forgotten.

"Uh, Jules, you know I can't make it for that day, right?" I asked, timidly.

She stopped and faced me.

"What?" she asked.

And just like that, her smile was sad again.

I felt my palms instantly grow sweaty, and my heart attempted to surrender for the both of us by jumping right out of my chest.

"Remember, we were going to celebrate it that second week after," I said to her.

My voice came out even more timid this time, as her hollow eyes stared a hole into mine.

Then, suddenly, a smile cracked across her face.

"I know," she said, in a much too cheerful voice.

I stared at her blankly.

"Did I scare you?" she asked, showing off a wide, toothy grin.

I took in a slow, deep breath and then let out a sigh and lowered my head as I tried to hide the smile fighting its way to my face. Then, after a few seconds, I looked up and met her little, devious gaze again. She winked a big set of eyelashes at me and then spun around on her heels. That was my silent cue.

As she spun, I dashed toward her and squeezed my biceps around her little body. Then, I scooped her up into my arms, as she screamed in surprise.

"There's no room for jokes like that in this house, pretty girl," I said, planting a wet kiss on her cheek.

She squealed again and wiped the back of her hand across her face, as I carried her to the living room and gently threw her onto the couch before I fell onto the surface next to her.

"You have just officially lost all your demanding privileges," I said, flashing her a wide but serious smile. "We're getting sausage pizza."

"No," she screamed.

I started tickling her side and planted another wet kiss on her cheek.

"Sausage pizza," I said again.

"Okay, okay," she said, giggling and trying her best to squirm away from my hands.

"What kind of pizza are we getting?" I asked, still running my fingers up and down her side.

She continued to giggle and squirm.

"Sausage pizza," she screamed, through her laughter.

I slowed my fingers and then rested my eyes in hers. I was pretty sure I had a smile as wide as the Missouri River planted on my face.

"I'll call it in," she said, suddenly jumping out of my arms and up from the couch.

She danced away, and I sat up and started to reach for the remote but then stopped.

"Jules...," I cautiously called into the other room.

When I didn't hear anything, I jumped up, ran into the kitchen and spotted her already on the phone.

"Yes," she said into the receiver, "one, large pepperoni pizza with extra cheese."

I scowled at her, and she smiled back. And I didn't even try to fight the smile returning to my face, as I realized in that moment that I would eat a million pepperoni pizzas for that girl. And she knew it. Damn it.

Chapter Twelve
Anniversary

"I'm sorry I had to be on-call tonight," I said to her.

She softly smiled at me and took my hand.

"It's fine," she said. "I'm here. Happy anniversary, Will Stephens."

I smiled and planted my eyes in hers.

"Happy anniversary, Jules," I said. "And if it's any consolation, I made a wish on one of those shooting stars of yours and asked for no calls tonight."

She lowered her eyes, shook her head and laughed.

"You're really bad at that," she said.

"What?" I asked, surprised.

"You're not supposed to tell me what you wished for or it won't come…"

"Don't finish that," I said, stopping her.

I watched as she tried to bring her turned-up lips back to a straight position again.

"I love you, Jules," I said.

A smile eventually won its way to her face.

"I love you, too," she said. "Now, what are we going to eat? I'm starving."

My eyes rested in hers for a second longer. She looked beautiful, as always. Her hair was down and fell perfectly around her face. And she was wearing a fitted, white top that hugged her in all the right places and tight blue jeans with little holes down the front of her thighs. The holes were put there on purpose, I had learned, unlike the ones that always occurred by accident in my old jeans. And tonight, she had on her favorite pair of boots—the ones that towered up her long legs. God, she was sexy.

Reluctantly, I forced my eyes to my menu and started scanning the items on the left side of the page first. But before I even got to the second item, I heard a succession of tones ringing on my belt loop. Immediately, my eyelids fell over my eyes, and my heart sank. *Of all nights.*

When I opened my eyes, Julia's knowing stare was already on me.

"I'm so sorry, Jules," I said.

They were the only words I had.

Her lips forced a half-smile, but I could tell it was sad. I slowly stood up and kissed her on the lips.

"I'll call Jeff to come get you," I said, reaching for my phone in my pocket.

"No," she said. "It's okay. I'll call Rachel."

I stopped.

"You sure?" I asked.

"Yeah," she said, nodding her head. "I need to talk to her anyway."

I slowly shoved my phone back into my pocket and found her eyes again. It broke my heart to leave her on our anniversary.

"Go," she said. "Someone needs you."

I tried to give her the best smile I could muster up. Then, I started to turn.

"Will," she said, stopping me.

I turned back around and faced her.

"Be careful," she said.

One side of my mouth lifted into a grin.

"I'll call you," I said.

Then, I turned again and made my way toward the small restaurant's exit.

When I reached the door, I pushed it open and flew across the parking lot and into my truck. Once inside the cab, I slammed the door behind me and then stopped and rested my head on the steering wheel for a split second. A deep sigh later, I spun around and searched for my light in the backseat. I found it on the floor, unrolled the window and stuck it to the roof. Then, I threw the truck into reverse and peeled out of the little, gravel parking lot.

I arrived at the station a few minutes later and rushed inside.

"Residential fire?" I asked the captain, as I slipped into my boots and threw on my gear.

"Yeah," he said and then quickly disappeared behind the truck.

I stopped for a second from adjusting my suspenders. There had been a look on the captain's face. And looks like that were pretty rare on a face that had seen all that you could fit inside twenty years on the department.

I tried to shake it off, then threw on my jacket and grabbed my hat.

Within a minute, there were four of us in the truck, with Bryan, our engineer, in the driver's seat. And Mike was in the tanker behind us. But I couldn't stop thinking about Jules. I wanted so badly to call her, even if it did seem ridiculous at the moment, but my phone was in my truck, back at the station, and with the sirens howling above me, I wouldn't be able to hear her anyway. Instead, I settled on staring out the window, as the truck breezed by stop signs—only making half-efforts to tap the brakes at each one—and praying that I'd make it back in time to still hang out with Jules some.

Suddenly, we all swayed to one side as the engine's wheels hit the blacktop that carved a path away from town. And soon, everything outside of the window turned black, and it stayed that way for the most part, until I would spot, every once in a while, a porch light on in a house at least a half of a mile or so off the road.

It was another ten minutes, though, before the engine slowed and took a turn at a place far enough outside of town that any other time would have taken a good fifteen to get to. And it was only then that I could see the smoke. It was illuminated in the dark by the flames beneath it. But even it was still a ways away, at the end of a long driveway. I swayed to the side as the engine turned sharply again and followed a bend in the path, finally revealing a clearing. Then, I could see the fire's flames threatening to reach above the tree tops on one side of the house. It was a pretty big house, but that one side looked pretty shot.

Adrenaline instinctively shot through my veins. Fire could be a pretty devastating creature on the life people worked so hard to create, and this blaze looked as though it was no exception.

We neared the house, and I could see a couple of people standing outside. A woman was crying. I recognized her, but I didn't know her well. Her kids went to the school in the town up the road. And there was another woman with her, and she looked as if she was dialing something on her phone.

The brakes on the truck squealed to a halt seconds later, thrusting my chest forward. And as if it were second nature, we all flung open our doors and jumped out. Bryan immediately went to the top of the truck, and I grabbed a line of the thick hose and threw it over my shoulder.

"Will," I heard my name shouted.

I glanced up and spotted the captain near the two women. At the same time, another volunteer grabbed the hose from my shoulder and took off with it toward the house.

"We've got a man inside looking for a dog," the captain said. "We need to get him out of there."

I nodded my head, and my oversized, hard hat moved with it. Then, the captain sprinted toward the house with an ax in his hand, and I followed after him, sliding my mask over my face.

The door to the house was wide open when we reached it. And inside, it was dark, and the air was thick.

The captain immediately bent down and started crawling along the floor. I did the same, trying to stay as close as possible to him as he tapped his ax against the floor to make sure it was stable. But with each foot, the air got warmer and thicker, and the popping and the cracking of the fire got louder in my ears.

I turned my head from side to side, looking in corners and down hallways, searching for the man through the smoky haze. I couldn't see the fire, but I knew it was slowly eating its way over to our side of the house and that with each inch forward, we were that much closer to its flames.

Suddenly, the captain stopped in front of an open door. I stopped too and peered inside. Beyond the doorway, there were stairs leading down to a basement, and there was clearly a light on in one of the corners.

We stood there motionless for a moment. Then, I thought I heard something.

"I think he's down there," I said, through my mask.

I watched as the captain first glanced down the hallway in front of us. The flames were popping out of the rooms on the far end of the house now. We could have minutes, or we could have seconds. Either way, it wasn't much time.

I eventually followed the captain's gaze back to the flight of stairs before he angled his face toward mine and nodded. That was my cue, I guessed, because our next steps were down the series of wooden planks.

As our boots hit each board, I gripped with my gloved hand the banister. And seconds later, we were both at the bottom of the stairs and standing on a concrete floor. To the far right of us, the ceiling had already started to give way. A wooden beam was sticking halfway out of the first floor. It was charred black at its end. And through the hole it had left, I could see the big, orange flames raging their chaos above us.

"I'm over here," called out a strained voice from the other side of the basement.

My Butterfly

The voice was faint, and I wasn't quite sure how I had heard it over the fire's havoc in the background.

I turned to see a man slumped over a box in a corner. He was conscious, but from the way it looked, he was barely conscious.

I patted the captain on the shoulder and then hurried over to the man. When I reached him, I took off my mask and put it to his face. I knew I wasn't supposed to, but it looked as if he could barely keep his eyes open. He was probably one breath away from passing out.

"Put your mask back on, Will," the captain yelled when he reached me.

He hastily removed my mask from the man's face and shoved it into my chest. Then, he took his mask and forced it over the man's nose and mouth.

"Here, help me get him up," he shouted.

I watched him bend low and throw the man's arm around his shoulder. I slid my mask back on and did the same on the other side, and together, we hoisted the man to his feet and started toward the stairs again.

But before we had even made it a couple of steps, there was a dog bark, and the man seemed to come to again and lift the mask from his face.

"My son's dog," he said, stopping and trying to turn back.

"It's all right," the captain shouted. "We've got to get you out of here."

"Please," the man cried, locking his heavy gaze on me.

I lifted my eyes and found the captain's stare, and I knew immediately what he was commanding me to do.

Then, suddenly, a beam crashed to the concrete floor on the other side of the big room, and the loud sound it made caught the attention of all three of us.

"Is there an exit down here?" the captain asked the man.

The man's eyes glazed over in fear. I looked up and caught the captain's stare again, and then we followed the man's gaze to a door now completely engulfed in flames.

"Come on," the captain shouted, pulling the man up the stairs.

The man hesitated but soon complied, allowing us to guide him to the door at the top of the steps. I stopped once we got there. The fire down the hallway was closer than it had been before we had gone down the stairs, but it looked as if there was still some time before the last exit to the basement was completely closed off by the flames. And I knew I was fast. I could do it.

The captain and the man made it a couple more steps before they noticed I wasn't by their side.

"Will, let's go," the captain yelled behind him.

I glanced at the fire down the hallway one more time, then at the captain. There was a brief second where our eyes met, and then I turned and flew down the stairs.

"Will," I heard him call out after me.

But I was already down the flight of stairs, and I couldn't turn back. In fact, I had gotten back to that small corner so quickly that I hadn't even realized the steps I had taken to get there.

Once in the corner, I shoved the box away. The dog was there in a tiny crawl space, whimpering, with its tail between its legs.

"Come on, boy," I said into my mask, squatting down and reaching out a gloved hand.

He was just far enough back there that only the tip of my glove could reach his fur.

I squatted down even more and squeezed my shoulders as much as I could into the crawl space. With my hand blindly reaching now, I felt the dog's leg and then its shoulder, and then in one, solid effort, I grabbed a hold of its skin. I pulled the dog closer to me until I could reach it with both hands. Then, I scooped it up into my arms and flew back to the base of the stairs. But when I looked up, my heart sank into my boots, and I stood there for a moment staring at the doorway, now covered in a thick cloud of billowing, black smoke. And behind it, was a fierce, bright glow.

"Shit," I said, into my mask.

I glanced back at the basement door on the other side of the room, but I could only see flames there—and not even any semblance of an exit. So, without a second thought, I charged up the wooden stairs and stopped two from the top. I couldn't see anything on the other side of the doorway through the smoke, and I knew the floorboards couldn't be stable, but I had no other option.

I charged forward, pressing the dog close to my chest. The air was hot, and the dog was shaking. Then suddenly, I felt my boots plunge through the floorboards. At the same time, the dog flew forward, and I instinctively reached for whatever part of the floor that was still able to hold me and caught myself under my arms.

I took a second to regain my bearings, and then I tried to pull my body back up from the floor. It was hot, and my head was starting to get foggy. I tried to block out the loud popping sound the fire made and pretend as if it weren't there. But I could still hear the dog barking. I managed to grab the corner of the wall, and I tried again to hoist myself up. It worked a little. I was able to get more of my waist above the floorboards. But the smoke was thick, and somehow, during the fall, my mask had gotten dislodged. And now, the fumes were finding their way into my nose and mouth. I retightened my grip on the corner of the wall again and tried again to pull myself to the surface. This time, though, I didn't budge. I breathed in another smoke-filled breath and gave everything I had to keeping my head up. The room was getting hotter, and there was a dog fading and reappearing again in the fog. I couldn't tell for sure if it were real or part of a dream.

I felt my hand loosen its grip on the wall. It shocked me, and I immediately retightened my hold. I was starting to take shallower breaths now, and my eyes were getting heavy. I felt my fingers start to loosen again, and it forced me to think about trying one, last time to pull myself up. But really, I just wanted to rest my eyes for a little while and try again later. And if it weren't for that dog shouting at me, I was pretty sure I would.

Then, suddenly, I felt something. It started tugging and then pulling on me. I lifted my head, and then instantly, my eyelids fell heavy over my eyes.

※

I awoke to Julia doubled over in tears at the foot of a tiny bed.

"Jules," I said, quickly sitting up but then being pulled back by a set of plastic tubes.

My words came out hoarse, and suddenly, I noticed my head wasn't fairing much better.

"Will," she said, turning to me and then rushing over to my side.

She moved, and then all of a sudden, there were way too many people in the tiny room. I noticed the fire captain first, and then I froze.

"You took a little fall," the captain said.

My Butterfly

I forced my eyelids over my eyes, and slowly, the memory came back to me. It was fuzzy and blurry, but it was there.

"You saved me," I finally said to the captain.

He smiled, gently.

"You saved the dog," he said.

A half-smile eventually found its way to my face.

"Just, uh, let's not make it that close next time," the captain said, giving me a wink.

My mouth turned up a little more at its corners, and then my eyes fell to the white sheets that I was covered in.

Julia grabbed my hand and forced it around hers and into her lap. I watched her intertwine her fingers in mine before I met her stare. Her eyes were so sad, and suddenly, I remembered the last words she had said to me before I had left her. And then it hit me—I hadn't been careful.

"Jules," I started to say.

She shook her head, stopping me, as her eyes started to fill with tears again.

"Jules," I said again. "I'm okay. I'm fine."

She was still shaking her head; a stream of liquid was now rolling down her cheeks. I reached up and brought her closer to me.

"Will, I can't do this...," I heard her start to mumble into my chest.

"What, babe?" I asked her.

She was quiet except for the sniffles.

I squeezed her tighter and stroked her pretty, long hair.

"It's okay, Jules," I said. "I'm okay."

I took in a deep breath and then slowly let it out.

"It's okay, sweetheart," I whispered again, closer to her ear. "Everything's okay."

Chapter Thirteen

Cold

"**H**ey," she said.

I switched the phone to my other ear. It had been a couple of weeks, but I felt as if I could still hear the cracking and the popping of that fire in one ear.

"Hey. How was your day?" I asked.

"Same old, same old," she softly replied. "How was yours?"

"You know, pretty much the same too," I said, as I kicked off, first, one shoe and then the other. "I had to get to class early because…"

I stopped. There was something off in her voice.

"Is something wrong, Jules?" I asked.

There was a pause. Pauses like that weren't ever good.

"It's just that...I can't...," she started and then stopped.

I waited for her to finish. Instead, there was silence.

"You can't what?" I asked.

I heard her take a breath.

"I just feel like we've grown apart," she said.

Her sentence was straight and to the point, and it completely derailed me.

"What?" I asked.

"I know that sounds really cliché, but I don't know how else to say it," she said.

I felt my heart momentarily take a break in my chest. Then, I took in a deep breath and then slowly let out a sigh.

"Jules, I know it's been hard, but...," I started to say but then let my words trail off.

"It has," she said.

There was another moment where there was only silence before she continued. I had no words, so I just listened.

"It's just that I've been busy with track," she said, "and you're doing your training, and when we do finally see each other, I feel like you aren't really even that excited, and..."

"Jules, is this about our anniversary?" I interrupted. "Jules, I'm really sorry, and it wasn't my intention to have us spend it in a hospital..."

"No, Will," she said.

Her words were soft and sincere.

"This is not about that," she said and then paused. "It is, but it's not."

My eyebrows darted to the center of my forehead. I could see them staring back at me now in the mirror as I started to take in shorter, shallower breaths.

"What?" I asked.

"It's nothing," she said. "It's just…It seems like it's a chore for you."

"What seems like a chore?" I asked.

"Us, Will," she said.

Her replies were getting shorter and shorter.

"I don't fit into your life anymore," she continued.

"Jules," I softly said and then stopped. "Jules, that's not true, and I'm always excited to see you. I'm just tired sometimes."

I took in another deep breath and then let it slowly escape past my lips before I continued.

"You don't have to answer to fire calls at two in the morning just to go back to bed and answer another one at five," I said.

"You're right, I don't, and I understand that," she said.

She sounded slightly irritated now.

"But since you've been doing that, you've never found a way to make it work," she said. "You've never found even the tiniest bit of energy for me. Will, I might not be answering fire calls, but I'm working my butt off up here. Plus, I'm the one driving home to see you every month. You're never here. I feel like I'm the only one trying anymore."

"I try," I said, my voice trailing off.

"How, Will? How do you try?" she asked.

"I stay up and watch movies with you," I protested.

I heard her sigh on the other end of the phone.

"First of all, you don't stay up," she said. "I know you're sleeping. Secondly, I don't want to always watch movies. I want to get dinner. I want to go dancing. I want to do things."

I felt my patience waning even as my heart was stabbing at the inside of my chest.

"I have a job, Julia," I said. "You'll understand how that works someday."

My words had grown cold, and I knew it. I was on the defensive, and at this point, I didn't quite know how to get back to the other side.

"Really?" she asked. "Will, this has nothing to do with me going to school or you having a job, and you know it—and I can't do this anymore."

Do what anymore? What was she talking about? Was she talking about us? She couldn't do us anymore?

"What does that mean?" I asked.

She didn't say anything. I took another deep breath, held it and then let it out, as a remnant of patience returned to my voice.

"Jules, it's us," I said. "It's us, Jules. You can do us. We know how to do us."

I heard her sigh.

"Maybe we should take a break or something," she said.

Her voice had grown so soft I could barely hear it now.

"You mean break up?" I asked her, slowly lowering myself to the mattress.

"Well, just to give us some time to think about it," she said.

"I don't need time to think about it, and Julia, you and I both know that there is no such thing as a break. There is only a breakup. Is that what you really want?"

There was that deafening silence again, and I couldn't believe what I had just asked her.

"Yes," she stuttered, eventually.

My heart started to sink deeper into my chest. She didn't mean that. She couldn't have meant that.

"Yes," she said again, more firmly.

"Jules, what are you saying?" I asked.

I waited seconds, but she didn't answer, and suddenly, I knew. She wasn't saying that she didn't fit into my life anymore. She was trying to tell me that I no longer fit into hers. She was saying she didn't want a firefighter; she wanted a lawyer. I let out a frustrated sigh. It had always been that. It will always be that.

"Well, I guess that's it then," I said.

The words stung even me, but I didn't care. She would figure out soon enough that no one could love her like I could—not even a fancy lawyer.

"I guess so," she softly said.

There was an awkward pause, and it scared me. I couldn't remember the last awkward pause I had had with Jules. In fact, I wasn't sure if we had ever had one. It made me nervous, and the nerves made me spit something out without even thinking.

"Take care," I said.

There was a quiet moment then—one of those quiet moments when you could hear the crashing and caving in of your world and nothing at all, all at the same time.

"You too," she eventually whispered.

Her last words came out sad, and immediately, I wanted to take everything back. I didn't want our conversation to end like this. I didn't want anything to end, and I didn't want to hang up. I pulled the phone away and looked at its display. She hadn't hung up yet either. I brought the phone back to my ear, and as soon as I had, I heard it go dead on the other end.

I tried to say her name, but nothing came out. And for the first time, I noticed I hadn't been breathing. I sucked in a quick gasp of air and tried again.

"Julia."

There was no answer. I slowly lowered the phone to my lap and stared at its display for a minute before my hand found my face in frustration. I rubbed my eyes, let my head fall back and then eventually forward, and then I habitually ran my fingers through my hair.

They might be college-educated and have fancy cars, but I knew Jules. I knew everything about her. I loved everything about her. That had to count for something.

I took a deep breath in through my nose and slowly let it escape past my lips. Then, my eyes rushed to the phone in my hand again. She would call back. She was going to call back any second. And she would tell me that she hadn't meant what she had said, that she wanted me and that she loved me.

Another five minutes passed with my stare frozen on the phone's display before I rested my finger on the button that would speed-dial her number. But just before I was able to follow through, I heard my tones go off in the other room. And what was left of my heart sank to the deepest pit of my chest.

"Damn it," I shouted out loud as I squeezed the phone in the palm of my hand and thrust it hard against my thigh.

Then, I hurled my hands to my face again and rubbed my eyes before standing up, shoving the phone into my jeans pocket and hurrying toward the tones.

Chapter Fourteen

Schemes

"Will, there's this girl from my class that I want you to meet...," Jeff began, even before I could get my jacket off.

"Uh-uh," I said, shaking my head.

"Come on, man," he said. "She's got long, brown hair. She's getting her nursing degree. She's sort of athletic. And have I mentioned, she's beautiful?"

I was still shaking my head when I pulled a can out from his refrigerator.

"What does 'sort of athletic' mean?" I asked.

"I don't know," he said, sending wrinkles to his forehead.

He sounded irritated that I had asked.

"Like she can throw you your keys, but don't expect her to throw you a football," he said.

"Aah," I said, smiling.

I pushed down the tab on the can and took a swig before I noticed Jeff had grown quiet. My eyes quickly scanned the room and found him in the corner staring at me.

"Well?" he asked.

"Well, what?" I asked. "Aren't you supposed to be getting some kind of an associate's degree or something and not checking out all the girls instead?"

"Hey," he said, "my parents want the degree, and I'll do it, but if I've gotta do it, I'm not gonna do it with a blindfold on."

I laughed.

"Okay, okay," I said. "But if she's so beautiful, why are you trying to set her up with me? Why don't you like her?"

He paused.

"Because she likes you, you idiot," he said, in a way that sounded as if he was annoyed to have had to say it.

"Oh, come on," I said, swinging over the arm of a chair in the living room and falling into it. "What's not to like about you?"

"Well, that's what I said. But she saw you last weekend, and now, all of a sudden I'm her best friend—but not in a good way," he said.

I turned my face back toward him and caught him rolling his eyes.

"She's friends with me only because I know you," he said.

"Last weekend?" I asked, under my breath.

He nodded his head and moved into the kitchen.

"Yeah, she must have seen you playing golf or something," he said, now taking out two slices of bread from the bag and slapping a piece of cheese on one slice. "She works at the golf course."

"Hmm," I said, flipping on the television.

"Anyway, what do you say?" he asked.

He was still fumbling around the kitchen.

"About what?" I asked.

"I don't know," he said. "I'm not a matchmaker. I'm just the messenger. What do I tell her?"

I glanced back and shot him a puzzled look. He caught my eye and stuffed half of the sandwich into his mouth.

"Dude, you have a really big mouth," I said, chuckling. "Has anyone ever told you that?"

"I'll t-ell her you'll c-all her," he said, sounding slightly exasperated.

I could barely understand him with his mouth stuffed full of sandwich.

"Jeff, I'm not gonna call her," I said. "Anyway, don't you like her? You call her."

"She likes you, toolbag," he said, sending the loaf of bread—bag and all—my way.

The loaf hit the can in my hand and spewed liquid all over my tee shirt.

"What the hell, Jeff?" I said, sitting up and whisking the drink off of my shirt.

"Look, you want Julia back?" he asked.

I stopped brushing off the liquid and looked up at him again.

"Invite this girl to the New Year's Eve party," he went on. "It doesn't have to be anything serious. Julia comes. She sees the two of you together. She proceeds to do the whole jealous-girl thing. Then, above-mentioned girl sees that you're a toolbag because you're still in love with your ex-girlfriend. Then, I look like a saint—next to you, of course. Ergo, I win. You win. We both win."

"Wait," I said. "Julia's coming?"

I sat up and watched him walk back into the kitchen.

"Yeah, she's coming," he said, opening the refrigerator door again.

"How do you know that?" I asked.

My questions for Jeff, nine out of ten times, were laced with suspicion. I could never tell if he actually knew what he was talking about or if he was just flapping his jaws.

"What?" he asked.

"How do you know Julia's coming?" I asked again.

He popped his head up from behind the refrigerator door.

"Oh, I think Rachel mentioned it last week or something," he said and then buried his head back into the refrigerator again.

I sat back in the chair.

"You never ended up calling her, right?" he asked.

"What?" I asked.

"Julia," he said. "You never called her? She hasn't called you? You guys are still broken up?"

I half came out of my trance and nodded my head.

"Yeah, I...," I stuttered. "What if I call her, and she says the same thing? I don't know if I could hear that again. And I still don't know what I could say to change her mind. I don't know. She sounded sad, but she wants..."

I looked up and found Jeff giving me a blank stare.

"She'll call," I said, giving up and turning back toward the television's screen.

"Yeah," he said. "She'll call after you show up to the party with Jessica."

I shook my head and started flipping through the stations. I assumed Jessica was the name of the girl he couldn't stop talking about.

"I'm not doing it, Jeff," I said.

I watched from out of the corner of my eye Jeff sprawl his skinny, lanky body across the couch.

"So, Julia is going to be there," I mumbled to myself.

Jeff ignored me, but I expected him to. I methodically flipped through the channels looking for a game, knowing full well that the only place my mind could possibly be was on Jules and on how much I missed her.

Chapter Fifteen

The Girl

"Hi," I heard a soft voice come from behind me.

I turned to see a brunette with a wide smile staring back at me.

"Hi," I said, slowly reaching down to pick up another ball.

"I'm Jessica," she said, extending her hand before I could reach the ball.

I stood up straight and met her hand with mine.

"Will," I said and smiled.

She stepped back, and I went back to the bucket of golf balls. Then, I set one of the balls onto the tee, positioned my feet and shoulders, cocked back my driver and swung.

"Not bad," she said.

I turned to see the girl still behind me.

"Thanks," I said, looking back at her with a modest smile.

"I think I'm friends with your friend, Jeff," she said then. "He's in one of my classes."

I took a second look at her. Jeff. Of course. This was the brunette who worked at the golf course that he had been blabbering about. Despite Jeff's endless chatter, I had never called her.

"Oh, yeah?" I asked, acting as if Jeff hadn't told me everything about her already. "Jeff's a good guy."

I turned back around and grabbed another ball.

"Do you need any more balls?" she asked.

I looked at my bucket, filled to the brim with little, white balls. Then, I glanced back at her and smiled.

"No, this should do it," I said.

She didn't say anything as I set another ball onto the tee, repositioned my feet and shoulders again, arched my driver back and then swung hard.

"Okay, well, if you need anything, just let me know," she said.

I turned back toward her and caught her grinning with that same, wide smile back at me.

"Thanks," I said.

Then, I smiled, picked up another ball and set it onto the tee.

"Hey, I think I saw that girl who you were talking about the other day—your friend that works at the golf course," I said when Jeff reached the steps of the porch.

"Yeah?" he asked. "Isn't she cute? You ask her to the party?"

"Whoa, slow down," I said. "I said I saw her. I didn't say I asked her to marry me."

"Wait, you didn't ask her out?" he asked.

He waited a minute as he stared me down with his goofy expression that I was pretty sure meant he was displeased with me. I laughed inside my head.

"Man, come on," he said, letting his head fall back. "Just get it over with. If you wait too long, you might lose your chance, and she's not going to want to hang around me anymore. And then, you'll have no one to take to the New Year's Eve party, and you'll lose Julia forever?"

I looked at him sideways.

"You really think that would work?" I asked.

"What?" he asked.

"Don't you think Julia would just get pissed if I show up at a party that we went together to for years with another girl all of a sudden?" I asked. "I mean, we just…"

"Broke up," he said, finishing my sentence.

"It's just a break," I said.

"Dude," he said, "you guys aren't together. And yeah, it'll work. Girls always get jealous of other girls when they see them with their exes."

I was quiet for a second. Then, I cocked my head in his direction.

"You reading one of your sister's magazines again?" I asked.

"Dude, this is a proven fact," he said.

"Proven fact," I repeated.

He stared me down with his goofy glare again, while I took in a big breath of cool air.

"Jeff, it sounds like a stupid idea," I said, shaking my head and letting go of the breath.

"A stupid idea that just might work," he said.

I paused for a moment and thought about it. If I had had a better idea, I would have used it by now. She wanted a fancy-pants lawyer boyfriend right now. How was I supposed to change her mind about that?

I put my thoughts on hold and glanced back at Jeff.

"But what about the girl?" I asked.

"Who? Jessica?" he asked.

"Yeah, that would be a pretty shitty thing for me to do to her," I said. "I can't do that."

"Will, I'm not telling you to be mean to her," he said. "She wants a chance. You're giving her a chance. She knows there's a chance you might not like her."

"But I'm not really giving her a chance," I said.

"Sure you are," he said. "Who knows, you might even fall for her."

He was proudly nodding by the time he had finished his sentence, but then he stopped and quickly cocked his head.

"But you're not going to fall for her," he said. "You're going to break her heart, and she's going to come running to her el-friend-o, me-o," he said, pointing dramatically at himself.

I glared at him with narrowed eyes.

"You're an idiot, Jeff," I said.

"But I've got a point, though, right?" he asked.

I walked into the house, grabbed a glass from the cabinet and filled it with tap water. I could hear Jeff's big footsteps trailing behind me.

"Jessica really wants to go to this party, and for some God-only-knows reason wants to go to it with you, and you want Julia back," he said. "And what's better to get a girl back than to use jealousy? It's perfect. You have to admit, I've got a point."

He walked closer to me and squared up to my frame. I knew he was waiting for me to acknowledge him. I wasn't sure if I wanted to, but I also didn't have another plan.

"Well...," he said, drawing out his *l*s.

"Okay, okay, you might have a point," I admitted, reluctantly.

"Yes," he shouted, spinning around and pumping his fist into the air.

I watched him eventually roll onto the back of the couch and hurl himself over it. Then, I took a drink and swallowed hard. I already knew his plan was a bad idea, but I just couldn't stop wondering: *What if it worked? Just what if this crazy idiot's plan worked?*

I set the glass down onto the counter and felt my chest rise as I sucked in another deep breath. The truth was that I missed her; I missed her too much not to try anything to get her back.

Chapter Sixteen

New Year

"Hi," I said, as she cracked the door and poked her head out of the small opening.

"Hey," she said, pulling a small, furry creature back and then opening the door wider.

I watched her take the fur-ball-looking thing to another girl sitting on a couch and then disappear into a dark hallway. The girl on the couch took the dog and cradled it in her arms. The door was still open, so I stepped in and closed it again behind me.

"Let me just get my purse," I heard a voice call out from some room in the back of the small house. "I'll be right there."

The girl on the couch glanced up at me.

"Hi," I said, rocking back on my heels.

The girl smiled and returned her attention to the television and the dog, now pawing at her lap.

I squeezed my fists together in my pockets. I felt nervous. I hadn't taken a girl out for the first time since Jules when we were sixteen. I counted the years quickly in my head. It was only three, but it felt like an eternity. She wore black on our first, real date—jeans and a tight, black top. God, I still remembered everything about it.

I glanced at a clock on a wall in the kitchen. Its loud ticking drew my attention. Eight o'clock. I touched my fingers to my palms. They felt sweaty or something, and I realized that I wasn't nervous because of Jessica. I was nervous because I really had a bad, sick feeling about this whole, stupid idea. I should have never let Jeff talk me into it. Julia was going to hate it, and she was going to hate me for it.

"Okay, I'm ready," Jessica said, emerging from the back room. "You look nice."

I paused for a second in mid-thought and then awkwardly smiled.

"Thanks. So do you," I said.

She was wearing a short, red dress—snug in all the right places. She really did look nice. And if I weren't already obsessed with a fiery, little blonde, I realized then that I might actually really like Jessica.

"Ready?" she asked, grabbing a coat from a tall coat rack behind the door.

"Yeah," I said and smiled.

Then, I lowered my face closer to hers.

"Does your roommate want to come?" I asked.

I watched Jessica's eyes travel back to the girl on the couch. The girl met Jessica's gaze and shot her an impatient look.

My Butterfly

"I've tried," Jessica said. "She says it's too cold to go outside in a dress."

I paused and shrugged my shoulders.

"She's probably right," I said, cracking a wide grin.

Jessica giggled and then slid her arms into her coat and reached for the doorknob.

"Bye, Sam," Jessica called out over her shoulder.

The girl on the couch looked up for a second, flicked her wrist and then went back to the sitcom on the television and to scratching the dog between its ears.

I followed Jessica out the door and down the sidewalk, leading away from the little, brick house. When we reached the truck, I leaned around her to open her door. She smiled and then slid in. I was pretty sure I flashed her an awkward grin before gently closing the door behind her. I quickly shook it off and sucked in a cool breath of air, then made my way to the driver's side.

Once behind the wheel, I felt for the key in the ignition and then purred Lou to a start before I suddenly noticed Jules's photo on the dashboard. I stole a quick glance at Jessica. She was searching for something inside of her purse. So, without a second thought, I hastily snatched up the photo, slid it into the inside pocket of my jacket and glanced back over at Jessica. She was still searching inside her purse.

I took in a deep, nervous breath and then felt it quickly escape past my lips. Then, I forced the gear shift into first but kept my foot on the brake.

"You sure you want to go to this party?" I asked her.

Maybe there was still a way out of this mess. Maybe there was still a way for Julia not to see my dumb mistake.

Jessica blankly stared back at me.

"Isn't everyone going to be there?" she asked.

The look on her face told me that there was no getting out of this one. Jeff was right. She really did want to go to this party. And I guessed I couldn't blame her. It really was the best New Year's Eve party around here, and it was always only locals who were invited. And tonight, she would be a local.

"Okay," I said and then gently smiled.

I took my foot off the brake and hit the gas.

"To the party we go," I said, taking in another deep, uneasy breath.

It was only half past eight, but the rooms in the big, Victorian house were nearly full. If Kathy knew one thing, it was how to throw a party. Jules always used to say that Kathy was a sixteen-year-old going on thirty-six every time Kathy would invite us to one of her elaborate shindigs back in high school. The thought and the perfect, sarcastic way Jules always used to say it made me smile on the inside.

"Will, I'm so pleased you could make it," Kathy said, throwing her arms around me.

"Wouldn't miss it, Kath," I said.

Kathy pulled away and then quickly forced her attention to Jessica.

"And who's this?" Kathy asked in a pleasant voice.

"Oh, sorry," I said. "This is Jessica. Jessica, this is Kathy. And this is Kathy's parents' house," I then said to Jessica.

"Hi," Kathy said, snatching up Jessica's hand with both of hers. "I'm so glad you could make it."

"The house is beautiful," Jessica said, with a timid smile.

"Oh, thanks," Kathy said. "It's been in the family for years. Are you from around here?"

"Chester," Jessica said.

Kathy immediately cocked her head and put on a playful smirk.

"Well, normally, we don't entertain Chester Eagles, but we'll make an exception tonight," Kathy said, as her smile grew warm again.

Jessica laughed.

"Thanks," Jessica said.

"Well, how do you two know each other then?" Kathy asked.

"I…we…," I stuttered but didn't finish.

I couldn't remember how I was supposed to know her. Was I supposed to know her from the golf course or through Jeff or somewhere else?

"I'm getting my associate's degree at West Central," Jessica said, saving me from my stumbling tongue. "Jeff is in one of my classes. And I saw him talking to Will one day…"

Jessica stopped and lowered her eyes, as if she had said too much.

"I see," Kathy said, giving Jessica another warm smile. "Well, let me take your coats."

Kathy put a hand on my shoulder and leaned dramatically to my side.

"Julia's coming tonight," I heard Kathy whisper near my ear.

I met her eyes. They were warning me, I knew. My lips immediately parted, and I felt my chest quickly rise and then fall. Then, I felt Jessica's hand on my arm, and my eyes dropped to the spot on my bicep that Jessica was touching.

"You want to go inside?" Jessica asked me after she had given her coat to Kathy.

I caught Jessica's hopeful gaze. It was making a direct path from the foyer where we were standing to the warmly lit room in front of us. Then, I stumbled onto Kathy's stare again. It was still burning a stern warning straight through my forehead.

"Uh, yeah," I said, taking a step forward. "Uh, thanks, Kathy."

"Make yourself at home," Kathy said in a way that sounded to me more like: *Make your own bed. You're the one who has to lie in it.*

Jessica and I made our way to the back of the house. She followed my every move, but then again, she knew Jeff and a couple of Jeff's friends from school, of which, only one had arrived. Everyone else was a new face.

"Do you want something to drink?" I asked her.

"Sure," she said, nodding her head. "I'll just take whatever you're drinking."

"Easy enough," I said. "I'll be right back."

I ventured back toward the kitchen but took the long way to get there. If Julia were there, I could find her and explain everything before she could have a chance to get the wrong idea. I searched in between and around the swaying heads. There was no sign of her, but there was, on the other hand, an awkward, lanky kid across the room. I made my way over to him.

"Hey," I said, coming up behind Jeff and grabbing his arm. "Have you seen Julia?"

"Hey, toolbag," he said, putting out his hand.

He started doing the stupid handshake he made up for us in the fourth grade. I humored him and forced my hand through the motions.

"Where's Jessica?" he asked me, ignoring my question.

"She's in the living room," I said. "Is Julia here yet?"

"Haven't seen her," he said, pushing past me and making his way toward the back of the house.

I took another glance around the room before ambling back toward the kitchen.

I got two drinks and then ventured back to the living room, where Jeff was already propped up beside Jessica, flapping his jaw. I saw him drawing the outline of a mountain with his hand, and I knew right away he was telling her the story of when he climbed some mountain in Colorado two summers ago. Jessica had that same look every girl had when Jeff was talking to her. I really hoped she wanted to come to this party as bad as Jeff said she had. If not, I really was going to have at least two girls hating me by the end of the night.

I walked over to the two of them and handed Jessica her drink.

She looked up at me, smiled and took the glass.

"Here," she said, "sit down. Jeff is telling me about his summer at Estes Park."

Her hand patted a small space on the couch beside her.

I stared for a couple of seconds at the spot where her hand had just been. Then, I looked up and caught Jeff's bugged-out eyes. I was pretty sure he was silently telling me to just do something, so that he could get on with his story. So, after a few more seconds, I reluctantly fell into the couch next to her.

"Estes Park, huh?" I asked.

"Yeah, Will hates this story," Jeff nonchalantly said and then went back to flapping his jaw.

Jessica knowingly glanced at me and smiled.

I laughed once and took a drink from my cup. I was nervous, but I played it off by sneering at Jeff. He paused for a second but then continued.

I took another drink from my cup. I didn't know if it were the sound of Jeff's unending story or the thought that Julia could come waltzing into the room at any moment that was making me claustrophobic. Someone had to go.

I motioned for Jessica to trade me my cup for her glass. She obliged without much nudging.

"Hey, Jeff, I think Jessica needs another drink," I said. "Can we put your story on hold for a minute?"

Jeff stopped talking just long enough to eye Jessica's cup.

"I got it," he said, snatching the cup from Jessica's hand and shooting up."

"No, it's okay…," she started and then stopped when she caught a glimpse of my shaking head. "Okay, thanks," she said instead and smiled.

"I'll be right back," he said. "Save my seat."

I watched as Jeff disappeared behind a group of people hovering around the doorway. Then, I looked back at Jessica to find her questioning stare.

"He likes getting girls drinks, believe me," I said, thinking of a way to move to a spot on the armrest of the couch without making it too awkward. "And he's a little wound for sound—his own, that is."

I glanced at the armrest and then back at her. I felt the anxious smile still glued to my lips. I wondered if she could see it too.

"Besides, I don't know about you, but I needed to get out of the Colorado wilderness for a second," I said.

Jessica laughed and then rested her hand on mine. I flinched slightly, as my eyes darted to her hand.

"You're my hero," she said, playfully tossing her long, brown hair behind her shoulder.

My Butterfly

Her hand was soft and kind, but it wasn't Jules's hand. *What the hell was I doing?*

I awkwardly smiled. I wanted to pull my hand back, but I couldn't. I had already brought her to this party as a decoy for the girl I really wanted to bring; I had subjected her to Jeff's loathsome hiking story; and if I took my hand back now, I would surely be the jerk I was turning out to be after all. I just couldn't bring myself to embarrass her.

"Jeff said that you are getting your paramedic's license and that you want to be a firefighter," I heard her say, as if her voice were coming from some distant world.

My eyes were temporarily locked on our hands.

"Uh, yeah, I am," I managed to get out, as I forced my gaze instead to her face. "I'm a, it's a…"

"My uncle is a firefighter," she said, saving me again from my stumbling tongue. "It's a tough job, but it's really honorable."

She slid her fingers around mine as she spoke, and suddenly, the room's temperature rose another ten degrees—as if it weren't already as hot as hell in the small room. I habitually pulled at the collar of my shirt.

"I mean, it's super dangerous," she continued. "My uncle has been trapped in a burning building and…"

She kept talking as I searched the room for Jeff. *What was taking him so long?* Now, all of a sudden, his stupid mountain story didn't sound all that bad. At least, it had distracted Jessica. And damn it, this dumb plan of his would surely be the end of me if Julia was to walk…

My thoughts stopped then. And my eyes came to rest on a thin blonde in a short, black dress, standing in the doorway. I met the blonde's fiery, green eyes as the words from the girl beside me quickly turned to mush before they reached my ears. Then, the blonde softly smiled and bit her bottom lip. She always did that when she was nervous.

God, she's beautiful.

I watched Jules take a step and then stop. Then, all of a sudden, her face went blank, and her eyes fell fast to the hardwood floor. I held my gaze on her, until her own eyes returned to mine seconds later. But she wasn't smiling anymore. In fact, now, her green eyes had turned sad. My heart sank as I remembered Jessica's hand still wrapped up in mine. I tried to pull my hand back, but it was numb. I couldn't move. I could hardly breathe.

God, what have I done?

I looked back up at Jules, and for a second, it looked as if she were going to run. *No, don't run. Yes. Run. Let's both run. Let's get out of here together.*

Instead, she took a step toward us, and then another, until she was standing in front of Jessica and me.

"Hey," Jules said, softly. "How have you been?"

I looked up at her, into her eyes. I felt as if I were dreaming. I wished I were dreaming. I expected her to be here. I wanted her to be here, but now, everything just felt wrong. It was all wrong.

"I've been good," I said, slowly nodding my head.

They were the only words I had, but it wasn't completely a lie. I felt good, compared to how I was going to feel after she slapped me across my face and told me that she never wanted to see me again. And how could I blame her? Yeah, we weren't together. But what did that really mean for two people who weren't meant to be apart?

"That's great," she said.

There was a smile on her face, but it wasn't a good one. I had seen that smile before. It wasn't one of my favorites.

My Butterfly

"So, did you go to Will's high school?" Jessica suddenly interjected.

Then, it all hit me like a massive wave to the chest. Sometime in the last few minutes, Jessica had stopped telling me about her uncle, the firefighter; Julia had found me in the living room, sitting too close to Jessica; and my hand had become even more intertwined with the brunette's.

My eyes fell onto Jessica's face for the first time since Julia had entered the room. Her focus was on Julia, and I followed her eyes back to the blonde.

Please, Julia, keep it short. Make this end. Please make this end quickly.

"Yes," Julia finally said. "I did. I went to New Milford."

I let out a deep sigh. *Thank you, Jules.*

"Julia," a voice suddenly called out from behind her.

It was Rachel. She had appeared seemingly out of nowhere, out from the swaying heads and idle bodies in the other room.

"Chris wants to ask you something about track and find out how outstandingly well you're doing," Rachel said in a loud, commanding voice.

She pulled on Julia's arm and gave me an *if-we-weren't-in-public, I'd-kill-you* look. Rachel was known for those, but I wasn't really known to get them. My heart sank further.

Julia willingly complied and allowed Rachel to guide her away from me.

"It was nice to meet you," Julia said, turning back in Jessica's direction.

Her words came out soft and gentle, and they weren't the words I was expecting.

At the same time, Jeff returned from wherever he had been and proceeded to distract Jessica again. My eyes followed Julia until she reached the doorway and shot a quick glance back at me.

"Thank you," I mimed with my lips because somehow I knew this could have gone even worse than it had.

She gave me a half-smile, and I felt the corner of my mouth edge up my face just a little, in a purely instinctive reaction to her smile because, in reality, I knew that I was as good as dead. There was no way that Jeff's plan ever had a snowball's chance in hell of working. Desperation will drive you to do things you know will never make you whole again and even to lose the very thing you're desperate for. And as if I had to live it first, I knew that now—a little too late.

I watched Julia's face turn until I couldn't see her pretty eyes anymore, and then her black silhouette faded away into the crowd. My heart shattered right then and there. I tried to stand, but I still couldn't feel my limbs.

"Will!"

My face instinctively turned toward Jeff.

"Dude, you all right?" he asked.

I blankly stared at him.

"I just said your name three times," he said.

"What?" I asked.

I looked at him and then glanced at Jessica. Both of their expressions made me feel uncomfortable. They looked worried.

"I just, um," I stuttered. "I'm going to get some more to drink."

I looked into the glass in my hand. I saw that it was full, and I remembered then that it was Jessica's. But I didn't bother changing my excuse for leaving. I simply took a quick glance at each of them, forced a smile and then pushed myself up from the couch and made a beeline for the room that Julia had just disappeared into.

But no sooner had I made it through the doorway, I ran straight into a brick wall. It was Rachel, and her pointy, narrow finger was digging into the muscles in my chest.

"Will, I don't know what messed-up act you're trying to play tonight, but you need to stay away from her," she said, in her very serious tone. "She doesn't want to talk to you."

She dropped her finger from my chest, sighed and then placed a hand on each of her temples.

"Seriously, Will," she said. "Who is that girl?"

"It's just a girl Jeff goes to school with," I said. "Really, Rachel, it's nothing. It's not what it looked like."

"Really, Will?" she asked.

Her voice sounded exhausted.

"Because what it looked like to me was that you were holding hands with a girl you just met, knowing that the love of your life would see it."

I grabbed the back of a chair pushed up against the wall as my knees slightly buckled under my weight. Rachel's eyes fell to my white knuckles gripping the chair and then narrowed back on my eyes, but this time, her expression seemed a little softer.

"What are you doing, Will?" she asked. "I know you, and I know you love her."

"Rachel, I just...," I said and then stopped and lowered my head. "I mean, this whole thing was her idea. She wanted the break. I just don't understand."

I lifted my eyes to Rachel's again, as she sucked in a big breath of air and let out a sigh.

"You just don't know everything about her like you think you do, and you might have just screwed this up for yourself, Will Stephens," she said, her eyes turning stern again. "You've just got to give her some space now."

She turned then, walked to the corner of the room, grabbed Julia's arm and escorted her to the door. I watched Rachel pull a coat off the coat rack and hand it to Julia before pulling one off for herself. Julia's eyes were sad. I could tell that much from where I stood, even though she never looked up at me. My heart stabbed at the inside walls of my chest. It took everything in me not to run after her, but I knew Rachel was right, and even if she weren't, there was no way I was getting past her and to Julia—not tonight anyway. Instead, I watched Julia walk through the door—and possibly out of my life forever.

An anxious breath quickly escaped past my lips as the hard, wooden door closed behind her and the room grew dark around me.

I wasn't sure how long I had been standing there when, seemingly by instinct, I charged toward the door. I swung it open, and a blast of cold air engulfed my body. I knew I should have felt it more than I had, but a part of me was still numb. I hastily scanned the street. The night was black, so the taillights of her jeep pulling away were easy to see.

I took a couple of steps, and I was off the porch and on the sidewalk. I reached for my keys in my pocket but then stopped. I couldn't chase after her. I couldn't leave Jessica in there. And chasing after Jules ultimately wouldn't get us anywhere tonight anyway. I wouldn't want to see me either. My heart stung my chest again, and at the same time, a chill ran up my spine, reminding me that I wasn't invincible. I shoved my hands into my pockets and leaned up against a porch beam. Then, I forced my head back against the beam's wood, as I took a deep breath, slowly let it out and then watched the fog it made disappear into the night.

After some time, I glanced at my watch. It was midnight, a new year. A set of headlights on the street in front of me caught my attention. I stood up and locked my eyes onto them. They slowed, stopped at the sign and then continued on.

I let out a sigh, as my eyes fell to the ground again and my hand found my forehead in frustration. She wasn't coming back. She was gone, and it was all my fault.

It was a little after one in the morning, and I was following Jessica up the walk and to her doorstep.

When she reached her door, she stopped and faced me. I, meanwhile, took in a deep breath of air through my nose. It was even colder than it had been earlier, and it stung my throat and lungs.

"You know, you disappeared before midnight, and I didn't get a New Year's kiss," she said, softly smiling.

I looked up from the ground, found her eyes and forced an awkward smile.

"Jessica," I said and then stopped.

Her eyes were planted on mine, and I knew she was waiting for me to say something else, but I just didn't know how to say what I had to say. I repositioned my feet in the spot where I was standing, shoved my bare hands into my warm pockets and lowered my eyes to the walk again.

"I'm, uh, not ready to do this yet," I eventually managed to get out.

I didn't hear anything, and my eyes soon rose to meet hers. She looked as if she had just been hurt, and she had been, and it was my fault.

"I thought that maybe I was," I lied.

Her big, brown eyes continued to stare into mine. Then, eventually, she nodded her head, and it seemed as if she tried to smile.

"Okay," she said so softly that I could barely hear her.

She stood there for a little while longer, then turned toward the door, placed her hand on the doorknob and paused. I waited for her to turn around, but she didn't. Instead, she turned the knob and slid past the door's frame and into the warm house. I watched as the door closed gently behind her, until all I could see was a wreath hanging from a nail at the top of the door. I quickly read the inscription underneath the wreath's big, red bow: *'Tis the season to be merry*.

I let out a deep sigh and then followed with my eyes the path my breath made escaping back into the cold air.

New Year's resolution—find a way to make things right again.

Chapter Seventeen

Gone

"So, how'd it go the other night?" Jeff asked as he sauntered into the room, one big foot after the other.

"What?" I asked.

I was finishing up a paramedic class assignment and would rather not hear Jeff's voice over it, but I knew we couldn't always get what we wanted.

"The party," he said.

I stared at the words on the page in front of me for a second longer before I looked up at him.

"You really have no idea?" I asked.

He was giving me a puzzled look.

"No, Jessica seemed kind of down at school," he said. "I figured she found out you were still in love with Julia."

I impatiently looked up at him, then leaned back in my chair and rubbed my eyes with my palms.

"Julia saw Jessica holding my hand, and she left the party early with Rachel," I said. "When I got up to get a drink that last time, I was going to talk to her, but Rachel stopped me. They left right after that."

"You were holding hands with Jessica?" he asked. "Dude, you weren't supposed to hold her hand."

"I know that," I said. "She just grabbed it, and then all of a sudden, Julia was there in the doorway, and I was screwed."

"She grabbed your hand?" he asked.

He had a disgusted look on his face.

I audibly sighed.

"Julia left, Jeff," I said.

"Well, has she called?" he asked.

I flashed him another impatient look.

"No, idiot, it turns out holding another girl's hand just makes the ex-girlfriend leave you quicker the second time," I said. "How did I let you talk me into that?"

"Well, they're supposed to call. They get jealous, and then they call," he said.

"Jeff, she's not going to call," I said. "She's not jealous. She's gotta think that I'm the biggest jerk in the world right now."

He planted his feet in front of me and leaned up against a tall stool.

"Oh," he said.

His face turned a little more sympathetic.

"Well, that doesn't sound all bad," he said. "It means she cares that you were holding Jessica's hand."

My Butterfly

He had a point—almost.

"But she never called," I said. "Jeff, I told her that I wanted to marry her, and then a month later, I'm sitting on a couch holding some girl's hand when she shows up in the doorway."

"I just don't get it," he said, shaking his head. "It always works in the movies."

"In the movies?" I exclaimed, letting out a frustrated groan, as I threw my head back and rubbed my eyes again.

"I'm doomed," I said out loud.

"Dude, it can't be that bad," he said.

"No, I really screwed this up," I said. "Rachel made that pretty clear."

I watched Jeff's eyes lower to the floor.

"She said something though," I said, suddenly remembering back.

Jeff's eyes traveled up toward mine again.

"Who? Julia?" he asked.

"No," I said. "Rachel. She said that I don't know Jules as well as I think I do or something like that."

Jeff's eyebrows furrowed together.

"Well, of course you don't," he said. "She's a girl. They think and feel things on a daily basis that we'll never think or feel in a lifetime."

A crooked smile shot to my lips.

"I guess you're right, buddy," I said.

Jeff paused for a second then before he opened his mouth again.

"So, you gonna call Jessica then?" he asked, hesitantly.

He was wearing two, sad eyes now.

"No, I told her I wasn't ready for a relationship," I said.

He seemed as if he wanted to smile but stymied it.

"I'm sorry, buddy," he said.

My eyes fell back onto the book in front of me.

"Actually, I was thinking about giving Julia a call in a little while," I said.

My eyes happened to catch Jeff's face in midsentence. His features had positioned themselves in a way that just looked strange to me.

"What?" I asked.

"Do you think that's such a good idea?" he asked.

"And I suppose you have another great plan," I said.

"No, no more plans," he promised. "I'm just...I'm not trying to suggest anything, but have you ever thought that maybe the two of you just aren't meant for each other?"

A scowl replaced my puzzled look.

"Weren't you the one who said, 'Take Jessica to the party. Julia will be there. She'll see the two of you. She'll get jealous, and then she'll come running back to you?' Wasn't that you?" I exclaimed.

He blankly stared at me.

"Hey, you admitted it was worth a shot," he said.

"I know, but now you're telling me to give up on her?" I asked.

The volume of my voice was rising.

"Listen," he said, "New Year's Eve was my fault. I'm man enough to admit it. In all honesty, I really thought it would work. I thought it would work for both of us. Instead, Julia hates you, and judging by her somber mood today, Jessica loves you even more."

He let out a big sigh.

"I'm sorry, man," he said. "It was a bad idea."

I cradled my face in my hands and let out a frustrated grunt.

"It's fine," I eventually said. "I knew it wouldn't work, but I did it anyway. Damn it! What do I do now?"

I directed my question not to Jeff but to myself, though I heard Jeff start to stutter.

"Um, I mean, I don't always have the best ideas or say the right things," he said.

My eyes, glazed over in sarcasm, found his.

"But I really am just looking out for you, buddy," he continued. "And no one would be happier than me to see you and Julia together—and Jessica finally wise up and fall for me, of course."

He stopped and cleared his throat.

"But have you ever thought that maybe Julia just isn't coming back?" he asked.

His voice had grown sheepish.

"I mean, they go off into that big, college world, and they don't come back, Will," he said. "They don't ever come back. I mean, name someone who's come back."

I paused and thought for a second, while names started scrolling through my mind. Most of the names were of people who had never "left" New Milford. The rest were names of people who had "left" and who had never come…

I stopped in mid-thought.

"Jeff, it's Julia," I said.

The words were gentle but deliberate.

Jeff paused and set his eyes on me again.

"Will, it could be Juliet, but the fact is, most times, they don't come back, and you know it," he said.

I sat back in my chair, as a dull pain began stabbing at the inside of my chest near my heart. Jeff kept talking, but I couldn't make out what he was saying. I was starting to feel sick.

"Will," I thought I heard him say.

"You all right, buddy?" he asked.

My eyes slowly turned up toward him. I must have had an uneasy look planted on my face or something because he was backing away from me and into the stair railing. I could always count on Jeff to run from trouble, even if it meant leaving me in it.

"Yeah, I'm fine," I said, finally.

Then, I was quiet. Jeff found the stool again in the meantime and slid back onto it. Then, we sat there, wallowing in our own thoughts for a reflective minute.

"I probably should have told you that you were never going to win Jessica that way either," I eventually confessed.

Jeff's eyes fell to the floor, and he shook his head.

"You always get the good ones," he said, starting to crack a smile.

He looked back up at me and then raised the glass of water he had been holding in his hand.

"Here's to moving on," he said.

I stared at him for a second, then picked up the bottle of soda that sat in front of me and brought it to his glass.

"To moving," I said, with a heavy half-smile.

Chapter Eighteen

The Call

I cradled my phone in the palm of my hand. There was only one light on—a small lamp. Otherwise, the room was dark. Lately, the station seemed to be the only place where I could concentrate—and maybe that was because I had no memory of Jules being there.

I used my finger to scroll through the contacts in my phone. Her number was still on speed dial—number *two*—only because *one* was already assigned to voicemail. But tonight, I skipped the speed dial. Scrolling through the contacts gave me more time to think—what I was going to say and how I was going to say it.

If time were what she needed, like Rachel had said, I had given her some time. She deserved that. And despite what I had let Jeff believe, I had no intentions of moving on. What I did plan to do, however, was move forward—do something, anything to get Jules back.

I finally found her name but wasn't any closer to figuring out what I was going to say. I stared at the phone's screen for five, solid minutes, then I closed my eyes and pressed the button that sent the phone dialing her number. A deep breath in and a slow, uneasy exhale followed.

I heard the first ring, and it sent my heart into overdrive. I anxiously waited for the second ring, and then it came just as the first had—unexpected but deliberate. My heart continued to race. But, oddly, the sound of the rings, one after the other, was comforting somehow—that was until the fourth ring. On the fourth ring, I started to panic. And by the fifth ring, the sound of the solid tone was shrilling and unsettling. By that time, I knew that I wasn't going to have the chance to talk to her. I took another deep breath and waited for her voicemail to pick up. Then suddenly, the ringing stopped, and a familiar, robotic voice poured through my phone's speakers.

"The caller you are trying to reach does not have a voicemail box set up yet. Please try again. Goodbye."

And with that, the other end of the line went silent.

I sat there on the edge of the cot, phone again cradled in my hand and my eyes locked on the phone's screen. I waited there for minutes, willing the screen to glow and for her name to appear in bold letters across it. But when the minutes passed in silence, I couldn't bear to hear the deafening sound of the quiet anymore. I lowered my head and cradled my face in my hands. I wasn't sad. It felt more like anger, but it wasn't anger either. It was like nothing. I felt numb. At least with sadness, I could mope

My Butterfly

away my sorrows. But with this strange pain, it was as if there was nothing I could do to make it go away.

I took another deep breath in and tried to collect myself. Then, I refocused my attention onto my phone, and it suddenly came to me: I could text her.

I started typing, but I only got to *"Jules, I need to"* when a sound at the doorway made me look up.

"Why are you still here?" asked a tall, shadowy man.

The man was the station's chief. He wore a New Milford Fire Department tee shirt—just like the one I was wearing—but he also had short, wavy, graying hair and a mustache. In fact, he kind of reminded me of Clark Gable from that long movie Jules always loved to watch.

"I, uh, was just working on some homework," I said.

He eyed the phone in my hand.

"In the dark?" he asked.

I glanced over at the small table next to the cot with the lamp and an opened book on it.

"I can't concentrate with too much light," I said.

He shot me a suspicious look, held it on me for a few seconds, then started to leave but stopped.

"Something on your mind, son?" he asked, turning back toward me.

I didn't say anything. I wasn't really in the mood to talk.

"Aah," he said. "It's a girl, isn't it?"

My eyes turned up.

"Why do you say that?" I asked.

"Because that's the only reason a young man, such as yourself, ever sits in this station in the dark with a frown that wide on his face," he said.

I tried to laugh.

"I'm right, though," he said, dragging a fold-up chair to the cot.

I smiled, but it felt unnatural.

"What did you do?" he asked.

I flashed him a puzzled look.

"Come on," he said. "I also know you did something stupid. I forgot to mention that every young man, such as yourself, that comes into my station with a frown that big on his face has also done something stupid to a girl."

I dropped my head and slowly shook it back and forth.

"I let her go," I mumbled.

My eyes locked onto the phone in my hand again.

"You let her go?" he asked.

"Yeah, I should have said something when she said it wasn't working, and I should have followed her that night on New Year's," I said.

After a couple of moments, my eyes turned up from the phone, and I realized he didn't have a clue as to what I was talking about.

"I let her go," I repeated.

"I see," he said, nodding his head.

"We're talking about Julia, aren't we?" he asked.

I nodded my head.

I watched his eyes travel to the lunch bag he had been holding in his hands. He turned it over a couple of times and then looked up.

"Sometimes, you just have to let go," he said. "She'll come back, when she's ready."

I sat there for a second in silence. Then, he reached over, patted me on the shoulder and chuckled.

"Happiness is like a butterfly," he said. "The more you chase it, the more it will elude you. But if you turn your attention to other things, it will come and sit softly on your shoulder."

By the time he had finished, my eyebrows were in a heap at the center of my forehead.

"It's Thoreau," he said, chuckling some more. "Didn't you ever learn that in school?"

I laughed.

"Can't say I did, sir," I admitted.

A moment passed, and my smile started to fade.

"Does that really work—the whole letting go and coming back thing?" I asked.

His eyes fell to the tiles on the floor before they found my stare again.

"Some of us spend our entire lives hoping it does," he said. "And for some of us lucky ones, it does. But, boy, I have a good feeling that for you, it'll work. Just be patient."

I smiled and lowered my head again as he got up and scooted the chair back to its place against the wall.

"And don't do anything stupid in the meantime," he said over his shoulder as he made his way to the door again.

"No," I said, shaking my head. "I'll try not to, sir."

"Oh, and by the way," he said, stopping at the doorway, "didn't you just get some big, fancy job on the department in St. Louis?"

I smiled.

"Yes, sir," I replied.

"That's no small feat," he said, shaking his head. "But if you'd ask me, I'd say they got the better deal. You're a damn good firefighter, Stephens."

My eyes traveled to the floor.

"Thanks, sir," I said.

"And Will," he said.

I looked up again.

"Turn some lights on. You're going to end up lookin' like me by the time you're thirty," he said, smiling and tugging on his glasses.

"Yes, sir," I said.

My stare remained on the dark doorway for a few seconds, even after the chief had disappeared through it. Then, eventually, I lowered my eyes to my phone's screen again, and I retraced the letters I had formed just minutes ago. Slowly then, I watched each one disappear as I backspaced the message out of the phone and repeated the chief's words in my head: *Just be patient.*

Chapter Nineteen
The Band

"Hey, so Will, I heard you can sing?" I heard a voice call out.

I looked up and saw Matt charging toward me.

"Where'd you hear that?" I asked.

"Through the grapevine, I guess," he said, panting and stopping in front of me.

"Geez, Matt, you ran five steps," I said, starting to laugh.

"I know," he casually said. "I didn't warm up first."

I smiled at him and went back to working on the hose.

"So, this band canceled at this bar my friend manages in The Loop," he continued. "And he can't get anybody last minute, so I said maybe we could do it."

I stopped and looked up at him again from where I was kneeling.

"We?" I asked.

"Yeah, Daniel plays the drums; Chris plays the bass; and I play the keys," he said. "We get together every once in a while, but our singer's always been a floater. None of us can sing."

He laughed and handed me a screwdriver. I cautiously took it, as I judged his face.

"Listen, I know you're new to the station and St. Louis and all, so if you don't want to, that's okay too," he added. "We're getting together to run through some songs tomorrow night at eight at my house. If you're there, great. If not, I've gotta a guy who I know will do it."

I watched him cup his hand around his mouth.

"He's just, you know, a filler—not the best songbird in the cage," he said.

He dropped his hand then and picked up a wrench.

"Just think about it, and let me know," he said, ambling back toward the door again.

"I've heard you've got some talent, Will," he called out over his shoulder. "You'll be doing us a big favor, and who knows, maybe you'll have some fun."

He smiled a wide grin and then disappeared into the breakroom.

I kept my eyes on the breakroom door, just in case he reappeared again to tell me that he was pulling my leg or something. Seconds drew on, though, and he never returned.

"Where'd he hear that?" I whispered to myself, as I went back to screwing on the nozzle.

My Butterfly

It was Friday night, and I couldn't stop thinking about her. I had already found her number ten times in my contacts only to set the phone down onto the TV dinner table and stare at it for another twenty minutes.

I finally snapped out of my latest trance and spotted the remote balancing on the edge of the couch. I quickly snatched it up and powered the television to life.

The next thing I knew, I was flipping through each channel, only stopping briefly on each one and then flipping to the next. And within seconds, I was already back to the beginning of the order. I let out a sigh and then hit the power button on the remote, causing the screen to go black again.

What was she doing now?

I stared at the black screen for a couple of minutes, lost in my thought, until my eyes eventually landed on my phone again. Something told me not to reach for it, but my hand went for it anyway. And just before I could touch it, its display lit up.

My heart instantly started a fast, rhythmic pounding against the walls of my chest, as I quickly snatched up the phone and peered into its glowing screen. Next, I forced my eyes into a frantic search for the sender of the message, until they eventually stumbled upon a name and stopped cold.

It wasn't her.

I let out an exhausted and heavy sigh. Then, I took a second before picking my heart up off of the floor and following over the words in the message: *You comin', buddy?*

I took a deep breath in and then forced my eyes shut and let out a frustrated groan. If I didn't know better, I'd swear I was going crazy in this little apartment.

When I opened my eyes again, my guitar was staring at me from the corner of the room. I cocked my head then and narrowed my eyes, focusing all of my attention on the six-string.

Moments passed. Then, I glanced up at the clock on the wall.

"What the hell," I said out loud, before standing up and shoving my phone into my jeans pocket.

I made my way over to the corner and snatched up the guitar. Then, I grabbed my coat from a chair and my keys from the kitchen counter. And within seconds, I was out the door and heading for Matt's.

*

"Will, you made it," Matt cheerfully shouted, as he swung open his door. "We've been waiting for you."

"Waiting?" I asked.

I watched his eyes fall to the guitar in my hands.

"You can play too? Great," he said.

He pulled me inside by my coat's sleeve.

"Guys, look who's here," Matt shouted into the garage.

I shyly entered the doorway and stood stiffly inside its frame.

"Will," Chris yelled out first.

"Hey, does this mean we don't have to call Jim?" Daniel asked no one in particular.

Chris burst into laughter.

"Okay, okay, let's get going," Matt said, raising his voice over Chris's laughter.

Then, Matt shuffled over to a keyboard and took his place behind it.

"Will, we play a lot of covers—all sorts of stuff," Matt said. "Do you know 'Brown Eyed Girl'?"

"Yeah, the girls love it," Chris shouted.

I lowered my head and smiled.

"Yeah," I said, nodding my head. "I do."

"Okay, we'll start with that, and if you got any, you let us know," he said to me.

I nodded my head again, then looked around.

"Is that where I go?" I asked seconds later, eyeing the microphone in its stand.

Matt and Chris laughed.

"That would be where you go," Matt said.

I awkwardly grinned and took my place behind the stand. My guitar was now swung across my body, sheltering me, as I played with its strings and tuning pegs.

"All right, here we go," Matt said.

The melody filled the room a short count later. I was a little nervous, but if I knew a song, I knew this one—thanks to Jules.

The part where I was supposed to come in came quickly, and my first words came out timid, but it didn't take long for it to feel as if she were the only one in the room again.

After several minutes, I sang the last words of the song and took a step back from the mic, still strumming my guitar. Then, eventually, the music stopped and the garage was silent again. I turned around and faced the guys behind me. I noticed first the goofy grin on Daniel's face.

"We've finally got a band," Daniel yelled.

A wide, toothy smile soon lit up Chris's and Matt's faces as well. And only then did I feel a grin start to edge up my face too. I quickly lowered my eyes and tried to calm my excited breaths. It was as if there were some kind of weird adrenaline rushing through my veins all of a sudden; it was strange. But at the same time, I tried to tell myself that it wasn't strange in a fun way because that would mean that she had been right all along.

"Oh, but Will," Chris said, interrupting my thoughts.

I looked up at him.

"You do know that it's brown-eyed girl, not green-eyed girl, right?" he asked.

I froze, as if I had been caught naked or something, then chuckled to myself.

"Yeah, sorry," I said, lowering my eyes again and shaking my head.

"Okay," Matt said. "It doesn't matter what he sings. They'll love it anyway. Let's just keep it going."

When I looked back up, Chris was staring at me, and he had a mischievous look glued to his face. I furrowed my eyebrows at him, then brushed off his look and returned my attention to Matt, as he rattled off a list of songs.

We played through the rest of the songs. They were mostly classics and country—oddly enough, the songs I used to sing to Julia—so I knew them well. Every so often, though, my heart would stab at my chest when a particular lyric sent me back to a summer afternoon with her in my arms. But then, not too long after, a slight smile would find my face when I realized that I couldn't escape her no matter what I did. It was like her to always find a way to win. At least now, however, I would be a little distracted. Here, the music forced me on to the next moment without too much thought. And really, these guys weren't bad.

"So, what do we call ourselves?" Chris asked, when the music stopped for the last time.

"I thought we had a name," Daniel said.

My Butterfly

The men froze—Daniel where he sat and Chris and Matt where they stood. I watched each one's face twist and turn into a puzzled mess.

"What was it?" Matt asked, finally.

A moment of silence passed again.

"Whatever it was, it mustn't have been that good," Chris said. "Let's come up with a new one. I feel like we're a real band now."

"What about WDCM?" Daniel asked.

"What?" Matt asked. "What's that supposed to mean?"

"It's our initials all squished together," Daniel explained.

"Vetoed," Chris yelled out. "What about Matt's Garage?"

"Matt's Garage?" Daniel sarcastically asked and then snickered. "Yeah, I can see us famous someday, 'Uh, hi, we're Matt's Living Room, uh, I mean, Matt's Bathroom. No, I mean, Matt's Garage. Can you guess where we started?'"

I laughed and so did Matt.

"This guy," Chris said, pointing at Daniel, "has already got us famous now. Daniel, you'll be lucky if Will remembers to introduce you tomorrow night."

Daniel hit the snare and then the cymbal and a ba-DUM ching echoed through the garage.

All three of them laughed.

"What about District 9?" I asked, shyly.

Their eyes slowly moseyed toward my corner and then rested on me for a second.

"You know, I like that," Matt said first.

"Yeah," Chris said, nodding his head. "We're firefighters first."

Daniel started a drumroll. It got louder as it continued until it finally stopped.

"District 9 it is," Daniel shouted.

"Okay, we've got a name," Chris said. "Shouldn't we have at least one song that's ours?"

We all looked at each other.

"We don't necessarily have to," Matt said. "Plus, are we really gonna learn a song in a night."

"Well, I think we could," Daniel said. "But it doesn't have to be for tomorrow. We can just have it ready for the next time."

"What next time?" Matt asked. "Do you know something I don't know?"

"Dude, we're a real band now," Daniel said. "We've got a singer."

He stopped, gestured toward me and smiled.

"And we've got a kickass name, and you know all those club people who thought we were okay without a real singer," Daniel continued.

His eyes were planted on Matt.

"Okay, okay," Matt said. "I'll see what I can do."

"Okay, so what about the song?" Chris chimed in.

"You gonna write one for us, Chris?" Matt asked. "None of us could write a song to save our lives."

I watched as everyone's eyes turned toward the floor. Then, after a moment, Chris's head suddenly popped up.

"None of us have ever written a song, right?" he asked the room, but he was only looking at me.

And slowly, Daniel's face and then Matt's face turned up as well, and before I knew it, all three of their sets of eyes were on me.

I stared back at them. I felt strangely nervous, as my lips started to turn up.

"I might have written a song," I confessed, hardly more audible than a mumble.

"What?" Matt asked.

There was a surprise in his voice.

"Let's hear it," Daniel shouted.

I shook my head.

"Nah, I don't think it's the kind of song you're looking for," I said.

"Will, we're looking for whatever you've got," Matt said.

"Nah," I said, shaking my head. "It's a slow song."

"Perfect," Daniel said. "I like slow songs. Girls like slow songs. Let's hear it."

There was silence then, as the three of them stared at me and I stared back at them. They were pleading with me out of pure desperation, I could tell. And suddenly, I realized I was just about to do what I would have been doing at home, except now, I had a live audience of my three, hopeless co-workers staring back at me.

"Damn it," I mumbled under my breath, as I repositioned my guitar in front of my body again.

The three men cheered and then settled back into their spots behind their instruments.

I turned my back toward them and stepped up to the microphone. Then, I rested my fingers on the guitar's strings and fiddled with a couple of the tuning pegs again. When I was sure I had her tuned, I planted my eyes on the garage door but then stopped. And the next thing I knew, I was shuffling around and twisting the microphone stand so that I was facing the guys again.

"Yeah, that's better," Chris said, chuckling.

I smiled.

"Yeah, I thought so," I said.

I repositioned my guitar.

"If you hate it, just stop me," I said.

Then, I cleared my throat as my fingers started a slow melody on the strings of my guitar. And seconds later, I parted my lips and started in:

"I'm famous in this small town
For a ghost I cannot shake
They all know I'm talkin' to you
But of it—I don't think they know what to make

But they don't see what I see
They don't see you dance on the river walk,
Underneath the street lamps
With those stars in your eyes

They don't see you
Lying next to me
Tellin' me your dreams,
Planted somewhere up in those big skies

No, they don't see what I see
Because I see
A rainstorm in June
Just before the sun
The black of night
Just before the stars
And, girl, I see your ghost
Just before our dawn

And tonight I'll see you again
Just like every night before
But they don't see what I see
What I see is more

My Butterfly

Because I see
A rainstorm in June
Just before the sun
The black of night
Just before the stars
And, girl, I see your ghost
Just before our dawn

And, girl, I see your ghost
Just before our dawn."

The room turned silent when my fingers stopped dancing on the strings. My eyes were planted on the floor. The song meant something to me, but they didn't need to know that.

Eventually, I heard a slow clap. I collected myself and slowly lifted my head. Another clap joined the first one, and then, the third set of hands started in.

"Will, man, that was amazing," Matt said.

"That's our song," Chris blurted out, pointing at me. "We can use that song, right?"

His gaze fell on me, and I bashfully smiled.

"Yeah, I wouldn't have sung it otherwise," I said, jokingly, all the while, trying to swallow the thought of the girl behind the song.

"The girls are going to love us," Daniel yelled, throwing his fists into the air.

"Okay, okay," Matt said. "Now, let's get to work."

Chris and Daniel were pulling out of Matt's driveway as Matt and I waved from our place underneath a basketball goal. We watched their headlights eventually fade and then disappear.

"How did you know that I might be able to sing?" I asked, as I turned back toward Matt.

"Your buddy, Jeff, right?" he asked. "The one who hung out with us a couple of weekends ago…"

I nodded my head.

"Yeah, Jeff," I confirmed.

"Yeah, I believe his exact words were that you have 'the voice of an angel,'" he said. "Of course, he was a little, you know…"

He tipped back an imaginary glass in his hand.

"Yeah," I said, smiling. "That sounds about right."

"Anyway, I believed him nonetheless," he said. "And I'm glad I did. What are you doing dressed in turnout gear anyway? Shouldn't you be in Nashville or something, gettin' all the pretty, country girls?"

I laughed once and shook my head. Then, I tipped my baseball cap and started out toward Lou on the street.

"So, I'll see you tomorrow night then at seven?" he called out after me.

I nodded my head and raised my hand in the air.

"I'll be there," I said.

I got to the driver's side door and pulled on the handle.

"Hey, Will," Matt called out from the driveway.

I looked back up in his direction.

"It'll be fun," he said.

I smiled and nodded my head. Then, I opened the door, set my guitar onto the backseat and slid behind the wheel. I found the key next and then stuck it into the ignition.

"Fun," I mumbled under my breath. "Yeah, I've heard that a couple of times before from someone else."

A wide smile battled its way to my face and eventually won.

My Butterfly

"And she just might have been right, damn it."

Chapter Twenty

The Gig

"**O**kay, you guys ready for a sound check?" asked a stout man propped up against the side of the stage.

I glanced over at Chris plugging the last cord into an amplifier and hesitantly nodded my head. We were on a tiny platform in a room a little bigger than New Milford's corner bar. But the ceilings were high and unfinished, and they gave the place a more modern look than the little bar from back home.

I watched the stout man take the three steps back down the stage and then make his way across the room again. He stayed as near as he could to the wall as he shuffled to his place in the far corner. There were people already sitting around tables and standing at the bar. They all seemed to be in their twenties and thirties mostly. Some were watching us, shielded behind their drinks and the darkness that filled the area below the stage. But most looked as if they didn't even notice us. My eyes eventually fell again onto the stout man, squeezing behind a counter, lit up with knobs and buttons. He played with some of the knobs and then finally looked my way and gave me a thumbs-up. I turned then and found Matt.

Matt caught my glance and paused from digging through a container full of electrical tape and pliers and whatnot.

"You can go ahead," he said. "I'll go next."

I faced forward again and stared at the microphone resting at the top of its stand. Then, I looked back up at the man behind the counter. His eyes were turned down; his fingers were busy dancing over the lights and the knobs. I caught a pair of eyes near the stage, and I smiled an awkward smile. She smiled back, and then I went back to the sound check that was evidentially already in progress. Suddenly, I felt as if I were seven all over again and playing rock star with the kids up the street. I shook off another uneasy smile and then tapped the top of the microphone. A dull sound bounced off the walls in the little room. It seemed to attract only a few more faces. I readjusted the guitar's strap around my body. Then, not really sure what to do next, I brought my lips to the microphone, remembering a movie I had seen once.

"Test, test," I said into the mic.

My words came out soft. I could barely hear them over the constant hum of voices in the room.

The guy behind the buttons and knobs pointed his finger in the air.

I nodded my head and waited.

"Test, test," I said again into the mic after a moment.

This time, I could hear myself.

"That sounds good," I heard Matt call out from behind me.

I gave the sound guy in the back of the room an *okay* gesture with my hand and nodded my head in approval.

"Song list," Matt said, setting a sheet of paper onto the stage at my feet.

I glanced down at the floor. The paper had a list of titles scribbled down the page.

"Okay, thanks," I said.

Then, I played with the strings on my guitar, acting as if I hadn't just tuned it, while Daniel tapped around on his drums and pedals and Matt and Chris worked with the sound guy. These guys were old pros at this stuff. I felt like a tadpole out of pond water.

When the guys were finally satisfied with their sounds, several more lights appeared in rays from the ceiling. Some were white; the others were red. They were bright and caused me to squint until I got used to them, which took me about a minute.

"You ready, Will?" I heard Matt ask.

I turned and found Matt. Then, I glanced at the mic and then back at him as if to say, *now?*

"Yep," he said. "We're ready."

I took a deep breath in and then felt it instinctively escape past my lips as a big smile edged its way across my face. I was pretty sure I thought the wider I smiled, the less my heart would race.

"Hello," I said into the mic.

Suddenly, the hum of the small crowd hushed.

"Hello," I said again, once the room was quiet. "How are ya?"

A few people clapped. One person whistled.

I swiveled around slightly, being careful to keep my lips near the mic, and glanced back at the band.

"We're, uh, District 9," I said.

Then, I turned back toward the crowd and the lights, trying my best not to squint my eyes.

"We're really, uh, firefighters, so even if you don't like our songs, feel free to clap anyway," I said, softly laughing into the mic. "You'd be doing some goodwill for the St. Louis Fire Department that way."

It took a second, but soon, a soft buzz, followed by enthusiastic applause, filled the little room. I let go of a wide smile then, and it instantly shot across my face. Then, I stepped back from the microphone and lowered my eyes to my guitar as Daniel started in on his drums. Immediately, I felt my hands fall into place on the guitar's strings, and I brought my lips close to the microphone again. The old melody was already taking me back to when I was a kid in the back of my grandpa's store singing my lungs out to the same song, and it helped to crush my nerves.

Soon after, I got the first words out, and the rest came easy. Then, the second song felt like a rush as this strange, adrenaline-like stuff shot through my spine. I had barely noticed that a line of people, mostly girls, were now pressed up against the side of the stage, dancing and singing. Every so often, I would look down to see if I could find Julia in one of their faces. I knew that she wasn't there, but that didn't stop me from trying anyway.

We finished the last song scribbled on the list before I knew it. And I let my guitar hang from its strap, as I grabbed the microphone's stand with both hands.

"Thanks so much," I said. "You guys were kind."

There was a loud applause, and I paused and smiled.

"Again, we're District 9, and remember to change those batteries in your smoke detectors," I said into the mic.

I heard laughter in the crowd, then more applause. And then, the stage went dark again. I narrowed my eyes trying to get them to readjust faster. I could barely see a thing again.

Still squinting, I turned and caught Matt's figure first. He was smiling. Then, I looked over at Chris and Daniel. They had wide grins planted on their faces too.

"Well done, boys," Matt finally said. "Well done."

※

Daniel, Chris and I were busy packing up the last of the gear into Chris's SUV when Matt came over to us and leaned his head near ours.

"So, listen, guys, my buddy said that he's got a friend who needs a band next week," he said. "You guys in?"

Daniel and Chris looked at each other and then at me.

I shrugged my shoulders.

"Sure," I said.

"See, what did I tell you, Matt?" Daniel shouted. "I knew you'd find us another gig."

"Can you guys be at my house on Sunday?" Matt asked. "We've got to practice. This place is bigger, and I think we should do Will's song."

We all looked at each other and nodded our heads.

"Sunday it is," Chris shouted, as he let out an excited howl.

Chapter Twenty-One

The Card

Weekly gigs kind of became a usual occurrence. I wasn't quite sure even how it had all unfolded exactly. One day, I woke up, and it just was. I was a firefighter most days, and I played in a band on the others. It made me laugh to think about it because it all seemed as if it were a dream—not like a career dream but like a real dream, as if I were actually sleeping while we were playing on some small stage in some other part of town. I was always waiting for a big, pink elephant to fly across the room or for a squirrel in the crowd to ask me why I was naked on stage or something. It felt like that kind of dream. I enjoyed it though. I seldom admitted it, even to myself. But when I was sitting alone on my little bed in the station, I thought about it. And I thought about if maybe sometime we got a gig in Columbia that I might see Julia. I always pictured her in the front row, with a happy smile on her face. I thought about that sometimes.

I picked up a cord leading to the stage and started wrapping it around my arm. I hardly got it wrapped around my elbow twice when a voice stopped me.

"Hi, Jesse Sovine," a man said, extending his hand.

I glanced at the man's outstretched arm and followed it up to his face.

"Will Stephens," I said, eventually meeting his handshake.

"You've got a great voice," the man said.

I smiled an awkward smile and went back to wrapping the cord around my arm.

"Thanks," I said.

"I've seen these guys play a couple of times, but I've never seen you before," he said.

"Yeah, it's kind of a side thing," I said.

"So, you're a firefighter?" he asked.

I glanced back up at him, and then my gaze fell onto the cord again.

"Yes, sir," I said.

"Well, have you ever thought about a career in music?" he asked.

I stopped and looked at him sideways.

"A career in music? Us?" I asked.

He nodded his head and smiled.

"Your band. Yourself," the man said.

I raised one eyebrow.

"Did a little blonde put you up to this?" I asked.

The man's smile faded, and his face twisted into a puzzled look.

"I'm kidding," I said, chuckling. "No, really, it's just a side thing."

He seemed to pause before he continued.

"Okay," he said. "Well, talk to your band. I'd love a chance to represent you guys."

"Represent?" I repeated.

"Yeah," he said, pulling out a clean, white business card from the inside pocket of his tailored jacket.

"If you change your mind, my number's on the card," he said, handing it to me.

I took the card.

"It's nice to meet you, Will Stephens," he said, extending his hand to me again. "I hope you change your mind."

I shook his hand again, and then I watched him disappear back into the crowd.

It was dark all around me, except for the neon light that flashed in my direction every once in a while. My eyes strained to see the bold lettering on the small business card as they searched each word:

Jesse Sovine, Talent Agent
Premiere Entertainment Management

I stared at the card for a second, then stuffed it into my pocket and continued again wrapping the electric cord around my arm.

"A career in music," I mumbled under my breath, while chuckling to myself.

I made my way into Matt's garage Monday evening. The guys were already there.

"Water, Will?" I heard Matt ask.

I turned toward him and held out my hands.

He tossed the bottle across the room. I caught it, opened it up and took a swig. Then, I set it onto the concrete floor and started to play with the strings on my guitar.

"Oh, guys, by the way, this guy gave me this the other night," I said, pulling the business card from my jeans pocket and tossing it onto Matt's keys.

"What is it?" Chris asked, snatching up the card.

His eyes scanned the words and then turned up.

"This is an agent," he eventually said.

His words were straight and to the point.

"What?" Matt asked, looking up.

"Where did you get this?" Chris asked me.

"The guy," I said, pointing to the card. "His name is on it."

"Dude, this is Premiere Entertainment," he exclaimed. "They're a big deal."

"What did you tell him?" Matt asked me.

"I didn't tell him anything, really," I said. "I just took the card."

"Guys, do you realize what this could mean?" Chris asked. "We could be famous."

"Let me see it," Daniel said, yanking the card out of Chris's hand.

Daniel's eyes followed over the words on the card.

"We've got to call him," Chris said, "and tell him we're interested."

"Whoa, whoa, whoa," Daniel said. "We've got to think about this first. I've got a kid and a family. I can't just run off with the band."

"Yeah, Chris, I agree," Matt said. "A lot of people have agents, but that doesn't mean they get anywhere. This isn't a ticket to fame and fortune, and we can't act like it is."

"But we can just see what he says," Chris said.

"I don't know," Daniel said. "I mean, playing on the weekends is fun, but…"

He shook his head.

"I need a real job," he continued. "One that pays the bills."

"Who said anything about quitting our jobs?" Chris asked. "We can just see where it leads."

"I don't know," Daniel said, still shaking his head.

"What about you, Will?" Chris asked. "He talked to you. What do you think?"

Suddenly, all eyes in the garage were on me.

I shook my head and laughed.

"I'm a firefighter," I said. "I don't know anything about the music business, and I'm not sure, beyond what we do Friday and Saturday nights, that I want to."

Chris tossed his head back and groaned.

"Look, guys, we don't have to give him an answer right now," Matt said, taking the card from Daniel's hand. "Here, Will, he gave you the card; you hold onto it. In the meantime, we can all think about it. Give it some time. Who's to say it'll even amount to anything. Let's think about if we even want to bother with it. Okay?"

Our eyes were on Matt. Then, they slowly strayed to Chris.

"Okay, okay," Chris said. "I'll think about it. You know what my answer is, but I'll think about it."

I chuckled and took the business card from Matt.

"Chris, if I didn't know any better, I'd think you had some secret dream of becoming a rock star," I said to him.

He held a sarcastic glare for a good, few seconds before he finally threw his head back again, and this time, laughed.

"Yeah, I might have thrown some leather pants on and a suede jacket and slung a guitar across my skinny, little chest for career day in the sixth grade," Chris said, slowly bobbing his head. "That might have been me. But let me tell ya, the girls loved it. The teachers—not so much. But the girls, they loved it. I knew before that day that I was destined to be famous, but that day in sixth grade, that day, I knew I wanted to be."

"For the girls?" I asked.

"Well, that day, it was just for Hailey Young," he said, his voice growing serious again. "But she moved away after junior high, and I never saw her again. Now, I guess…"

He paused for a second and stared off into space. Matt, Daniel and I just looked at each other, waiting for him to finish.

"Now, I guess," Chris started again, "I guess, it's still Hailey Young."

Chris's eyes were glazed over now as he continued to stare off, seemingly, into a different world or a different time. I glanced over at Daniel in the back corner of the garage. He was rubbing his eyes now, out of what looked as if it were boredom.

"Are we done?" Daniel chimed in. "MY Hailey Young has dinner for me at home, and I'm starving."

"Yeah, we're done," Matt said.

Daniel got up first and shuffled to the door, as a loud ring suddenly came from inside the house, and Matt scurried up to retrieve his phone.

I looked back at Chris. We were the only two left in the garage. His head was down now, and he looked as though he was thinking. I walked over to him and patted him on the shoulder.

My Butterfly

"We're all chasin' after our own Hailey Youngs," I said to him. "Hang in there, buddy."

I watched him nod his head, and then I slowly made my way to the door.

"You got one, Will?" I heard him ask.

I turned back around and caught his sad eyes. Then, I slowly nodded my head.

"Yes," I said, softly.

I watched him try to smile. It was a perceptive smile, as if he had already known my answer. I forced the corners of my lips up slightly. Then, I turned again and made my way out of the small garage.

Chapter Twenty-Two

Angel

"Hey," I heard a soft voice call out from behind me.

I turned to see a brunette staring back at me.

"Jessica," I said.

I knew I had to have sounded a little thrown off.

"My uncle was the speaker," she said, smiling softly and pointing toward the stage.

"Oh, that was your uncle?" I asked.

She nodded her head.

"Wow," I said, running my hand through my hair. "That was one, close call he had there."

I watched her eyes turn toward the floor at our shoes.

My Butterfly

"Yeah, he's had a couple of close calls," she said, returning her eyes to mine.

I caught her gaze, then lowered my eyes and slowly bobbed my head, as the conversation grew silent.

"You look great," she said.

I chuckled and looked down at my black slacks and white, button-up shirt. I felt overdressed.

"Thanks," I replied.

My eyes then caught her silhouette in her snug, blue dress.

"Uh, so do you," I said.

Jessica's wide smile beamed back at me. I smiled but then suddenly spotted in the back of the room a thin blonde, in a short, yellow dress. My heart nearly stopped, then restarted, only to almost beat out of my chest, but I kept my eyes on the girl in the yellow dress, until she noticed me.

"Uh, Jessica, there's someone I see that I've got to talk to," I stuttered.

I wasn't even sure if half of the words had come out as words, but Jessica smiled and nodded all the same. Then, I glanced back up at the blonde. I hadn't been imagining things. She was still standing there, watching me. But this time, her eyes cast down to the floor when I met them, and she started fidgeting with something in her hands. I felt Jessica's stare follow my gaze. I probably should have felt bad for Jessica—for cutting her off—but at the moment, I couldn't feel anything but happy.

"It was, uh, good to see you," I said, as I flashed Jessica another smile and then stepped to her side.

"Yeah," she said. "It was good to see you too."

I barely heard Jessica's last words. My mind had been set onto one track, and suddenly, I was useless for all other purposes.

I rushed over to the blonde and stopped just a foot away from her slender frame and met her eyes.

"Hi, Will," she said, softly smiling.

"Julia," I finally managed to get out.

A smile came with her name. It felt good. It had been a long time since that had happened.

"I was home for the weekend, and there was a note on my calendar, and I thought...," she said and then paused.

"I thought I'd stop by," she finished.

I kept my eyes in hers.

"I got you a gift," she said, handing me a small box.

I took the wrapped package into my hand and sent a wild smile her way. I couldn't help it. This girl was so unpredictable, it made me crazy. But somehow, I loved it.

I turned the small package over in my hands.

"I just happened to run across it one day, and I don't know, it was force of habit or something because the next thing I knew, I was at the counter, handing the woman my debit card," she said, softly laughing. "It's just something small, and because I think it was made for you."

"Sounds like I love it already," I said, sending her a wink.

She turned her face away, but I had already seen the red in her cheeks.

"You can open it later," she said.

"You know what?" I said, through a wide smile. "I've got a better idea. Let's get lunch."

She looked into my eyes as if she was asking me a question but damned if I knew what it was.

"Come on," I said. "There's this place that has the best cheeseburgers in town. I know you can't pass that up."

My Butterfly

"But your family?" she asked.

"Them?" I asked her, as if she were crazy. "Mom's doing this little shindig at the house later. She's already told me that she's ditching me after this to get ready for it."

I watched a smile crawl across her pretty face.

"Here, let's go tell 'em I'm leaving, and then we'll get outta here," I said.

I grabbed her arm, but she gently pulled away.

"No, you go," she said. "I'll just wait outside."

I stared at her for a second, as I fell back down to earth. There was something different about her, and my heart stabbed at my chest because of it.

"Okay," I said, as I cleared my throat and slowly nodded my head. "I'll, uh, I'll just go tell them I'm leaving, and I'll meet you out there."

She smiled, nodded and then turned toward the doors that led out into the hallway.

I watched her walk away. My breathing was starting to get shallow, and I swore the temperature in the room just rose a couple of degrees. *What was she hiding?*

We gave the waiter our orders and our menus. Then, I planted my eyes on Julia.

She sent that same, irresistible smile that only she could give my way. God, I missed that smile.

"Open it," she said, gesturing toward the small box, now sitting on the table in front of me.

I found her eyes again and smiled. Then, I slowly started pulling away the paper that covered the box. But before I got all of it off, I stopped and looked up at her.

"I can't believe you're here," I said.

Her eyes turned down before they met mine again.

"Well, I know this is a big day for you, and I had the gift," she said.

"I wasn't expecting this—the gift or you," I said. "And it's just my paramedic certification."

She smiled.

"It's a big deal, Will," she said.

I held my gaze in her eyes for a moment longer. Then, I tore off the rest of the wrapping and pulled out a metal pin from a small box. It was an angel pulling up a firefighter who had fallen.

"It's your guardian angel," she said, before I could say anything. "Wear it. She'll keep you safe."

I looked up at her and gently smiled.

"I will," I said. "Thank you."

Her eyes immediately cast down, so I took the moment to study the soft features on her face before I returned my attention to the guardian angel in my hand.

"So, how long are you in town?" I asked.

"Just today actually," she said.

My smile instantly faded.

"Well, maybe I could come up and see you some time, and we could go get dinner or something," I said.

I lifted my head just as her eyes were starting to light up, but then something happened. And I watched the green in her eyes grow dim and her smile too start to fade. My heart sank.

"It could be just as friends," I quickly said.

Her expression didn't change, and my heart sank even further into my chest. I knew she wanted to tell me something—that thing she had been hiding.

"What is it, Jules?" I asked, too impatient to wait for her to get it out on her own.

"I just don't think dinner is such a good idea, Will," she said, tossing her stare to the table's surface.

I furrowed my brows.

"Why not?" I asked.

She seemed to pause, and then she found my eyes again.

"I'm seeing someone," she said.

Just like that, the words had come out as if they were a death sentence.

"What do you mean you're seeing someone?" I asked.

I slid back into my chair and tried to replace a dagger to the heart with a smug smile.

"You mean, like you see someone every day in a line to get coffee or something or like you're seeing ghosts or something?" I asked.

She sarcastically batted her eyelashes.

"I mean I'm dating someone," she said. "His name is Brady, and he's on the track team, and he…"

"Okay, okay," I interrupted her. "I get it."

She stopped short, and after a long moment, I slumped back in my chair, then brought my elbows to the table and rested my forehead in my hands.

"Sorry," I said, lifting my head from my hands. "So, what does he do?"

"What?" she asked.

"What does this guy you're 'seeing' do?" I asked, making sure to use my fingers as quotation marks in the appropriate place.

"He's a sophomore," she said. "He's pre-med. He wants to be a doctor."

I let my head fall back at her mention of the word *doctor*.

"A doctor, Jules?" I asked. "Of course," I said, under my breath.

She shot me a puzzled look.

"You know the divorce rates for doctors?" I asked. "You don't want to marry him."

I watched her dramatically sigh.

"Will, no one said anything about marrying anyone," she said. "And besides, like your job's much better. I can't even count the number of times you left me somewhere when your tones went off or the hours we missed because of them."

"I always left you with someone we knew, Jules," I reminded her. "You make it sound like I left you on the side of the road somewhere."

I watched her take a deep breath, close her eyes and then smile.

"Will," she said, "we don't have to fight like this anymore."

"Anymore?" I asked. "Jules, we never fought, and we're not fighting now. We're just discussing our differences, like how you're fond of doctors, and I'm not."

She took another deep breath, and her smile turned soft.

"Really?" she asked. "Because it sounds a lot like a certain night that I remember not so long ago."

I stared at her, trying desperately to find the meaning in her riddle.

"Come on, Jules, don't even bring that night up," I eventually said, recalling our breakup, and at the same time, running my hand through my hair. "I hate that night."

"That makes two of us, so let's just agree to not fight anymore," she said.

She was still wearing a smile, but it looked fake.

I stared into her eyes for a minute and then finally forced a grin too.

My Butterfly

"Fine," I said, "no more fighting. Let's talk about you instead."

A sincere smile came to life on her face again.

"What about me?" she asked.

"Well, how's school?" I asked.

"It's good," she said, nodding her head. "It's just prerequisites and electives. Nothing too exciting."

"What about track?" I asked.

She smiled wider.

"What is it?" I asked.

"My time dropped two seconds," she said.

"I knew it," I exclaimed, as I leaned back against the chair and smiled. "What did I tell you?"

"I know," she said, starting to laugh.

"What about you?" she asked.

"Well," I said, trying hard to censor the parts where I sulk most nights thinking of her, "I got a job on the department in St. Louis."

"Wow, that's great, Will," she said, smiling wider.

I followed her stare to a spot on the table then and watched as her smile started to fade. It looked as if she were thinking about something.

"What?" I asked her.

Her eyes quickly flashed back to mine.

"Oh, nothing," she said. "It's just that it went by so fast."

I nodded my head as her eyes lingered for a second in mine.

"Do you still play sometimes?" she asked.

I pushed my lips together, thinking about the band and our weekend nights.

"Sometimes," I said.

"Good," she said, smiling again.

I locked my eyes in hers then.

"You know, I bet doctors come home smelling worse then ashes," I said, cracking a smile. "Have you ever smelled the inside of a hospital?"

"Will," she playfully scolded.

"Okay, okay," I said. "But don't say I never warned you."

She shot me that cute, pouty face that she stored in that arsenal of expressions she owned. She must have known that she was killin' me. I let my eyes linger in hers a second too long, but she didn't seem to mind. Jules was still in there somewhere. I took a deep breath in and then gradually let it out, as a knowing smile found its way back to my face.

Chapter Twenty-Three

Fall

"**Y**ou were on his emergency contacts," I heard a voice say on the other side of the curtain.

I felt my heart speed up, and my eyelids instantly fell shut. *Emergency contacts*. I had forgotten about that. I sat up straight and tried to make out my reflection in the black, television screen. I probably looked like hell.

I combed back my hair with my fingers and then listened for Jules's voice, but for several moments, there was only silence. My eyes darted back and forth from the curtain to the only piece of the door that I could see, as I anxiously rubbed my palms against the white blanket, subconsciously smoothing out its deep wrinkles. Then, finally, her thin frame emerged from the temporary wall. And her eyes instantly caught mine.

"Hey, are you okay?" Julia asked.

Her voice was soft and shaken. I was pretty sure I was expecting her to be pissed that I had uprooted her from doing whatever she had been doing more than a hundred miles away.

"I'm fine," I said. "If I would have known that they were going to call you, I would have told them not to."

"No," she said, shaking her head. "It's okay. I mean, they really couldn't tell me anything on the phone. What happened?"

"Just an unlucky step, which led to an unlucky fall, that's all," I said. "In reality, it's all kind of a blur. I remember feeling the heat from the flames. I remember stepping backward, and the next thing I remember is being here, in this bed."

"They said that it knocked you out, and your wrist...," she started, her eyes falling to the cast on my arm.

"Yeah, it's broken, but it should heal pretty fast," I said.

I watched as she tried to force a smile.

"Listen," I said, "I'm really sorry that you had to drive all this way. It's stupid. I'm fine. And it's stupid that I even have you on the list. You were just the first person I thought of. It was a while ago, out of habit, I guess," I lied, "and you never expect to ever have to need that list..."

"Will, stop," she said and then rested her hand on my good arm. "I'm just happy that you're okay. You could've been..."

I met her gaze.

"But I wasn't," I said.

I rested my eyes in hers and took a deep breath, then slowly let it out. Moments passed before either one of us spoke.

"The nurse said that you were wearing this when you came in," she eventually said, opening her palm up to me.

Inside, was the silver pin with the angel pulling up the firefighter. I took it from her hand. My eyes traced every line that made up the metal pin, trying to recall, first, the moments that led to my fall, and second, the percentage of good men and women who didn't make it past a fall like that. And after a minute, I looked back up to find Julia's eyes clouding with tears.

"Jules," I said, trying to reach for her but getting pulled back by the IVs still attached to me. "I wear it all the time. I'm here because of it. I'm fine because of it."

My eyes followed over the sad lines in her face.

"Come here," I said then, gesturing her closer to me.

I scooted over as much as I could in the tiny bed and used my good arm to pat the small space on the mattress I had just made for her.

She seemed to hesitate at first, but then eventually, she climbed onto the bed and nuzzled into the small place between my chest and the bed's railing. I wrapped my good arm around her shoulder and brought my hand, still cradling the pin, to rest on her opposite arm. I could tell that she was a little reluctant to rest her head on my chest, but she did it anyway, as I squeezed her still closer to me and smiled.

"I'm not keepin' ya from any big plans tonight, am I?" I asked.

I heard her laugh once and then felt her head move back and forth.

I smiled wider and then rested my cheek on her head.

"I'd offer you something to drink, but the drink selection in here is awful, and the service isn't much better," I whispered into her ear.

She laughed that pretty laugh of hers again.

"That's okay," she said. "I'm hitting up another hospital after this, and it's supposed to be like five stars or something AND have live entertainment."

I raised my head up from hers.

"Live entertainment, huh?" I asked her.

"Mm hmm," she said, nodding into my chest.

One side of my mouth started to lift into a grin.

"Baby, you're not going anywhere else tonight because this place might be lacking in other areas, but it is definitely not lacking in the entertainment department."

She giggled.

"I got songs—lots of songs," I continued. "What do you want to hear?"

I heard her mumble something, but I couldn't quite make it out.

"Hmm?" I asked, lowering my ear closer to her lips.

"'Brown Eyed Girl,'" she said, a little clearer.

"Oh," I said, smiling. "You mean 'Green Eyed Girl'?"

I felt her playfully tap my chest with her hand. And I brought my cheek to rest on her head again. It felt so good for her to be next to me. I squeezed her still closer to my body and breathed in the sweet smell of her hair.

It sure wasn't my intention to fall through a ceiling and down a story, but it sure wasn't ending that badly either.

"'Green Eyed Girl' it is," I softly said, as I smiled wide and made sure to keep my thoughts to myself.

Chapter Twenty-Four

Breakfast

I opened my eyes to white ceiling tiles and what sounded like a loose wheel on some type of cart or something rambling past the room. I closed my eyes again and tried to recall how I had gotten there. There was a call, a fire and then...there was Julia. My eyes shot open. She was still asleep on my chest, and my arm was still around her. I tried to rest my hand on her arm, but I couldn't feel my hand. It must have fallen asleep. My eyes darted back to her face as I watched her nuzzle her head deeper into my chest. I froze then and became conscious of my every movement out of fear that the slightest flinch would wake her. I couldn't help but want to watch her sleep. She looked so peaceful. She always looked peaceful when she slept, and while I wasn't quite convinced that this would be the last time I would ever get this moment—to watch her dream—I had learned something yesterday—that no moment was guaranteed.

I caught her head move again, and then I noticed her eyes flutter open. I quickly forced my eyelids over my eyes again and pretended to be asleep.

She was still for a few more seconds, but then she quickly sat up. I peeked out of one eye and saw her reaching for something on the floor. It looked as if it might be her shoes maybe. *Where was she going?*

"Good morning, sunshine," I said, pretending to wake up.

I stretched my good arm toward the ceiling and started to sit up but then fell back with a groan.

"God, what happened to me?" I asked, faintly smiling.

Her face angled back toward mine.

"You'd think I had fallen through a burning building or something," I continued.

She laughed once.

"Careful there, Spider-Man. You're probably going to be a little sore," she said, as she sent a smile my way and then went back to putting on her shoes.

"Where are you going?" I asked.

"I am going to get us some breakfast," she said, in a way that made it sound as if it were an announcement.

She paused for a moment, glanced back at me again and then softy smiled. It didn't seem like a happy smile.

"And then, I've got to get home," she said.

My heart sank, but I forced a smile anyway.

"This hospital bed not homey enough for you?" I asked.

Her lips started to edge up her face just a little more, as she sarcastically batted her eyelashes at me.

"You have bed head," she said then, snickering.

I playfully narrowed my eyes but then smiled as I noticed the long second that her gaze lingered in mine.

"There's a doughnut shop across the street," she said, eventually dropping her eyes from mine and then grabbing her purse from a table at the foot of the bed.

I watched her make her way to the door, but before she disappeared behind the curtain, she stopped and turned toward me.

"Chocolate Long Johns with sprinkles?" she asked.

I flashed her a wide smile, which I guessed was all the confirmation she needed because she turned then and escaped past the tall curtain and out of the room.

I waited for almost a minute, staring at the door, just in case she had forgotten something and popped back in. Then, my eyes darted toward the television at the front of the room. I had to strain my neck a little in order to see my reflection in its black screen and even then, I was still just a shadowy outline. But it would have to do. I quickly ran my fingers through my hair, then suddenly, I felt a muscle in my back pull tight, and it made me flinch. I groaned and then returned to the same position on the bed in which I had been for the last twelve hours or so and raked over my hair one, last time.

After I had done the best I could with my bed head or whatever she liked to call it when my hair spiked up every which way, I spotted a glass of water on the table next to my bed. I picked it up, took a big swig and swished it around my mouth. Then, I looked around the room for anything that resembled toothpaste or a toothbrush. Nothing. My eyes eventually landed on a small bouquet of flowers on the little table. I guessed they were mine. *Could I eat a flower? Would that even help?* Thankfully, I spotted a bag of mint chocolate candies next to the vase and scooped it up. I popped a couple of the chocolates into my mouth and chewed them. Then, I took another big swig of water and set the glass back down.

The room was quiet and still without Jules in it. My eyes began a slow scan of the space around me. There was a window to my right, and there was a little sliver of light pouring through it. But the only view out of it and to the world was the empty side of a red, brick building. Besides that, there was a chair near the window, a small table at the foot of the bed, the television and then a trash can near the big curtain to my left, but that was it.

I let out a breath of air, as my eyes lowered to my hands again. And just then, I got an idea. I quickly rolled the candy wrappers into tiny balls. Then, I sent them, one at a time, flying toward the trash can across the room. But I missed both times, and both times, the foiled paper rolled to a final resting place on the tiles near the basket. I sighed and then looked around the room for something else to do to kill the time until Julia returned. Besides the few standard things, the tiny place was empty and mostly dark, and the air smelled kind of stale. I was happy that I hadn't had to spend the night alone in it.

My mind got stuck on that thought, as I replayed in my head waking up next to Jules. I wasn't sure how many more buildings I could fall through and still be all right, but if that were all it took to get Julia Lang next to me again, I also wasn't sure I'd think twice about doing something stupid the next time.

I heard the loose wheel on that cart again outside the room. It sounded as if it slowed when it reached my door and then continued on. When I couldn't hear the sound of the wheel any longer, my gaze fell to the white sheets that were turned every which way at my feet. Then suddenly, a shiny object near the middle of the bed caught my eye. It was the guardian angel. I cautiously reached for it, being conscious of my sore back. Then, when I was close enough to touch it, I clasped my fingers around it and brought it close to my heart. And after several seconds, I rested my head back against my pillow and stared up at the white tiles, until eventually, my eyelids fell over my eyes.

"Two chocolate Long Johns with sprinkles and some milk."

Startled, I forced my eyes open. Then, I watched Jules make her way over to my bedside and set a paper bag and a small container of milk into my lap.

I smiled.

"Thanks, dear," I said, grabbing at the top of the bag.

I stole a quick glance at her. She was staring at me sideways, just as I had suspected she would be. I watched her eyes do that playful, sarcastic thing, which drove me wild, and I held out for what I knew was coming next. Wait for it. Wait for it. There it was—a smile.

"I mean Jules," I said, finally.

I went back to rummaging through the doughnuts in the bag as she took a seat on the bed next to my midsection and faced me.

"So, how long do you have to be here anyway?" she asked.

"Uh, I think they'll let me go today," I said, starting to grin. "I'm pretty sure they were just waiting to make sure nothing else was wrong with me."

She slowly nodded her head.

"Good," she said, through a soft smile.

I watched her then, as she lowered her eyes and reached her hand into her purse. Her hair was pulled together, and it sat in a pile near the top of her head. It looked kind of messy, but it had always been my favorite look on her.

She eventually found what she had been looking for inside her purse, I guessed, because she pulled out a short stick and smeared its contents onto her lips.

"Jules," I finally said, setting the bag of doughnuts and the milk onto the bed beside me.

She lowered the Chap Stick from her lips and met my eyes.

"Thank you," I said.

I rested my hand on hers. Her eyes darted toward my hand, but she didn't move.

"I lied last night," I said.

I watched her head tilt a little to the side, as if she might be interested in what I had to say.

"I didn't just put you as my emergency contact out of habit," I went on. "I did it because…"

"Where is that lucky bastard?" I suddenly heard a familiar voice come from behind the curtain. "Better be decent. I brought your girl."

My eyes rushed toward the door, and within seconds, the curtain flew open, revealing a tall, lanky guy and a petite brunette. Almost at the same time, I felt Julia's hand quickly escape from underneath mine, and before I knew it, she was standing at the bedside, fidgeting with the hair on top of her head.

"Oh, hey, Julia," Jeff said, stopping short and staring at her with big eyes.

Julia looked up for an instant and bashfully smiled at him.

"I didn't know you had company," Jeff said, meeting my stare.

I didn't say anything. I just stared back at him with a defeated expression. And after a moment, he swallowed hard and carried on.

"Well, you dead yet, buddy?" he asked.

I found Julia again. Her eyes were searching the floor at her feet, but she eventually caught my stare and sent me an awkward smile. My eyes traveled back to the curtain then, but Jeff had already made his way over to a monitor near my head and was now poking at buttons. And Jessica was standing at the foot of the bed, looking shy, with flowers clutched within her small fingers.

"No, Jeff, not dead...yet," I mumbled.

"I heard what happened," Jessica said. "Are you okay?"

Her voice was timid but sweet. And suddenly, it felt like New Year's Eve those years ago all over again—with Julia and Jessica in the same room. Only this time, I hadn't been holding the brunette's hand when Julia had entered the doorway. This time, it had been Julia's hand and Jessica had appeared, but somehow, it didn't seem to make a difference—not to Julia anyway.

"Yeah," I said, looking up at Jessica. "It's just a broken wrist. I'll be fine."

My eyes left Jessica when I noticed Julia in the corner of the room, rifling through her purse again. I watched her pull out a set of keys and then turn back toward the three of us—me; Jeff, playing with some cords at my head; and Jessica, now sitting in the spot on the bed next to me where Julia had been just moments ago.

"I should be going," Julia said.

Jeff stopped playing with the cords and looked up.

"What? No. Stay," he said, stuffing a Long John into his mouth. "We were just about to see if Will needs all of these cords to live."

Julia's eyes fell onto mine, and she sweetly smiled. Then, she looked back up at Jeff.

"I really need to get going," she said, starting toward the curtain.

"Jules," I called out after her.

She stopped and turned.

"You don't have to go," I said.

A half-smile slowly found its way to her face.

"I do," she said, nodding her head. "Take care, Will."

Then, she turned again, disappeared behind the curtain and was gone.

Chapter Twenty-Five
The Note

I stared into the steering wheel for a few moments before grabbing the note from the passenger's seat. Then, I climbed out from behind the wheel and gently closed the door behind me.

The parking lot was full of cars. It was three thirty in the afternoon. I made my way over the gravel and to the pavement and planted my eyes on the track up the hill. I could tell that there were people up there, but I couldn't make anyone out.

"Whoa," I suddenly heard a voice come from behind me.

I stopped as a guy with shorts and a cutoff tee shirt breezed past me, brushing my shoulder.

"Sorry," I said.

"No problem, buddy," he said, continuing his jog up the hill.

"Uh, hey," I called out after him.

The guy stopped and looked back at me.

"I don't want to mess up your, uh, running…," I started.

He laughed before I could say anything else.

"It's fine. I wish more people would stop me," he said. "I could use the breaks."

I hesitated, as my mouth lifted into a grin.

"I was just wondering if the whole team was practicing up there right now," I said.

He took a second.

"Should be," he said. "It's Monday. We're usually all here toward the beginning of the week. It only gets pretty thin toward the end."

"Aah," I said, nodding my head.

He started to turn but hesitated.

"You need help finding someone?" he asked.

"Uh, no," I said, shaking my head. "It's okay. Thanks though."

"No problem," he said.

I watched him turn again and trot up the hill and eventually disappear onto the track.

The note in my hand was getting crumpled and sweaty. I tried to smooth out its wrinkles as I continued my trek up the hill to a set of tall, metal gates.

I reached the entrance about a minute later. The gates were open, so I walked in. And a few steps later, I stopped at a shorter fence that looked as if it wrapped all the way around the track.

I quickly scanned the whole place first. I was looking for a blonde with those little shorts she always wore. But there were so many people in one, small area, and they all seemed to be wearing the same, little shorts.

My eyes eventually got stuck on the grassy field inside the track. There was a guy there throwing a long spear. I watched as the spear left his hands and landed in a spot in the grass almost a hundred yards away from him. Then, my gaze ventured to my right, and I spotted a girl catapulting herself high into the air and over a bar. The thought of being that high in the air on top of that narrow of a stick made me cringe.

I quickly forced my eyes away from the high bar then and scanned the rest of the track until I stumbled onto her. There she was, at the far end of the field. She was stretching. She looked beautiful. Maybe she would come to dinner with me tonight. Maybe she'd even ask me to stay. I smiled and let go of an excited breath. Then, I gripped the note tighter in my hand and stepped even closer to the fence. But I kept my eyes planted on her. She was wearing her little shorts and a tee shirt with the university's mascot on it. And she looked as if she was talking to someone behind a big mat, but I couldn't tell who it was. She was smiling, though, and it made me smile wider.

I watched her for a few more seconds. Then, someone stood up from behind the mat. It kind of looked like the guy I had just run into. He was wearing the same shorts and tee shirt, and he had that blondish, reddish hair. My eyes followed him as he walked closer to Julia. She must have been talking to him—and she was still talking to him. I felt my smile start to fade.

I narrowed my eyes and watched as Julia stood up too. She played with her hair for a second and then positioned it on top of her head again. Her playing with her hair forced a grin back to my face.

I watched then as she walked over to the fence nearest to her and pulled something out of it, while I nervously tapped the note in my hand with my thumb and thought about what to do next.

Eventually, my eyes left Jules and went to the note. I stared at it for a second. Then, I forced it open and read over its words one more time:

Jules,

Thanks for making a night in the hospital a night I never want to forget. Not surprisingly, you're a part of a lot of those kind of nights for me. Jules, I'm sorry I don't always know what to say or when to say it. I'm sorry I didn't give you what you deserved when I had the chance. But, Jules, I just want you to know that I love you with everything I am—a million times a million and to the moon and back. Forgive me, Jules, and give your life with me another chance.

~Will

I finished reading the last, few words. Then, I folded the note, tightly clutched it inside my sweaty palm and looked up.

Jules was talking to that guy again. I hesitated as my head instinctively tilted to the side.

The guy who she had said she was dating a while ago, did she say he was on the track team? Could she still be dating him? I narrowed my eyes and focused my attention on the guy. He was smiling—at Julia. I shifted my weight to my other leg and gripped the fence in front of me. I watched as he took a step closer to Julia. My fingers clutched the fence tighter. He was still smiling, but now, he was suspiciously looking around. What was he doing? I narrowed my eyes even more, praying that it would help me to see into his plan. It didn't work.

My Butterfly

My stare followed him as he took one more, quick glance around the track. And then he moved in, attacking Julia on the lips. My body stiffened, and my breaths stopped. *Hit him, Jules. Hit him.*

I let go of the fence and started quickly around its perimeter toward Jules. But I only got several yards before I stopped. She didn't look angry. In fact, she was smiling. She was acting as if him kissing her were normal, as if it were just another day or something. My heart plummeted to the ground at my feet as I squeezed the note in my hand. And suddenly, the earth started spinning. I grabbed hold of the fence again and allowed my eyelids to fall over my eyes for several moments. And when the earth had finally stopped careening and had come to a halt again, I opened my eyes. But now, I felt as if I were in some kind of weird vacuum, though it appeared as if nothing around me had changed. Everything seemed the same. Everyone looked normal— each person doing the same thing he or she had been doing before the earth had spun out of control. In fact, each figure looked as if it belonged exactly where it was. I was the one who didn't belong. My eyes fell back onto Jules. She was laughing. I took in a deep breath and held it in my chest for as long as I could. Then, I cautiously let it slip past my lips. *I was the one who didn't belong.*

And in the next moment, I found the note again in my hand and quickly shoved it into my back pocket. Then, I turned and made a beeline for the parking lot. At the same time, I battled back the mist in my eyes, which worsened with each stride.

Chapter Twenty-Six

Haunting

"Julia."

I stopped suddenly and slowly set the can of chili back onto the shelf. The voice had come from an aisle over. I rushed to the end of the row, stopped and took a quick check of myself. I looked pretty rough, but what could I do now? I took off my cap and refit it over my head again. Then, I sauntered casually into the aisle, as if I were looking hard for something. And when I couldn't take it anymore—several seconds later—I looked up and spotted a woman and a young girl. My heart sank.

"Hi, Will," the woman said.

"Ms. Evans," I said, tipping my baseball cap.

She smiled at me and then glanced at the girl next to her.

"Oh, Will, I don't think you've ever really met my daughter," she said. "Sweetie, this is Will. He's the firefighter that came to our house that one time."

The girl blankly eyed me. I could tell she didn't remember me. She was only a little girl back then.

"Will, this is my daughter, Julia," the woman continued.

I swallowed hard.

"Nice to meet you," I said.

The girl smiled wide, though she seemed a little nervous. I watched as she tossed her hands behind her back and then tried to shove them into her pockets before finally crossing her arms in front of her. I guessed she was maybe in junior high or some age around it.

My eyes eventually traveled back to the woman.

"How have you been?" I asked.

"Oh, great," she said.

She moved closer to me and squeezed the part of my arm near my bicep.

"You've been stayin' safe, right?" she asked.

Her eyes seemed more like they were commanding something rather than asking it.

I smiled and nodded.

"Good," she said, releasing my bicep and continuing down the aisle. "Tell your mom I said 'hi.'"

"I will," I said, softly, as my eyes turned down to the white tiles on the floor.

I took a deep breath in and then let it out before I looked up again. The girl was still there, and she flashed me another wide smile.

I smiled back, then tipped my cap and hastily made my way down the aisle, past the registers and out the doors. I didn't stop until I was back in my truck.

Once I was behind the wheel, I grabbed it with both hands. I wanted to curse as loud as I could, but I didn't. I knew enough to know that the walls had ears, as did my sixth-grade teacher putting groceries into her trunk two cars down from mine.

I fought for my keys inside my jeans pocket, and after a brief struggle, shoved one into the ignition.

She wasn't just a name attached to a face—although, I was pretty sure she was never just that. But even so, now she was also a memory, the worst kind of memory—the kind that pulled you to your knees at just the sound of her name.

I backed Lou out of the spot faster than I should have and sped out of the parking lot. And I sped all the way to my house and eventually landed in the driveway. Jeff's truck was already there. I sighed and made my way into the house.

"You're out of chili," Jeff informed me when I entered the room. "And everything else. Are you hiding all your food from me at your apartment in St. Louis?"

He was lounging on a chair in the living room; his legs were sprawled out over its arms. I didn't answer him. Instead, I charged straight through the house and out the back door.

Within seconds, I reached the two, wooden lawn chairs at the edge of the lake and fell into one. Then, I immediately threw my elbows to my knees and used my hands to bury my face.

Minutes went by, though it had felt like hours, before I heard Jeff's voice behind me.

"Uh, hey, man."

My Butterfly

I cocked my head to the side and glanced up at him. Then, I sat back and let my eyes fall onto the lake.

"You all right?" he asked, still hovering over me.

I listened to him fumble around behind me and eventually find a seat in the chair next to mine. Jeff was never really good in situations like this, and I really wasn't in the mood.

"I, uh, looked at Lou, and I'm guessin' ya didn't hit a deer," he said, sheepishly. "And I, uh, checked your refrigerator. I didn't leave your milk out again."

I angled my face slightly toward his again.

"And your dad called, so I answered it, and he just wanted me to remind you that you're supposed to help him with that barbeque tomorrow at the store," he said. "So, I figured, it didn't have anything to do with your family."

There was silence for a moment as I studied him with a puzzled look plastered across my face.

"You did all that in the little time that I was out here?" I asked.

He shrugged his shoulders.

I chuckled to myself and returned my eyes to the lake.

"It's not any of those things," I said.

There was a quiet pause.

"Then what is it?" he asked, in a way that made me think he believed there couldn't possibly be anything else that was "wrong" with me.

I took a deep breath and then tossed it back out into the soft breeze.

"It's Julia," I said and then sighed.

He sat up in his chair.

"What about her? You know she's back in town, right?" he asked.

I slowly bobbed my head.

"I know," I said. "I know."

He was quiet for a second again.

"Oh," he said, finally.

His word was short and sad.

I glanced back at him. And I couldn't help but smile.

"Oh what?" I asked.

He shot me an impatient look.

"Well, do you or do you not still have a thing for her?" he asked, staring back at me with big eyes.

I held my own stare on him for several seconds before I picked up a flat rock, swung my arm back and then skipped the rock onto the water. It bounced several times on the lake's surface before it eventually dived into the lake and disappeared.

"Well, why don't you just go tell her you still like her?" he asked.

I looked him in the eyes.

"Why don't you go tell Jessica that you like her?" I asked.

His face turned sour, and he shifted his weight in his chair.

"It's not easy for me like it is for you," he said.

I furrowed my eyebrows at him. I shouldn't have known what he had meant by that, but because I knew Jeff, sadly I did. Everything was harder in Jeff's world, apparently.

I found another rock and sent it flying onto the surface of the lake.

"Besides, the last thing I knew, she was still with that doctor," I said.

"Wait, he's a doctor?" he asked.

"He might as well be," I said.

"So what?" Jeff asked. "You had her first."

My Butterfly

I laughed.

"Buddy, I wish it worked that way," I said. "Plus, if she wants one of those types, maybe she should have it. The heart wants what the heart wants, right?"

I glanced back at Jeff. He was shaking his head, and it seemed as though he was frowning.

"Well, maybe she'll get bored of him," he said.

I laughed again.

"Jeff, girls don't just wake up one day and say, 'You know what? I'm tired of all these nice things and smart people. I want to go live in a one-horse town with a guy who leaves her with guys like you every time his belt starts singin'.'"

I eyed Jeff. He only shrugged his shoulders, so I kept going.

"'And you know what? I've suddenly discovered that I love the smell of ashes. Instead of nice cologne, I want a guy who comes home every night smellin' like ashes,'" I said.

Jeff was making his you-got-a-point face by the time I had finished.

I sighed and skipped another rock across the lake.

"But she's not just any girl, Will," Jeff said, sheepishly.

I turned in my chair and looked back at him, and suddenly, I felt a smile fighting its way to my face.

"You know, you're not always very good at giving advice," I admitted to him, patting his knee. "But every once in a while, you are."

He gave me a proud, goofy smile, and I sat back in my chair and locked my gaze onto the water.

"You're right, Jeff," I said, smiling. "She's not just any girl."

Chapter Twenty-Seven

Promise

"Will."

I turned in my chair and caught a thin blonde standing a lawn away from me on my porch. She looked like an angel, and instantly, a smile crept to my lips as I thought about Jeff's words from a week ago: *She's not just any girl.*

"Hey," I said in a surprised voice as I set my fishing pole onto the ground as quickly as I could get it there.

My heart had sped up by a couple of beats per minute, but I managed to make my way over to her in record time.

"Your aunt said you would be here this weekend," Jules said.

My Butterfly

I reached her and wrapped my arms around her little body. There was a big part of me that couldn't believe that she was standing on my porch. And I still didn't know why she was there, but it didn't matter. She was there.

I tightly squeezed her, and after a long moment, I pulled my body away from hers and smiled. I was pretty sure that I had that wide, stupid smile I got sometimes—mostly when she was around—planted on my face.

"Well, here I am. Pull up a chair," I happily said, gesturing down the wooden porch steps and toward the lake.

She walked with me to the water's edge, and I watched as she fell into the chair next to mine.

"Are they biting?" she asked, pulling her knees up to her chest.

I met her eyes and smiled, then grabbed my fishing pole again.

"A little, but I haven't caught any yet," I said, falling into the wooden chair. "I heard you were back in town. For how long?"

She seemed to hesitate before she spoke.

"A month," she softly said. "I'm substituting up at the school."

I let her answer sink in. Then, I nodded my head. I knew I had asked the question; I guessed I had just hoped the answer would have been a longer period of time, maybe even forever.

"I don't mind it actually," she continued. "I kind of like it. It gives me something to do for now."

"The substituting?" I asked, now somewhat distracted by the thought of her leaving again.

"Mm hmm," she said, nodding her head.

"I see," I said. "Then where are you going?"

I kind of dreaded that answer too.

"California," she said.

I choked on my own breath.

"California?" I blurted out. "What for?"

She gently smiled.

"School," she said.

I watched as she paused and fiddled with the zipper on her jacket for a second.

"Law," she continued.

"Law," I simply repeated, as I nodded my head and forced a smile. "Well, that's your dream."

Silence crept into the conversation, but I squashed it within seconds.

"But why California?" I asked. "That's like a whole, different country. You know there's no grass or trees out there. Isn't there something closer?"

I watched her toss her head back and laugh. I had forgotten how much I missed her laugh.

"It's warm though," she said, with a grin.

I paused for a second, lowered my head and then met her eyes again.

"So, you're telling me that if I find a way to get rid of the winter here, you'll stay closer for once?" I asked.

I felt one side of my mouth lifting into a grin.

"I'll stay forever," she said, laughing.

"What about palm trees?" I asked.

She smiled and shook her head.

"Yeah, I didn't think so," I said, still grinning.

We grew silent then, as we both stared off into the lake. I tapped my fishing pole a couple of times against a cattail and watched the bobber bounce on the surface of the water. And for the first time, I noticed the air smelled like old maple trees and the last cut of hay. I tugged at the pole some, then spotted some butterfly weeds off in the distance on the other side of the lake and remembered what the chief had told me.

"Happiness is like a butterfly, you know?" I mumbled to myself.

Out of the corner of my eye, I saw her face turn toward mine.

"What?" she asked.

I shifted in my chair, then met her gaze.

"Happiness is like a butterfly," I said again. "The more you chase it, the more it will elude you, but if you turn your attention to other things, it will come and sit softly on your shoulder."

"It's Thoreau," I added.

She held her stare on me for a little longer. Then, she returned her gaze to the lake.

"Hmm," she said, in what seemed like reflection, as she slowly nodded her head.

"So, how have you been? What have you been up to these days?" she asked moments later.

I shifted restlessly in my chair.

"Working, golfing, fishing," I quickly rattled off.

I was trying not to sound frustrated, but deep down, I knew I had already lost that battle.

"You're looking at it," I added, just for good measure.

"How's living in St. Louis? I heard you got an apartment. Do you like it?" she asked, seemingly unfazed by my detached state.

"It's fine," I said. "It's all fine. Are you seeing anyone?"

I kept my eyes on the water. I was afraid of this answer even though I already knew it.

"I am," she said. "I'm still seeing Brady."

I mumbled what could have almost been a word under my breath. She didn't seem to notice.

"What about you?" she asked.

"What about me?"

"Well, how's Miss New Year's Eve?" she asked.

My gaze shot back toward her. A second later, I was searching her eyes to gauge her seriousness.

"You still remember that?" I asked.

I was still hoping that she hadn't—that the night had just miraculously disappeared from her memory.

Her eyes faltered and fell to the ground.

"Jules, that whole thing was just a bad idea," I said and then stopped.

I searched her features then with narrowed eyes and furrowed brows, until she found my eyes again, and my expression softened. Surely, she hadn't thought that I had been with Jessica this whole time.

"Jules, I'm sorry about that night. I...," I started.

"Will, it's fine," she said, stopping me. "You had a date. So what? We weren't together. Plus, it was a long time ago. I don't even think about it anymore."

I tried to say something, but instead, the word *anymore* bounced around my mind, interfering with my speech functions. *She didn't even think about it anymore.* The thought made me sigh both because there was a part of me, I guessed, that still hoped she did think about it—about us—and then there was another part of me that wished I could say the same. Most times, I wished I couldn't remember it either. I let my eyes linger in hers for a few more seconds before I gently smiled and returned my attention to the lake again. Then, I refit my baseball cap around my head and tried to clear away the ache in my throat. That ache meant I had to act fast. I had to get her or me away before that damn mist in my eyes returned.

"Well, I have to go to my parents' house for dinner tonight," I said, as I reeled in my line and stood up from my chair. "Mom's making her specialty. I promised her I'd be there."

I watched her grow still and then nod her head.

"Okay, yeah, can't miss that," she said. "I'd better get going then. It was nice seeing you again, Will."

I caught her awkwardly fidgeting with the zipper on her jacket again, and it helped me to smile.

"Come," I blurted out.

"What?" she asked.

Her voice was soft and hesitant.

"Come with me," I said again.

Her eyes fell toward the ground, then returned to mine a couple of seconds later.

"Okay," she said, starting to smile and to slowly nod her head again.

"All right, let's go," I said, turning to leave.

I took a couple of steps, then looked back at her. She hadn't moved.

"You coming?" I asked.

I watched as her pretty lips lifted into a grin. Then, she nodded her head and followed after me.

"Dinner was okay, huh?" I asked.

She met my gaze and smiled.

"Dinner is always more than okay here," she said.

She kept her eyes on mine for a couple of seconds. Then, I noticed her stare venture over to my guitar, propped up against the porch railing.

"Do you still play?" she asked.

I smiled a wide grin at her, then got up, grabbed the guitar and laid it across my lap.

"This song is all yours," I said, swinging the guitar's strap around my body.

She flashed me a puzzled look. I, in turn, gave her a confident smile and then went to playing with the guitar's strings for a second.

"Mine?" she asked.

"Yep, all yours. Everyone needs a song—this one will be yours. I'll never use it for anyone else," I vowed.

She lowered her eyes and laughed.

"Okay," she said, peeking at me from behind her long eyelashes.

I got lost in her stare for a moment. Then, I took a deep breath and reluctantly tore my eyes from hers. Seconds later, I started in on a soft melody, and then, added its words:

"It's a summer night
And I can hear the crickets sing
But otherwise, all the world's asleep
While I can only lie awake and dream
And every time I close my eyes
A butterfly comes to me

It has soft, green eyes
A sweet soul
Brave wings
And each time, it hears me sing…"

I stopped singing but continued to tickle the guitar's strings, until eventually, my fingers ceased their dance altogether, and silence filled the air around us again.

My Butterfly

"That's it?" she asked. "Where are the rest of the words?"

My eyes fell to the wooden floor beneath us.

"I'm...I'm still working on the rest," I said.

I was trying not to smile.

"You can hear it again when I'm finished with it. I promise," I said.

I returned my eyes to hers. Her suspicious glare was burning a tattoo into my forehead.

"Well, when will it be finished?" she asked.

I paused and allowed the corners of my mouth to slowly rise.

"I'll find a way to get it to your ears," I said. "Don't worry."

She playfully pursed her lips. Her eyes were still narrowed, and she was still giving me an apprehensive look.

"Okay," she said. "I'll wait if I have to, I guess."

I watched her take another sip of her lemonade.

"You should play for people—you know," she said, setting the glass back down onto the porch boards. "I might even do you the honor of being your biggest fan."

I laughed once.

"You never give up, do you?" I asked.

My eyes caught hers and rested in them for a little while.

"Nah," I finally said. "Work keeps me pretty busy. Besides, I don't mind just playing like this—for friends, for you."

She smiled, and then her eyes ventured off to somewhere in the distance. I followed her stare to a couple of street lights starting to come alive in the darkness that threatened to engulf us.

"Will," she said.

Her soft voice attracted my full attention again.

"You know you've got a piece of me always, no matter what this crazy world has planned for us, right?" she asked.

I nodded my head as a smile pushed its way to my face. I knew I probably should have been thrown off by her confession, but I wasn't. It was the truth. The truth rarely surprised me.

"Yeah, I know, and you've got the other half of me, damn the luck," I said, chuckling.

I watched her tilt her head back, as a soft laugh fell from her lips.

"How can we ever function separately?" I asked, silently stroking the strings of my guitar.

She caught my stare and smiled a wide grin.

"I'm sure we'll make do," she said.

Her eyes lingered in mine just a little too long—long enough for me to imagine kissing her again. My heart sped up, and I could feel my chest rising and falling in short blips.

"I probably should be going," she said, suddenly throwing her gaze to the hard floor.

I froze for an instant, my eyes still locked on her.

"Okay," I said, eventually forcing a sound.

I didn't agree that she should be going, but I knew that I couldn't force her to stay either.

Then, suddenly, she started to get up. I followed with my eyes a path from her pretty lips to her hand that now rested on the arm of the chair. And then, without another thought, my own hand instinctively went to hers.

"Jules," I said, placing my hand on top of hers.

I felt her soft skin under mine, and I squeezed my fingers around hers. She stopped and sat back in her chair, as her eyes darted first toward her hand and then to my eyes.

"Promise me you'll come if I ever change my mind about the singing gig," I whispered. "Promise you'll come and listen to the rest of the song."

She looked a little caught off guard, of course. I would have too. I followed her eyes as they moved back and forth from my hand on hers to my eyes. And then, she smiled.

"I promise," she said, in almost a whisper.

Then, she pushed up from her chair, slid her hand out from underneath mine and made her way back into the house.

My body was frozen, but my eyes followed her into the kitchen. And I watched her through the glass as she set her drink into the sink and then made her way to the front door.

I quickly got up then and scurried inside after her but stopped when she turned back toward me.

"Thanks for tonight, Will," she softly said.

I forced a smile.

"Don't mention it," I said.

She held her gaze in mine for a moment, and then without another word, she turned and escaped back into the night on the other side of the door.

Chapter Twenty-Eight

Deal

"**Y**ou should sing—for people," she said, through her pretty laughter.

The sound of her laugh echoed off the walls in the empty room.

I shook my head, but a smile lingered on my lips.

"No, Will, I'm serious," she said. "You should."

Her smile was soft and confident, but then it faded. And I watched as she turned and started to walk away.

"Where are you going?" I asked.

My smile had disappeared as well.

"I have to go," she said.

I could hear a certain longing in her voice, as she stopped and faced me again.

My Butterfly

"Dreams don't wait, Will," she said, with a sad look in her eyes.

"You'll like it," she assured me.

I traced the features of her pretty face, as a smile slowly returned to life under her sad eyes.

"And I'll come back. I promise," she said.

Her gaze lingered in mine, and her longing stare made my heart crumble into a billion pieces. I didn't know her thoughts, but I knew they carried with them some amount of sadness. I kept my eyes on the green in hers, until I blinked, and then she was gone.

"Julia," I yelled, running toward the door.

I pulled on its knob when I reached it, but the door didn't open. I pulled harder with both hands, but it still wouldn't budge. I turned and thrust my back against its wooden surface. Then, I cradled my face within my hands out of frustration mixed with a pain that made my knees buckle. I felt my body slowly slide down the door then, and I sat there kneeling until a noise made me look up. It sounded as if something had just fallen to the floor, but nothing was there. Then all of a sudden, I noticed something. She must have dropped it. I picked myself back up and shuffled toward the object. It was a card—a business card. I read the name at the top: *Jesse Sovine.* Then, my eyes followed over the words below the name, but as I got to a word, its letters quickly disappeared, until the card was just blank, except for the name at the top.

Then, suddenly, there were hundreds of the same card all raining down from heaven. I lifted my hand to shield my face from them. And as soon as I had, I noticed there was something else now on the card in my hand. I squinted my eyes in order to read the tiny text. Now, instead of the name, there was one, small sentence: *I Promise.*

I turned my face over on my pillow and felt something hit my forehead. I quickly shifted again and then pulled the sheet up so that it was covering most of my face. A second later, I felt something else hit the top of my head. Then, I opened my eyes and saw a big peanut resting on the pillow next to me.

"What the hell?" I exclaimed, as I quickly sat up.

"Dude, are you going to sleep all day?"

"What?" I asked, noticing Jeff in the doorway, a can of peanuts in one hand. The other hand was feeding handfuls of peanuts into his mouth. "What time is it?"

I rubbed my eyes and searched for the glowing numbers on my alarm clock.

"Umm, seven maybe," he said.

I shook my head and rubbed my eyes again.

"Why are you in my house?" I asked.

"Dude, I've been standing here trying to get you up for ten minutes now," he said. "You sleep like a bear."

"Wha…," I stuttered, still shaking my head.

I didn't even bother finishing my sentence.

"I was wondering if you wanted to go fishin'," he said.

I found the clock. It glowed six twenty in its neon numbers.

I took a breath in and then let out a sigh.

"All right," I said.

"Good, I've got the poles in my truck," he said.

Just then, my eyes fell onto the business card sitting on the chest across the room.

"Just put some pants on. Let's go," he squeaked.

Another peanut hit my face and broke my stare from the card.

"Is there something wrong with you?" he asked.

My Butterfly

"What?" I asked, returning my attention back to him. "No...I just remembered this crazy dream I had."

He threw his head back and laughed once.

"Buddy, your life's a crazy dream," he said. "Now, let's go."

My eyes eventually settled onto the card again.

"Okay," I said. "Just give me a second, and I'll be out there."

I glanced back at him. He was giving me that dumb, puzzled look he does best. I didn't say anything.

"Okay," he eventually said.

I watched him turn and leave the doorway. Then, I pulled the sheets back and walked over to the chest. I picked up the business card and held it carefully in between my fingers. I read over its words, then spotted my phone sitting on the chest next to a bottle of cologne. I reached for it, picked it up and cradled it in my other hand. Silent moments passed with the business card in one hand and the phone in the other. Then, finally, I took a deep breath, slowly let it out and then pressed number six on my speed dial.

"Hey, buddy," I heard a voice answer on the other end a few rings later.

"Hey, Matt. I didn't wake ya, did I?" I asked.

"No, no, we just got back from a call," he said. "What's up?"

"Uh, you still want to give this agent a shot?" I asked.

He was quiet for a second.

"Uh, yeah," I eventually heard him say. "Do you?"

I smiled to myself.

"I think I do," I said. "Do you think you could talk Daniel into it?"

"Daniel's in," he said. "He just needed some reassuring that it wasn't quite the craziest thing we've ever done."

I laughed.

"Okay," I said, taking another deep breath.

"So, we're really going to do this?" he asked.

I could hear a smile in his voice.

"I'll give this Jesse Sovine guy a call, and we'll see what happens, I guess," I said.

"All right, great," he said. "I'll tell the guys."

"Okay," I replied, nodding my head.

My finger lunged for the button that would end the call but stopped when I heard his voice again.

"Wait, Will?"

"Yeah?" I asked.

"What made ya change your mind?" he asked.

A smile started to slowly etch a path across my face, as I let a silent moment pass.

"A girl," I said.

I heard him laugh on the other end.

"I should have known," he said.

"Hey, call me after you talk to him," he said.

"Okay, I will," I said.

I hung up and found the number on the card still cradled in my hand. Then, I methodically punched into my phone each number, until all ten digits were displayed on the phone's screen. And after another deep breath, I counted to three in my head and then hit the *call* button.

Five, long rings later I heard his voice telling me to leave a message. I contemplated hanging up, but I didn't and instead, waited for the beep.

A second went by after the beep before I said anything. Then, I cleared my throat.

"Uh, hi, Mr. Sovine, this is Will Stephens from District 9," I said into the receiver. "We talked at the Home of Blues a while back. And I don't know if you're still interested, but we'd like to talk about you possibly representing us."

I hesitated for a second.

"Uh, you can call me back on this number. Thanks."

I stopped, ended the call and carefully set the business card back onto the chest. Then, I felt something small hit the back of my head, and I watched as a peanut rolled to a spot on the floor.

"Dude, I thought you went back to sleep or something," Jeff said in his whiney voice. "Why don't you have pants on?"

I looked down at my boxers, then turned around and shuffled back over to the other side of the bed without even acknowledging him. I found a pair of jeans I had worn the day before lying on the floor and stepped into them. Then, I reached for a shirt from an open drawer and squeezed it on over my head.

"Voilà," I said, turning and facing Jeff with my arms out to my sides. "Ready."

"About time, loser," he said, as he turned on his heels in the doorway again. "The fish have probably all hibernated or frozen in the time it took you to do that."

I smiled and shuffled toward the bedroom door. But on my way, I took one, last glance at the business card staring back at me from the chest. It forced me to suck in another big breath of air.

"Girl, the things you make me do," I mumbled in my next exhale.

Chapter Twenty-Nine

Wedding

"**W**ill, I've been looking for you."

I turned around in the bench to see a young woman, dressed from head to toe in white, and immediately, it made me smile.

"Hey, Mona, do you need something?" I asked her.

Mona had always been like a little sister to me, and now, she seemed all grown up all of a sudden.

"No, no," she said, laughing. "I just saw you talking to that girl over there."

"What girl? When?" I asked.

"Taylor," Mona said. "The petite girl, auburn hair, you know? She's a friend from college."

"Oh," I said, habitually rubbing the back of my neck.

"Uh, yeah, she's requesting a song," I said.

My Butterfly

Mona flashed me a mischievous grin.

"She asked if I would dance with her when it plays," I continued.

"And you said?" she asked.

"I said I would, but it's just a dance, Mona," I said. She shook her head.

"She's the one," she said, pointing at me. "Taylor's a really nice girl, Will."

"I just met her, Mona," I said, through a patient smile.

"She's the one," she said again.

I gave her a disbelieving look.

"Just give her a chance, Will, for your little cousin on her wedding day," she said, with a pleading smile.

"Mona, Taylor's the one…," I started but stopped short, as my eyes caught a familiar silhouette and my heart momentarily took a break from its beating.

"Julia," I said, quickly sitting up.

"Hi, Will," she said.

Jules planted her eyes in my gaze for a moment and then turned her attention to Mona.

"Hi, Mona," she said. "You look beautiful."

Mona shot me a suspicious look and then set her eyes on Julia. I, in the meantime, tried to relax my shoulders and to not look so obvious.

"Thanks, Julia. I'm so glad you made it," Mona said, wrapping Jules into a big embrace. "And we'll have to catch up, but right now, I've got to find the groom. They're making us take more pictures, and this guy's been holding me up," she said, pulling away from Julia and gesturing toward me.

I sent Mona a puzzled look, but it didn't seem to faze her as she hurried off to somewhere else and left Jules and me alone.

I took a second before I spoke.

"I wasn't sure you'd be here," I said.

"I wasn't either," she replied.

She smiled and caught my stare.

The shock of my heart suddenly stopping moments ago was starting to fade, and my smile was returning.

"How long are you here?" I asked.

"Just tonight," she said.

I glanced around.

"You here with anyone?" I asked.

"No," she said, shaking her head.

I cocked my head to the side.

"No," she quickly said again, seeming to read my mind. "Brady had to work."

"Oh," I said. "You two still..."

I couldn't even finish the sentence, damn it. I felt my mood changing fast. I tried to hide what I was sure was obvious disdain, as she nodded her head in confirmation.

Of course.

I sucked in an audible breath and then sat back.

"How is everything?" she asked.

I met her eyes again. *Did she want me to be honest?*

"It's fine," I lied.

She nodded her head again as her lips went back to a straight position on her face. But she held her eyes in mine. I could tell she was thinking something, but I couldn't tell what it was.

Then, I watched her carefully slide off her shoes and then tiptoe over the grass toward the bench I was sitting on and take a seat.

I glanced at the space in between us. It wasn't the close I was used to associating with Jules, but it was a couple thousand miles closer than I got these days. So, in the end, the ten inches that separated us made me smile again.

"You look nice," I said.

She looked up at me, and I watched as her lips broke into a sweet, sideways smile.

"Thanks," she said. "You don't look so bad yourself."

I felt my grin growing wider, and suddenly, it didn't matter that she was leaving again the next day. At least I had tonight.

I thought of something then—something I had been waiting to tell her.

"Hey, remember prom night our senior year and you said that you only had one wish in life?" I asked her.

She laughed.

"For New Milford to get a pizza place," she said, bobbing her head.

Her gaze was straight ahead, and a pretty smile lingered on her lips.

"Well...," I said.

"No," she exclaimed, quickly angling her face back toward mine.

"Yes," I confirmed.

She shoved my shoulder. It moved me only slightly, but it did cause my smile to grow wider.

"I can't believe it," she shouted.

"Believe," I said.

"Where?" she asked.

"Downtown, next to the movie theater," I said.

Her mouth was slightly frozen open. It looked sexy and playful all at the same time.

"Have you been?" she asked.

Her excitement made me laugh.

"I have," I said, nodding my head. "It's good."

"I have to go," she exclaimed and then paused.

I watched her stare fall to the shoes dangling from her fingertips.

"Next time," she said, as her wide smile began to fade.

I nodded my head and felt my grin vanishing too.

"Next time," I softly agreed.

There was silence for a moment again. And my eyes fell onto the dress she was wearing. It was green. It matched her pretty eyes. But it also reminded me of the green dress she wore to homecoming our junior year. We stayed up all night that night—her in my arms—and watched the sun come up in the morning.

"You're in too many of my memories, Jules," I said, as a grin fought its way back to my lips again.

Her eyes instantly fell into mine. And then, slowly, her eyebrows drew closer together and one corner of her mouth faintly rose.

"I have that same problem," she said, softly laughing into the subtle breeze.

I held my gaze in her eyes, until her stare broke and returned to her hands and her shoes, now slowly swaying from side to side. Then, I sucked in a deep breath of cool air, and at the same time, felt my smile wane.

"How do you like it out there?" I asked.

I watched as her chest rose and then fell.

"It's beautiful," she said, sending me a quick glance.

A wide smile had returned to her face.

"But a different kind of beautiful than here," she continued. "I mean, there's a lot of traffic and a lot of people. But the ocean is perfect, and there are mountains, and there's an orange tree in my neighbor's front yard."

"An orange tree, really?" I asked.

Her pretty eyes were big.

My Butterfly

"I know, that's what I said," she exclaimed, nodding her head.

She looked so happy all of a sudden.

"And school?" I asked.

She laughed.

"It's school—on steroids," she said. "I just never thought that I could cram this much stuff into my brain at one time. It's so much stuff."

She emphasized the *so*, but she was smiling as she said it.

"You like it though?" I asked.

She nodded again.

"I do," she said.

She paused then.

"What about you?" she asked. "How's the job going?"

I nodded my head before I spoke.

"It's great," I said and meant it. "There's always something going on. I like that about it."

"Please, God, tell me there hasn't been any more close calls," she demanded.

I watched her eyelids fall over her eyes and her hand rush to her chest and cover her heart. Then, I softly chuckled to myself.

"No," I reassured her. "No close calls, knock on wood."

I knocked on the wooden arm of the bench.

"But I've also got my guardian angel," I said, touching my hand to my heart.

She found my eyes again and smiled.

"There you are," a voice suddenly called out from behind us. "You ready? You promised. This song."

My eyes traveled toward the voice, as a girl with auburn hair planted her feet directly in front of Jules and me. She was smiling wide, and her head was cocked playfully in my direction. I glanced back at Julia and then back at the girl. And in that time, the girl's eyes had fallen on Jules.

"Uh, Taylor," I stuttered, trying to remember her name again. "This is Julia. Julia, this is Taylor."

I watched as Julia's eyes widened a little and her lips fell slightly open.

"Taylor," Julia repeated then, as if she were remembering something.

Taylor extended her hand.

"Nice to meet you," she said, in a Missouri-Bootheel twang.

Julia raised her hand to meet Taylor's. Her smile was poised.

"You ready?" Taylor asked again, quickly redirecting her attention to me.

Everything in me was shouting *no*, as I stumbled onto Julia's eyes again.

"Go," she whispered, so softly that I was sure Taylor couldn't hear it.

"The next one?" I asked her.

Jules smiled.

"Next time," she said.

I hesitated. There was something in her voice that made me feel as if there wouldn't be a *next time*. A sudden sadness took hold of my chest then and squeezed it tight. I almost told Taylor that I couldn't leave Julia, but I didn't. Julia was happy; I could tell. And there was a part of me that wondered if my interference would somehow shatter that happiness.

I reluctantly returned my gaze to Taylor. She shot me a wide grin, and then I slowly lifted myself up from the bench. But when I was on my feet again, I turned back

My Butterfly

and met Jules's eyes one, last time. She smiled her beautiful smile, and I tried my best to force a smile too. Then, I begrudgingly followed Taylor to the dance floor.

The song ended, and immediately, I searched the faces on the dance floor for Julia. I didn't see her, but I did see Rachel.

"Rach, have you seen Jules?" I asked, when I got close enough for her to hear me.

Rachel turned and met my eyes.

"She had to go," Rachel said. "She's got an early flight tomorrow—gotta get back to her big-city life. She doesn't have time for us small-townies anymore."

She elbowed my arm and giggled.

"God love her," she went on. "Maybe she'll take me with her next time."

She eyed her boyfriend and deviously smiled.

Jon stared at her for a second. Then, without warning, he shrouded her in a big bear hug and squeezed her close to his side

"You're not going anywhere," he said.

Rachel giggled again and then dramatically sighed.

"Maybe another life then," she said, staring back up at me.

I tried to force a smile, but in the end, I just didn't have the strength. Everything in me was focused on Julia and on the one thought that was swirling endlessly around in my mind: *How could I have let her get away again?*

Chapter Thirty

One Step

"Is this the first time you boys have ever been inside a recording studio?" the thin man asked in a half-serious, half-joking tone.

We all looked at each other.

"Yes, sir," I eventually said, nodding my head.

"Okay, well, you ready to record a song then?" he asked.

"Yeah," Chris excitedly yelled.

The rest of us only nodded our heads and smiled wide.

My Butterfly

"All right, let's do it," he said. "Drums first."

We each took turns recording our own tracks, until it finally came to the vocals.

I stood there playing with the big headphones that threatened to engulf both sides of my head. I couldn't hear anything in them except for the thin man's voice, which would muffle through every once in a while.

My eyes eventually turned down, and I caught a glimpse of metal peeking out from in between my fingers. Her guardian angel was tightly pressed against my palm.

"Okay, Will," I heard the man's voice again. "I'm going to start the track."

I looked through the glass to where the thin man was sitting and nodded my head.

A few seconds later, the music trickled through the big headphones, and I slowly brought my lips to the funny-looking microphone. I felt the words then grow in my stomach and then climb into my chest. They stayed there for a moment and then finally fell from my lips one by one—just like they had a hundred times before:

"I'm famous in this small town
For a ghost I cannot shake
They all know I'm talkin' to you
But of it—I don't think they know what to make

But they don't see what I see
They don't see you dance on the river walk,
Underneath the street lamps
With those stars in your eyes

They don't see you
Lying next to me
Tellin' me your dreams,

Planted somewhere up in those big skies

No, they don't see what I see
Because I see
A rainstorm in June
Just before the sun
The black of night
Just before the stars
And, girl, I see your ghost
Just before our dawn

And tonight I'll see you again
Just like every night before
But they don't see what I see
What I see is more

Because I see
A rainstorm in June
Just before the sun
The black of night
Just before the stars
And, girl, I see your ghost
Just before our dawn

And, girl, I see your ghost
Just before our dawn."

My lips hovered in front of the microphone as the last words of the ballad hit the black mesh and disappeared. But the music still played inside my big headset and filled my ears. I closed my eyes and took in each note, as a deep breath invaded my lungs. The song meant something to me, and I couldn't sing it without feeling something too. I fought back the tightness in my chest as the small room eventually grew quiet again.

"That was great, Will," I heard a muffled voice say into my ears. "I think we've got your single."

A smile scurried to my lips. Those words sounded better together than I had ever imagined they could. I squeezed my fingers tightly around the guardian angel in my hand again, and suddenly, I felt one step closer.

Chapter Thirty-One

District 9

"What's this all about?" Chris asked when he entered the room.

"Not sure," Matt said.

Daniel, Matt and I were already seated around a big desk in a small office. There was a window that overlooked the street behind the desk. And on the desk, there were office gadgets resembling every piece of the music industry you could dream up—including a guitar that was also a tape dispenser and a microphone that moonlighted as a lamp. I took a deep breath. The room smelled like a mixture of that cologne Jesse always wore and some kind of weird smell that came from an air freshener contraption on a shelf filled with little glass trophies. The contraption made a noise every couple of seconds and then puffed out a misty fog. I watched the fog now as it followed a path to the desk and then eventually disappeared. Then, I caught Matt's stare. He held his gaze on me until I shrugged my shoulders and sat back in my chair.

Jesse flew into the room seconds later in perfect Jesse fashion—quick and dramatic. He looked as if he were in a rush; but then again, he always looked as if he were in a rush.

"How's it going, guys?" he asked, falling into the leather chair behind the big desk.

He always asked the same question. But we knew not to answer it. There was never enough time from when he asked it to when he started talking again.

"I've got this band that's interested in having you guys as the guest artists on their album," he quickly went on. "Have you guys ever heard of Ren Lake?"

We all looked at each other like this guy was suddenly going to grow a snout and wings and fly out of the room and take the dream with him. This went on for a few seconds.

"Is that the knock-off of the real Ren Lake or something?" Chris eventually asked, chuckling to himself and sending us a quick glance.

We all kind of snickered, but Jesse just smiled and lowered his eyes to a spot on the surface of his desk.

"Good guess, but no," he said, lifting his eyes again.

"Wait, you're not telling us it's the real Ren Lake?" Daniel asked.

Jesse's mouth started to slowly turn up at its edges.

"I'm telling you there's only one Ren Lake, and they want District 9," he said.

The room instantly grew silent then. We all seemed to be studying the slender man facing us. Even I watched his every move: his every eye blink, the way he kept biting his bottom lip and furrowing his brow—as if he didn't quite know what to make of our silence.

"Wow," Chris eventually shouted. "Well, what did you tell them?"

Jesse paused for a moment.

"Well, I told them that I would have to talk to you guys first but that I think it would be a great fit."

"Hot damn," Chris shouted again.

He held his hand up in the air in front of Daniel, and Daniel high-fived it.

"So, what does this mean exactly?" Matt asked.

"Well, it means that you guys will be a part of Ren Lake's new album, which means a lot more exposure for you. And we can never tell for sure where that exposure might lead, but the hope is that there will be more and bigger gigs, and in the future, possibly an album."

"An album!" Chris shouted.

"Now, it would also most likely require significantly more time from you guys," Jesse continued. "And I know you have the firefighter gig. I don't know if, need be, you could take a leave of absence or something like that or even think about music as a career."

Jesse sat back in his big, leather chair and smiled. I found Matt's stare and then Daniel's. Then, Jesse sat back up and shuffled some papers around his desk.

"But we can cross that bridge when we get there," he said. "So, you guys in?"

We all looked at each other one more time. I tried to hold back a smile, but I couldn't. And Chris and Daniel were already smiling when the corners of Matt's mouth started to twitch upward.

"This only happens maybe once in a lifetime," Chris said, his eyes big.

My Butterfly

Matt shrugged his shoulders.

"We can figure the rest out as it comes, I guess," Matt said.

I glanced at Daniel. He was nodding his head in agreement.

My eyes fell back onto Jesse, who had since abandoned the papers on his desk and now seemed to devote his full attention to the four of us.

"I think we're in," I said to him.

Jesse slowly nodded and then smiled.

"I thought you would be," he said.

Chapter Thirty-Two

Reunion

"I mean, really, is this really necessary?" Rachel asked, as she elbowed me in the arm. "I see these people almost everyday. And if I wanted to see them at night, I could do that too. The keyword here is *if*."

"Oh, come on, Rach," I said. "It isn't that bad. Your five-year high school reunion only comes around once in a lifetime."

She glared at me with narrowed eyes.

"The invitation said, 'no guests,'" she continued. "What kind of a party do you go to that you can't bring any guests?"

I shrugged my shoulders.

"I didn't make the rules, Rach," I said.

I grabbed two drinks from the counter, and at the same time, noticed a big guy in the opposite corner of the room.

"Wait, Rach, isn't that Jon over there?" I asked.

"Hmm?" she asked.

She seemed disinterested.

"Jon," I repeated.

"Oh, yeah, I brought him anyway," she said, flipping her hand in the air.

I stared at her for a second as she walked away. Then, I smiled and followed her to a table in the corner of the room. We sat down, and I slid her a drink. She took a big gulp of it and then set the glass down.

"Great," she exclaimed then, under her breath.

"What?" I asked.

"Don't look back," she said. "Maybe she won't see us."

"What?" I asked.

"Rachel! Will!"

I turned in my chair, but before I could get all the way around, a woman was already wrapping one arm around my back and hooking her hand onto my shoulder. She smelled of strong perfume.

"Janette," Rachel said, in a hollow and unenthused tone.

I caught Rachel's glare and smiled, knowingly.

"I didn't know you two were going to be here," Janette exclaimed, pulling up a chair and squeezing in between Rachel and me.

Rachel looked at me sideways. I shrugged my shoulders and smiled back at her.

"It's our class reunion, Janette," Rachel said. "Who did you expect to see here?"

Janette hadn't seemed to have heard Rachel's question, and if she had, she ignored it.

"Now, what are you two up to these days?" Janette asked in a high-pitched voice.

Rachel let out an exasperated puff of air.

"I'm teaching...," Rachel started.

"That's right," Janette interrupted, as she tossed back her head and laughed. "That's a silly question. You're in Hartsville, and Will, are you still fighting those fires?"

She winked at me, and at the same time, she dug her long, red talons into my bicep.

"Yes, Janette," I said, smiling up at Rachel.

Rachel scowled at me.

"Have you heard that my boyfriend just got a job at the bank?" she asked. "He's in the accounting department. I don't think you've met him. He went to Northwest Missouri, graduated near the top of his class."

I watched as Rachel's lips twitched but then finally formed a fake smile.

"He's probably going to propose to me at any moment now," she continued. "We've already talked about buying a house here in town, and he wants two kids. But we're going to start off with a dog first, you know. We're going to skip the plant. God knows we can take care of a plant," she said, laughing up into the air. "That's just a waste of our time. Time's a tickin', you know."

Janette paused and smiled at Rachel.

Rachel forced her fake smile higher up her face and slowly shook her head back and forth.

"It's a tickin'," Rachel repeated. "But sadly, not fast enough," she added under her breath, while flashing me an impatient glare.

Suddenly, Janette's purse burst to life then with the help of some off-beat tune, and immediately, Janette's attention flew to the bag. I watched her root in the purse for a second before I noticed Rachel's eyes on me again. They were big and telling, and I just knew she wanted to strangle Janette or run or something. I chuckled to myself and lowered my eyes.

Janette eventually rescued her phone and pulled it from her purse.

"Oh, it's just my mom. She probably wants my recipe for those blueberry muffins I made the other night," she said, still staring into her phone's screen.

Rachel's narrow eyes flashed back to Janette. I quickly cleared my throat and garnered Rachel's attention again. She met my eyes and gave me a pleading look but then eventually forced another counterfeit smile.

"By the way, Will, where's Julia?" Janette asked, after poking a button on the phone and throwing it back into her purse.

Rachel's eyes fiercely darted back toward Janette, and this time, there was nothing I could do to stop her. Instead, I just swallowed hard and uncomfortably shifted in my chair.

"Uh, Janette," Rachel said, regaining Janette's attention. "I heard that Ben, uh, knows a guy who went to Northwest and might know your boyfriend."

I furrowed my brows at Rachel. She caught my gaze and shrugged her shoulders.

"Does he really?" Janette asked.

She sounded excited.

"You know, I bet they were in the same fraternity," Janette said. "They're all so close, you know?"

Rachel smiled and lifted her shoulders again.

"You know, that's probably it," Rachel said.

"Where is Ben?" Janette asked, as she pushed herself up from her chair and craned her neck around.

Rachel pointed to a burly-looking guy across the room, and just like that, Janette was gone.

"Thanks," I softly said.

"Don't mention it," Rachel said.

There was a silent moment then as Rachel and I both watched Janette run over to Ben and say something and then Ben look at her as if she were crazy.

"Priceless," Rachel said, proudly smiling.

"So, how is everything going?" Rachel asked, planting her eyes on me again. "What do your parents think about the band and everything?"

I smiled.

"They seem to be getting used to the idea," I said. "I really don't think they knew what to think of it at first. But you know them; if I'm happy, they're happy."

Rachel shook her head and smiled.

"I bet your mom's ecstatic," she said.

I chuckled a little to myself.

"Yeah, I guess it was Dad that I had to more or less convince," I said.

"Oh, I'm sure it didn't take much convincing once he heard you guys play," she said.

I smiled, bashfully. Then, it was quiet for a moment again.

"So, have you talked to Julia lately?" I asked.

Rachel found my eyes and gently smiled, kind of like a mom would smile at you right before she told you that your hamster didn't make it through the night or something.

"She's doing well," she said, slowly nodding her head. "She has a test or something and couldn't make it tonight, but she's doing well."

I nodded my head too as my eyes turned down and searched for a spot to rest on the table's surface in front of us.

"Can you believe Janette?" Rachel asked, quickly changing the subject. "I mean, you're practically a rock star, and she's sitting here talking about her accountant boyfriend like he just found some medical cure."

I lowered my head and laughed.

"I'm not a rock star, Rach," I said.

"Well, you're gonna be, and Little Miss Tickin' Blueberry Muffin is going to drop one of her two kids into her perfect recipe's batter when she sees you on television someday," she said.

I chuckled some more.

"Rachel, you've got a wild imagination," I said.

Rachel laughed, found my gaze and then rested her hand on mine.

My eyes darted to her hand and then met her eyes.

"Call her," she said, softly. "There's no reason you guys should be strangers."

I forced a smile and nodded my head. Then, I felt her hand slowly pull away from mine again.

"Rachel," I said and then stopped.

I glanced around us. Nobody was within an ear's shot, so I continued.

"It's been five years, and it just doesn't seem like we're ever in the same place," I said. "There have been times when I've wanted to say things to her."

I paused and looked around again.

"But it just never happened," I went on. "There's a part of me that feels like she might prefer that we just be strangers."

Rachel softly smiled.

"Her dad was a cop," she said.

My eyes instinctively narrowed. She had said the words as straightforward as you could say words. I cocked my head and furrowed my eyebrows. Then, I watched her close her eyes briefly and nod her head.

"St. Boni Police Department for fifteen years," she said. "He quit the force when Julia was eight."

I was speechless for a second.

"What?" I eventually asked.

She sighed and met my eyes again.

"Evidently one night, he didn't come home, and Julia's mom went crazy trying to find him," she said. "Eventually, she found out that he had been shot by some guy he had pulled over that night. The guy had a warrant and thought shooting her dad was the only way to get out of going back to jail. Her dad was in the hospital for a week, until he recovered and went back to work. Julia's mom, on the other hand, never really recovered. Julia told me that she remembered waking up to her mom screaming the nights following the accident. He retired soon after that."

I sat back in my chair and stared up at the wall.

"Why didn't she ever tell me this?" I asked.

Rachel softly smiled.

"Because she doesn't talk about it—no one in her family talks about it," she said. "I just so happened to stumble across a photo with him in a uniform one day, and I forced her to explain. It wasn't a very happy time for Julia, and her dad must have loved the force, but he must have loved her mom more."

She met my eyes again. I knew my face was some kind of blank, and my lips were stuck on a word my mind couldn't seem to think to form.

"I'm only telling you because I think the eight-year-old girl inside of her is running from you," she said.

My Butterfly

She took in a big breath and let out a sigh.

"But you can't ever tell her I told you," she said, in a pleading voice.

I shook my head.

"I won't," I softly said.

I slid farther back into my chair and let its back catch me.

"Rachel, what guy do I know that knows Janette's boyfriend?" Ben interrupted, as he pulled a chair to our table.

Rachel flashed me a sly half-smile before she turned her attention to Ben.

"I just needed a break," Rachel said to him. "Wait, how did you get over here so fast?"

Ben chuckled.

"I just told her Jeff's the one who knew him," he said.

Rachel and Ben laughed. I was too preoccupied.

"How's Jon?" Ben asked Rachel, after their laughter had faded.

I pushed my chair back and stood up.

"Well, I think I'm going to take off," I said.

I didn't even try to make up an excuse.

"Oh, okay," Rachel said.

The pause in her voice told me that she understood.

"You leaving already, buddy?" Ben asked.

"Yeah, I think so," I said.

"Okay, well, have a good night," he said. "I'll be taking off here soon anyway. I swear I'm having déjà vu. I mean, didn't we just see all these people Friday night?"

Rachel dramatically nodded her head and found my eyes.

"See!" she exclaimed.

I forced a smile and tipped my cap to Rachel, and her proud smile turned soft again. Then, I walked to the door, pushed it open and hastily made my way to Lou in the gravel parking lot. My pace picked up with each step, but it was still as if I couldn't get behind the wheel and out of there fast enough.

Within a few minutes, I pulled in front of the high school and turned off my truck. I could see through the windows that the lights were off and that no one was inside. I got out, closed the door behind me and made my way around the building and to the back. When I came to a couple of metal doors, I reached above them and found a key under a layer of dust on the ledge. I slid the key into the door and pushed it open. Once inside, I closed the door behind me, shoved the key into my jeans pocket and took in a deep breath. It smelled like a mixture of unwashed basketball jerseys, old books and that wax they used on the gym floor every year. I waited for my eyes to readjust to the darkness inside. Then, I shuffled to the gym and switched on a light that illuminated the path in front of me. Four concrete steps later, I was on the stage. It was empty except for a couple of stray balls, a questionable ladder and an abandoned sweatshirt. I walked over to the far side and pulled on a narrow rope, which forced the heavy stage curtains to part. When the rope wouldn't move anymore, I hurried over to the edge of the stage and looked out onto the court. The light from behind me was just bright enough that I could see what I needed to see. My eyes immediately fell onto a rafter in the corner of the gym near the stage. And in the rafter, I spotted two balls.

A disbelieving laugh fell off my lips next.

"She was right. Nothing ever leaves the rafters," I said to myself.

My Butterfly

I swiveled around on my heels and spotted the ladder first. It was clearly not tall enough to get me directly to the ball, but if I stood on it and used one of the other balls lying on the stage, I just might be able to knock it down.

I rushed over to the stepladder, picked it up and carried it down another four steps to the other side of the stage. Then, I positioned it slightly under the ball imprisoned high in the ceiling and then ran back and grabbed two, rubber balls.

Once I reached the stepladder again, I carefully climbed up its wooden planks. The old ladder had definitely seen some better days. I got about three quarters of the way up, waited for it to stop swaying, and then I balanced my weight against its frame. Next, I took the first rubber ball, arched it back and sent it flying into the air toward the volleyball. It hit the ball but then fell right beside it, and in the end, only helped to wedge the volleyball even tighter into the rafter. I took the second rubber ball then, arched it back and then sent it into the air as well. It hit the volleyball and knocked it so that the volleyball was now balancing on both the beam of the rafter and the other ball. I waited for the second rubber ball to come tumbling back down to the floor. Then, I carefully scurried down the ladder and over to where it had rolled into a dark spot under the bleachers. My hand felt for the ball under the wooden seats, then quickly recovered it. And before I knew it, I was hurrying back to the ladder again. Then, one more arch and a launch later and the rubber ball and the volleyball were both plummeting back down to the hard gym floor.

"Yes," I yelled, pumping my fist into the air.

The ladder rocked, and I quickly grabbed each side to steady it again. Then, I watched the volleyball roll to the opposite side of the gym before I flew down the ladder.

Once my feet hit the floor again, I jogged over to the volleyball and scooped it up. Sure enough, her name and number were still tattooed to the ball. I ran my fingers over the letters in her name.

"You lasted some years up there, ball," I said, smiling to myself. "Don't worry, though, we're gonna finally get you home."

Chapter Thirty-Three

New York

I put my arms through my grandpa's old military jacket. His name and division were still etched on the tag inside. I had worn the jacket for every gig and show that I could tolerate its extra warmth under the bright lights. It made me feel as though I had a piece of him and a piece of home too, I guessed, everywhere I went.

I adjusted the jacket over my shoulders and arms while I stood in front of the tall mirror. The dressing room was nicer than any hotel I had ever stayed in. I was alone but only because Daniel, Matt and Chris were in the other room making a big stink about the food they had left us.

I started to fix the collar of my jacket but then stopped when I noticed the scar on my wrist. It had become a constant reminder of the night I had broken it. But what was funny about it was that I didn't remember the fire or the fall or the trip to the emergency room anymore. Now, the only thing I remembered was waking up next to Julia in that little hospital bed. The scar had become something of a little souvenir of sorts from our last night together.

I felt my lips start to slowly turn up as my mind got stuck on Jules. I was pretty sure she didn't know about the crazy events that had led up to this moment, unless Rachel had told her. And I guessed Rachel hadn't because this seemed as if it would have been something Jules might have went out of her way to mention—unless she really had forgotten about us, like Rachel always joked she had.

I looked at my reflection again in the mirror and took a deep breath and closed my eyes.

I let a moment pass before I opened my eyes again. I would look for her out there—just like I had every time I had stepped onto a stage. Though, I was pretty sure I wouldn't see her. I reached into my jacket and pulled out a small pin from its inside pocket. It was a guardian angel, her guardian angel. I ran my fingers over its metal surface. She promised she would come back someday, and I believed her.

"Hey, Will," Matt said, as he poked his head into the room.

I turned and faced him.

"They're calling us up," he said.

"Okay," I replied. "I'll be right there."

I turned around again and glanced one more time into the mirror and then at the angel in between my fingers.

My Butterfly

"I feel like I can't get to you fast enough," I whispered under my breath.

Then, I slid the pin back into my pocket and pressed it against my heart.

"Good morning, New York City," I yelled into the microphone.

Just then, a roar of screams echoed off the tall buildings that surrounded us. It was loud—louder than I had expected. And there was a row of people pressed up against the stage below us—girls, guys, kids.

I looked back at Chris and smiled.

He nodded his head once and smiled back.

"This is our first time in New York City," I yelled into the microphone again.

The crowd screamed louder.

It seemed as if every time I said the words *New York City*, the volume of the place increased ten times. I waited for the cheers to die down a little, and then I continued.

"We're just some small-town, Missouri firefighters who decided one day to start a little band, and we're happy you invited us into your little town," I finished.

I smiled then and lowered the mic as the crowd seemed to erupt. And within seconds, Matt started a count, and a melody came pouring through the speakers surrounding us. I readjusted the strap across my chest; my guitar was slung behind me. Then, I casually touched my heart, feeling for my guardian angel, before I gripped the mic with both hands and brought it to my mouth. And just before my first words pushed past my lips and out into the crowd, I thought about her.

Chapter Thirty-Four
Jessica

I had just gotten the last of the cords wound up and off the stage, and Daniel and Chris were taking what was left of the equipment to the truck. Matt had already taken off. His cousin was getting married in Springfield the next day, and he was driving through the night.

I stuffed the final cord into a plastic container and hoisted the container up into my arms when I heard my name. The voice was soft and kind of timid.

I turned, and through the dark with only glimpses of red and white stage lights, I made out a girl.

"Jessica," I said.

I watched her shy face grow a smile.

"You're back in Missouri," she said.

My Butterfly

I lowered my eyes, as I felt a smile creeping to my face. *It felt good to be home.*

"Yeah, we got back earlier this week," I said.

"Well, I was in the area, and I saw that you were playing, and I just thought I would stop by," she said.

Just then, Daniel came in through the back door and stopped in between us. He looked at me and then at Jessica and then back at me again.

"Uh, I think we've got everything loaded," he said. "Is this the last one?"

His eyes were planted on the plastic container still in my arms.

"Uh, yeah," I said.

He grabbed the container.

"We're going to go ahead and take off," he said, looking back at Jessica and then at me. "You've got your car, right?"

"What?" I asked.

"Your car—to get home," he said.

Daniel flashed me a cheesy grin.

"Oh, yeah," I said, nodding my head.

"Okay, I'll see you tomorrow then," he said.

Then, he bobbed his head at me, smiled at Jessica and then hurried again toward the back door.

My eyes followed him until he disappeared.

"You guys are really good," Jessica said.

I met Jessica's gaze again.

"Thanks," I said, smiling and tossing my eyes to the floor.

There was silence between us for a moment.

"Look, I know this place is closing, but I saw a diner at the end of the street," she said. "Maybe we could catch up."

I looked up and caught her soft stare.

"Uh, sure," I said, nodding my head.

For some reason, I felt strangely awkward around her all of a sudden. She didn't seem to be with Jeff. I wasn't used to her showing up without him.

"Okay, well, let's go this way," I said, eyeing the back door.

She smiled and then walked toward the exit. I followed after her but then reached out and pulled the door open for her.

"So, this is how you avoid all of your adoring fans," she exclaimed.

A coy smile was planted on her face.

I laughed.

"Of course, didn't you see the ten people that were in there?" I asked. "It would have taken us at least two, whole minutes to get to the front door."

Jessica's smile widened. She seemed confident again—a little closer to how I had remembered her from that New Year's Eve night years ago.

"You are crazy," she said. "Will, I don't know what you could see from where you were standing, but from where I was standing, the place was packed, and they were all loving it."

My eyes darted to the ground again, as we rounded the outside of the bar and made our way to the sidewalk in front of it.

"So, what brought you to this side of town tonight?" I asked her.

She seemed to hesitate before she spoke.

"Oh, you know, stuff," she said. "So, how have you been? It's been awhile."

I slowly nodded my head.

My Butterfly

"It has," I agreed. "I've been doing well. I took a leave of absence from the station. They were surprisingly pretty cool about it. We're doing this tour thing now."

She softly laughed, and I turned to examine her face.

"What?" I asked.

"It's nothing," she said. "I just...you're such a big deal, and there's a part of me that feels starstruck, but then there's that other part of me that doesn't even realize I'm talking to someone who was just on national television not too long ago."

I caught an almost bashful-looking stare beaming from her face, and I smiled.

"The TV thing really wasn't that big of a deal," I said. "Honestly, I just wanted to get out of the dressing room before Chris broke one of the fancy decorations in there and we had to use our money we needed to get back home to pay for it. Really, though, it doesn't feel any different."

She laughed to herself.

"It's just kind of surreal, I guess," she said.

I felt my smile grow a little bit wider.

"I guess," I admitted.

We reached the diner minutes later, and I opened the door for her again. Then, we found a small table in the back of the room and slid into it. A waitress, maybe in her sixties, sauntered over soon after, flipped open a pad of paper and grabbed a pen from behind her ear.

"What can I get ya, honey?"

She didn't even bother looking up. Jessica smiled at me and then glanced at her menu.

"I'll just have a cup of coffee," she said.

The waitress's pen didn't move.

"What about you, hon?" she asked, turning her face slightly in my direction.

"I'll just take some water," I said, turning over the menu in my hand. "And maybe some of your cheese fries."

The woman scribbled something onto her pad.

"Thanks," I said, attempting to hand her the menu.

She gestured toward the end of the table where a stack of menus already sat and then sauntered off without another word.

I smiled to myself and then slid the menu behind the ketchup bottle. And when I looked back up, Jessica's eyes were on me.

"This is a no-nonsense diner, Will," she said.

"I see," I said, chuckling.

"So, Jeff said you got a job in South County," I said.

She nodded her head.

"I did," she said. "Turns out, they were looking for nurses."

"How do you like it?" I asked.

She smiled.

"I love it," she said. "It took a little while getting used to the shifts, but now, I can't imagine working a nine-to-five."

"That's good," I said.

The waitress returned then with the coffee and water. She set the two onto the table and disappeared again.

"So, what's Jeff doing tonight?" I asked. "Isn't he usually bumming around with you if he's not with me?"

She started to smile, but then it kind of faded.

"I don't know," she said and then stopped.

"Listen, Jessica," I said. "I know he likes to talk, and most of the time, he doesn't know when to stop, but he's really a good guy."

I watched a smile finally find its way to her lips.

My Butterfly

"I know," she said.

"Cheese fries," the waitress said, sliding a platter of fries across the table.

"Thanks," I said to the woman, who quickly vanished again without a word.

"Cheese fry?" I asked Jessica, giving her my best enticing face, while holding out a soggy fry covered in the yellow stuff.

She laughed.

"I'm fine," she said.

I popped the soggy fry into my mouth.

"Will," she said.

Her voice had changed, and it instantly got my attention. I met her eyes just before they left mine for a spot on the table's surface in between us.

"I wasn't just in the area," she confessed, returning her eyes to mine. "I heard you were playing here, and I decided to come see you."

She paused, but I didn't say anything. She had gotten serious all of a sudden, and I was trying to figure out why.

I watched her take a breath and then let it out.

"I've been holding onto something for quite a long time now, and I just can't hold onto it anymore," she said.

I swallowed the fry and sat back in the booth.

"Remember New Year's Eve years ago?" she asked. "The night you said that you weren't ready for a relationship yet?"

I wished I didn't, but unfortunately, I did remember it.

I nodded my head.

"Well, I didn't understand until later," she said. "I put the pieces together, and Jeff, without telling me outright, helped me fill in the holes along the way."

She paused for a second.

"And I guess I'm just wondering if you're ready yet," she said.

Her eyes remained in mine. I shifted my weight in the booth and struggled to take a staggered breath and then to say something. But I had no words.

After a moment in my eyes, Jessica found the spot on the table in front of us again.

"It was Julia, wasn't it?" she asked, so softly I almost didn't hear her.

Her eyes turned up, and I met her gaze again.

"The girl on your dashboard and the girl from the party," she said. "And she was the one at your ceremony and with you in the hospital that day—that was her, wasn't it?"

I swallowed hard. All the things I thought she hadn't seen, she had.

I lowered my head and then slowly nodded. Then, I heard her softly clearing her throat.

"It still is, isn't it?" she asked.

I gradually looked up and met her eyes. Then, I nodded a second time.

"Do you think she'll come back?" she asked.

I sat there motionless for a moment. That question always made my heart sink. Eventually, though, I shrugged my shoulders.

"I don't know," I said, shaking my head.

I watched a sad smile form on her lips.

"You must really love her," she said.

I took a deep breath and then slowly nodded my head once again.

"I do," I simply said.

🙵

I paid the bill and walked Jessica to her car a block over from the diner. I waited as she unlocked the door and slid behind the steering wheel. There were tears in her eyes. I hopelessly watched as she tried to wipe them away with the back of her hand.

This was all my fault. If I could go back and change that night and the days that led up to it, I would. I would do everything differently.

"I'm sorry, Jessica," I said. "I never meant…"

She waved her hand and stopped me short.

"It was worth a shot," she said, smiling up at me. "But I should have known that I couldn't compete with her memory."

She paused for a moment then before she spoke again. I could still see the tears in her eyes.

"Take care, Will," she said.

I gently smiled. Then, I watched as she planted her eyes straight ahead and then pulled away.

The walk back to Lou was full of thoughts, but there was only one of those thoughts I just couldn't shake.

Once I was back inside my truck, I let out a deep sigh and then stared into the steering wheel.

What was I doing?

I was waiting. I was waiting for Jules, on her own time, to realize that she still loved me. Damn, that sounds crazy. But, somehow, I truly believed that she still did, and that in time, she would realize it. Does that make me crazy?

If she could just set aside everything that came with life for just one moment, I believed that she would see what I see. If she could just hear the song—if I could just get the song to her ears—maybe she would stop and remember us. *Maybe.*

I broke my stare from the steering wheel and anxiously started searching for my phone in the pocket of my jeans. My heart was racing by the time my fingers touched its rounded edge. I quickly pulled it out and glanced at its screen. Then, I rested a finger on the second number. I held it there for long, drawn-out moments before I just simply couldn't take it any longer, and I sent the phone dialing her digits.

Another second went by before I slowly brought the phone to my ear and took a deep breath and held it hostage inside my lungs. Then, when I heard the first ring, I allowed the breath to steadily escape past my lips. There was a second ring, and my heart sank lower. A third ring rattled through the phone, and my mind prepared for the message I would most likely have to leave. And after another ring, I heard a recording of her sweet voice pick up. Then, all too soon, I heard the screeching sound of the beep, and I froze. I didn't know if a second had gone by or four or five when my eyes finally fell shut and my mouth opened.

"Julia, I love you," I said into the phone.

Long moments ambled by before a woman's voice poured through the speaker and asked me if I was satisfied with my message. I took a second and stared into the phone's screen. Then, I pressed a number on its dial pad.

I heard the woman's voice again: "If you would like to delete your message and rerecord, press three."

My finger hovered over the keypad and then finally forced down a number.

"Your message has been deleted," the woman's voice said.

I threw the phone at the passenger's seat and slammed my palm hard against the steering wheel. Then, I took a deep breath and tried to swallow years' worth of regret. Knives stabbed at my chest, and I felt a warm liquid collecting behind my eyes as I collapsed onto the wheel. It had been so long, and now, I felt as if I were falling apart at the seams. *What if she didn't come back? What if she didn't remember her promise? What if I had already lost her?* I hated those thoughts, but in reality, none of them compared to the thought of losing her twice.

Chapter Thirty-Five

Even

I opened the screen door and let it swing back into its place behind me as I stepped into the tiny bar. There was music playing on an old juke box, as usual, and the place smelled of burgers and fried food—as usual.

"Hey, Annie," I said, when I planted my feet at the bar.

"Oh, hey, Will."

The round woman in her late fifties turned and glanced up at me.

"I've got your cheeseburger comin' right up," she said.

I smiled at the woman, then turned my attention to the rest of the bar. The room was dimly lit. It always was.

My Butterfly

"Hey, man," Ben called out from behind the bar. "You off tonight?"

"Yeah," I said. "Is Rachel here? I saw her car outside."

Ben's eyes locked on mine.

"She's not the only one here, buddy," he said, so quietly I almost didn't hear him over the music.

I followed his stare to the other side of the room. Then, I saw her. Her face was cast down. I didn't know if she had seen me. I felt my heart jump, and I grabbed the edge of the bar top as my eyes wondered back to Ben.

"I'll, uh…," I said, not even bothering to finish my sentence, as I nodded and took my first step toward her.

Each step after that was like a small journey in itself. My feet were heavy. I couldn't get to her fast or slow enough. I wanted time to think of what to say, but I also just wanted to get to her.

"Jules," I said, right before I reached her.

Her name just fell off my tongue, absent of any real brain function, I was sure.

"What? When? How have ya been?" I asked.

I felt the words pile up in my mouth and then just stumble off my lips.

She stood up from the table, and I leaned in and then wrapped her up into my arms.

"I got in today," she said.

I pulled away and held her shoulders in my palms. She was smiling. It seemed as if there were something behind her smile, but bottom line, she was smiling, and it made me smile too.

I pulled her close again and squeezed her body against mine for another several seconds. It was probably out of character, but damn it, I didn't even know how to act normal around her anymore.

I spotted Rachel out of the corner of my eye and then slowly released Julia.

"Hey, Rach. How are ya?" I asked, turning my attention to Rachel for a few seconds.

"Good, Will," she said. "Doing well. Jon says 'hi,' by the way."

"Where's he tonight?" I asked her.

"Hunting trip," she said. "Canada. Needless to say, I sat that one out."

Her eyebrows arched to the ceiling of the tiny bar, and then, a sound from the juke box made me stop. I met Julia's eyes again. They were already smiling.

"You want to dance...for old times' sake?" I asked.

I watched her glance back at Rachel.

Rachel found her stare and then found Ben on the other side of the room.

"Ben, get your two, left feet over here and ask me to dance," Rachel shouted.

Ben looked up from the juke box and smiled in Rachel's direction.

"You two, go ahead and catch up," Rachel said, gesturing toward the small dance floor.

Julia looked back at me and smiled. I put out my hand, and she met it with hers.

"If I had known you were going to be here, I would have put on a clean shirt and shaved and maybe worn some of that deodorant stuff," I said, grinning wide.

She smiled that little, bashful smile of hers.

"You look great," she said.

"So do you, Jules," I said.

I watched her face angle toward the floor, but when she looked back up and found my eyes again, she had a pretty smile stretched across her face.

"It's good to see you," she said.

My Butterfly

I couldn't help but just stare at her.

"I heard your song on the radio the other day," she said.

I tried to hide my shy smile, as my eyes darted to the floor.

"Well, what have you been up to these days besides becoming famous?" she asked.

I laughed.

"If I'm famous, it doesn't really feel any different," I softly muttered, as if it were a secret.

"That's probably because you were already used to it," she said. "You've been famous here since I've known you."

I laughed again. It had been awhile since I had really laughed. It felt good. And it felt good to be holding her hand. *God, if this were all a dream, I'm beggin' you, don't wake me up. Just let me rest.*

"Isn't everybody famous in a small town?" I asked.

The sides of her mouth lifted into another pretty grin.

"I guess you're right," she said.

She was quiet for a moment. I listened to the words from the juke box as they hit my ears, and I closed my eyes and remembered back to the first night I had played her the same song. On the back of my eyelids, I saw her green eyes lit up by the fire's flames and her wide smile tempting me to kiss her.

But suddenly, the sound of her voice forced my eyelids open again, and the image was lost.

"How's work?" she asked.

I took a second before I answered her.

"It's been good," I said. "I worked the last couple of days. It's good to be back—a little break from traveling. Though, I'm not complaining."

"I know," she said, smiling into my shoulder.

"So, you like it?" she asked.

"Like...?" I repeated.

"The lights, the fans, the entertaining?" she continued. "You like it, right?"

"Oh, that," I said, nodding my head. "I like parts of it. I like playing the guitar and that sometimes people get the words you're singing—makes 'em smile, you know?"

She nodded her head.

"Now, the lights, on the other hand," I continued, "I could do without them. They're bright, and they're hot and just unnecessary."

She didn't say anything for a minute. She just stared at me with those temptress eyes of hers.

"I told you so," she said, finally. "Well, minus the lights, I knew you'd like it."

"You were just itchin' to say that, weren't you?" I asked her.

"Maybe," she confessed.

A smile started to carve its way up my face and then stopped.

"You never liked the firefighting idea, did you?" I asked.

"What?" she replied.

She looked surprised.

"Why do you think that?" she asked.

"I don't think," I whispered near her ear. "I know, Jules."

She stared into my eyes. I watched her pupils dance back and forth as if they were searching for something.

"Will, you had to have picked the most dangerous career," she eventually said. "I wasn't exactly thrilled, but I was sincerely happy for you."

"I know. I know," I said, starting to laugh.

"And Will, I would have done anything to make you happy," she said, catching me off guard. "I still would."

My smile somewhat faded, and my feet grew heavy on the floor. I had just now noticed that there was a different song coming from the juke box, and I locked my eyes on hers as I moved my hand up the small of her back, forcing her an inch closer to my body. She seemed to notice but didn't stop me.

"I mean, we were best friends, Will," she continued.

"Are best friends, Jules," I said.

"What?" she asked.

"Jules, we are best friends," I said again.

She paused but then slowly nodded her head.

"Are," she said, smiling up at me.

She rested her head on my shoulder then, and I squeezed her hand in mine. Her hand was soft and warm and perfect. And I couldn't believe I hadn't told her yet. *God, how many years had it been, and I hadn't told her that I loved her, still love her—that I would quit fighting fires for her, that I would do anything for her?*

"Jules," I blurted out, causing her to lift her head from my chest. "I've, uh, been doing some thinking, and I…"

I reached for her other hand and cradled it in my own. Then, I closed my eyes for a moment, lowered my head and took a deep breath as I ran my thumb in a gentle motion over the tops of her fingers. But after several seconds, something stopped me. It was hard and jagged. I forced my eyes open, and the first thing I saw was a big, shiny object glaring back at me.

I swore my heart stopped right then. Which was her left? Which one was her left hand? *It was the one the ring was on.* I tried to tell myself I had her hands mixed up. I tried to tell myself that it wasn't a diamond ring—that it was only the grass ring I had given her years ago when I had asked her to marry ME someday. I closed my eyes again and gently squeezed her hand in mine.

"Jules, please tell me that this is just a pretty ring," I pleaded, with every last bit of pleading I had in me.

I opened my eyes and caught another glimpse of the shiny object on her finger before I found her gaze. She was searching in my eyes for something. There was a word on her lips, but she remained silent for the longest moment of my life.

"It's not just a ring, Will," she eventually said.

Her voice was almost a whisper.

I swallowed hard and softly cleared my throat. I felt the pain rising into my chest. I tried to shove it back down.

"The doctor?" I managed to get out.

I was looking at the ring on her finger again.

"Yes," I heard her say.

I tried to laugh, but it came out sounding too labored to resemble laughter.

"And I'm guessing this means you said *yes*?" I asked, trying my damnedest to smile.

She slowly nodded her head. There was a half-smile on her lips.

"Well, I guess congrats are in order then," I said, swallowing hard again and still trying to muster up that smile that just might not exist anymore.

"Thanks," she softly said.

My eyes fell onto her lips as she finished the word. Then, they returned to her eyes.

"Just tell me one thing, Jules," I said.

My voice had a serious tone to it now.

"Is he the one?" I asked her.

She continued to stare into my eyes. Her expression didn't change, and she didn't look thrown off or insulted. I expected to have to explain myself—to tell her that I only had her best interest in mind, even if I believed fully that it was in her best interest to be with me.

"He's good for me, Will," she said, finally.

I held my gaze. If there were such a thing as an out-of-body experience, I was pretty sure that this would qualify as one. I took another deep breath and then slowly forced it out, still keeping my eyes locked in hers.

It was another long moment before my stare fell to the hard floor at our feet. I tried to say something but nothing came out the first time, so I tried again.

"Well, that's what matters," I whispered. "That he's the one."

I raised my eyes to the rest of the bar then for the first time since we had started dancing. And I watched as heads simultaneously whipped in the other direction, until no one was looking at us anymore. Did they all know? Had they all known that this dance would end with my heart shattered into tiny pieces on the floor?

I met Jules's eyes again.

"It was really good to see you again," I gently said.

She seemed to hesitate.

"It was nice to see you too," she said.

Then, she swung her arms around my neck. It surprised me. I almost didn't know what to do; but eventually, I wrapped my arms around her and squeezed her body against mine. Then, I closed my eyes, breathed her in and held her. I held her for all the moments I had missed and for all the moments I was about to miss too, as if me holding her now would keep her from marrying that guy—would keep her in my arms forever. An image from the night she had come to see me in the hospital suddenly appeared in my mind, and I wished I could go back to that day.

I opened my eyes, and I was still holding her. I spotted Rachel in the back of the room. Her expression looked pained, and I wondered for a second if it were just my pain reflecting back at me. I felt a warm liquid forming in the back of my eyes, and I knew I had to go. I cleared my throat and pulled away from her.

"Take care, Jules," I said, starting to turn.

"You leaving?" she whispered, quickly resting her hand on my shoulder.

I stared at her hand and the rock on her finger. She seemed to notice my find and hastily retrieved her hand.

"Yeah, I'm helping out at the station early tomorrow morning—the call of duty," I said.

I tipped my baseball cap in her direction and forced what I had left of a smile. Then, I turned and pushed through the screen door. I heard Annie say something about a burger as my feet hit the gravel, but I didn't stop. I got around to the side of the bar and threw my back up against its wood paneling. I felt weak, as if I might pass out. Then, without a second thought, I felt my body slide down the wood until all my weight was on the back of my heels. I tried to think of something—just to make sure I was still conscious. The first thought that came to me was of Julia marrying that guy, and it sent my heart into another race.

I covered my face in my hands and took a deep breath. Then, eventually, I let both hands slide down past my eyes and my nose until just my fingertips were pressed up against my lips. And I just sat there and thought about her, about us, about an ending I wasn't ready for yet.

Then, after a minute, I finally felt okay to stand again. I forced myself to my feet and then sauntered over to Lou. I pulled open the door and slid behind the wheel. Then, for several moments again, I stared into the darkness on the other side of my windshield, until eventually, I closed the door and searched in my jeans pocket for my keys. I recovered them seconds later, then shoved one into the ignition and purred the engine to a start. Then, I forced my fingers tightly around the steering wheel as I peered into my rearview mirror and then froze.

There was a ball staring back at me. I thought for a moment, then spun around and scooped it up and started searching in the glove box for something to write with.

Before I knew it, I was hovering over Rachel's car and allowing the moments to pass by as I stared at Jules's name and her old volleyball number with the help of the porch light from the bar. And suddenly, we were sixteen and sitting around a bonfire, and her soft words were touching my ears for the first time: *You get the ball down for me someday, and we'll call it even.*

I smiled, then took the black, permanent marker that I had found in the glove box and wrote an inscription on the volleyball. Then, I balanced the ball on the hood of the car, against the windshield, and stepped back. Now, on the volleyball was her name, her number and the words: *Now we're even.*

I tried to smile again, knowing she'd remember and that it might make her smile too, but my lips refused. This wasn't the way I thought I would feel when I finally returned her ball. Instead of a new beginning, it felt more like letting go. There were so many years wound up in that ball—so many *I love yous* and smiles and laughter and tears and *goodbyes*. And there was so much I never said.

I sucked in a deep breath of cool air and then slowly let it pass over my lips.

"So much I never said," I whispered to myself before I turned and made my way back to Lou.

Chapter Thirty-Six

Ticket

It was five o'clock in the morning. I was staring into a laptop's screen; my hand was on the touchpad; my finger was hovering over its little, right button; and an arrow on the screen pointed to a box that read: *confirm*. I had been in the same position for forty-five minutes straight.

I sucked in a deep breath and then forced it out. I didn't know if it were my watch's incessant ticking that was driving me mad or the fact that I hadn't pushed the button yet.

I knew I couldn't let her marry him. *Maybe she loved him.* The thought made me swallow hard. But what if there were still a part of her that loved me too? I couldn't rely on my plan now. I would never be able to live with myself if it didn't work out and she married him without me taking the chance that I might very well lose her twice. I needed to talk to her. I needed to tell her everything I never told her in all the years that we had been apart.

I quickly pushed another breath of air past my lips, and without a second thought, I forced my finger down. And suddenly, the word *confirm* lit up on the screen.

The flight was in a week and a half. I glanced at my watch. It was five after five. I looked toward the back of the bus. Daniel was sprawled out. His legs were stretched the length of a seat, and he was knocked out with his mouth open. I was surprised he wasn't drooling yet.

I closed down the computer and set it onto the floor underneath me. Then, I readjusted my pillow, shifting it so that it rested up against the side of the bus. We were opening for Ren Lake in Memphis the next day and driving through the night to get there.

I lay on my back and stretched out my legs. The seat wasn't long enough, and part of my legs and my feet hung off, but it worked. The little bed compartments on the bus made me feel claustrophobic, so I preferred the seat instead. And I never thought that I would ever long to be on one of those old beds in the fire station, but compared to this bus, I'd take them any night.

I pulled the seatbelt clip out of my back and shifted in the seat again. Most times, there was a *comfortable enough*, and I thought I just might have found it. I rested my head back onto my pillow and closed my eyes.

A week and a half.

I felt my lips turn into a smile. In a week and a half, she would know everything.

"How was Memphis?"

My Butterfly

I looked up to see a brunette coming out of the gas station. I slid the nozzle into the tank and secured the lever to the handle.

"Rachel," I said. "Just the person I wanted to see."

She planted her feet in front of me, threw her hip into the side of my truck and crossed her arms. She had a questioning look on her face, but she seemed to shake it off before she spoke again.

"Well, how was it?" she asked.

I smiled.

"It was great," I said.

"How many numbers did you get this weekend?" she asked.

My eyes darted to the ground, and I shook my head, feeling a little bashful all of a sudden.

"I knew it," she said, grinning. "Thousands, huh?"

I laughed, and she narrowed her eyes again.

"Now, why did you want to see me?" she asked.

"Oh," I said and then paused. "I bought a ticket."

She cocked her head a little and drew her face closer to mine.

"A ticket?" she asked.

"To San Diego," I said.

Her puzzled look started to melt into something else. I waited for her smile—that one she got while meddling in someone else's business and not caring who saw her enjoying it. But that smile never came. Instead, her lips parted, and her eyes fell into some kind of sad state or something. Then, I watched as she sucked in some air through her teeth and shook her head.

The lever from the gas pump suddenly flew up and made a thud. My eyes fell for an instant onto the lever but then immediately returned to Rachel.

"I don't know if that's such a good idea, Will," she said then, sounding strangely uneasy.

I angled my head slightly to the side. At the same time, my heart started this slow, methodical beating, as if it were preparing for bad news.

"Well, she is always throwing out invitations, and I thought, I've never been to San Diego; I might as well go now before she graduates and moves somewhere else, you know?" I half-lied.

Rachel's eyes remained in mine. She was making me nervous. I watched her take a deep breath and then let out a sigh.

"You should probably give her some time," she said.

She looked at me as if I were some abandoned puppy or something. And Time? What the hell was all this talk about time? Is it never the right time for anything? I was beginning to think that waiting was nothing but a fool's game—either that or it was genius. But either way, it sure wasn't fun.

"Wait," I said. "What?"

She stared at me with a blank expression.

"You do know, right?" she asked.

My eyes narrowed.

"Know what?" I asked.

My heart almost couldn't take the suspense. *Know what?*

She continued to stare at me for a few more seconds, and then suddenly, her lips started to turn up into a smile.

"Wait, why did you buy a ticket to San Diego?" she asked.

My puzzled stare was turning bashful fast.

"I, uh, thought it might be nice to see San Diego, and it might also be nice to have someone show me around that knows it," I lied again.

My Butterfly

I shifted my weight to my heels. I did really hate lying to her, and I had been prepared to tell her everything, but that was before she had scared the hell out of me with that depressed look of hers at first.

"Hold on," I said. "What don't I know?"

I watched her quickly draw a half circle around us with her eyes. Then, she brought her face closer to mine.

"She broke off her engagement," she whispered near my ear.

My mouth fell open.

"What?" I asked.

She leaned back and simply nodded her head.

A smile tried to push its way to my face, but I quickly hid it as best as I could by throwing my gaze to the ground.

"Why?" I asked her, lifting my eyes again.

Rachel took in a deep breath through her nose.

"I'm not quite sure exactly, except that he just wasn't 'the one,'" she said, holding up quotation marks with her fingers.

I thought about it for a moment—let it process—before I lowered my eyes and found the asphalt near my feet again. And within seconds, I felt Rachel's hand on my shoulder.

"Give her some time, Will," she said.

I started to smile to myself as Rachel walked away.

There was that *time* word again. But this time, it didn't bother me nearly as much.

I watched Rachel get into her car and pull away, and when she was out of sight, I let the sides of my mouth turn up until they couldn't turn up anymore. So, it would be more than a week and a half before she would know everything now. That thought sobered me up a bit. But now, at least, I had time to get my plan together.

"Time," I said, under my breath, as I shook my head.

Time seemed as if it were the answer for everything these days.

Chapter Thirty-Seven

The Song

"**Y**ou ready, Will?"

The muffled voice hit my ears as if it were asking me if I were ready to go into battle or something. There was a weariness in the tiny recording studio. But it wasn't coming from the thin man or the thicker, bald man who moved buttons up and down on the other side of the glass window in front of me. And it wasn't the fact that they were staring at me either. I had somehow gotten used to them over the last couple of years. What I hadn't gotten used to, though, were the big headphones that swallowed my ears and the weird microphone that threatened to devour my face. They were still strange, but they also weren't the cause of my anxiousness. No, the anxiousness wasn't a guest of the present—but of the future, I guessed, as I stepped closer to the mic. It was more like that uneasy feeling of not knowing if you've spent the good majority of your life doing the right thing or the wrong thing. It was that feeling of finally having reached the top of that river bluff but then not knowing what to do when you got there.

I nodded my head in the direction of the thin man behind the glass.

"I'm ready," I said into the mic.

My eyelids slowly fell shut then, and I lowered my head. I had one chance to tell her what I should have told her years ago. In my head, I recited a silent prayer: *Lord, get this to her ears.* Then, I heard the music, and gradually, the words of her song began to instinctively fall off my lips:

> *"It's a summer night*
> *And I can hear the crickets sing*
> *But otherwise, all the world's asleep*
> *While I can only lie awake and dream*
> *And every time I close my eyes*
> *A butterfly comes to me*
> *It has soft, green eyes*
> *A sweet soul*
> *Brave wings*
> *And each time, it hears me sing:*
>
> *Where have you been?*
> *I've missed you so*
> *Tell me of your travels*
> *Tell me you've seen the world*
> *Now, you've come back home*
> *Tell me you've carried me with you*
> *That you've held me close*

My Butterfly

Tell me you've missed me
Or that I'm not crazy for waiting 'cause
Of all the butterflies that chose to stay,
I'm in love with the one that got away

Then in my dream it turns to me
And that butterfly smiles
And whispers in my ear:
Where have you been?
I've missed you so
My wings are tired
For I've carried you home
I've carried you through the mountains
I've carried you over the sea
Everywhere I went
I carried you with me

Then instead of spreading those brave wings
And flyin' far away again
That butterfly stays near instead
And whispers back to me:
Tell me again what you never said
And I sing again:
Where have you been?
I've missed you so
Tell me of your travels
Tell me you've seen the world
Now, you've come back home
Tell me you've carried me with you
That you've held me close
Tell me you've missed me
Or that I'm not crazy for waiting 'cause
Of all the butterflies that chose to stay,
I'm in love with the one that got away."

I sang the last words of the song and then lowered my head. And eventually, the music faded back into my headphones.

"That'll do it, Will," a voice hit my ears then. "That'll make the girls happy."

An anxious smile slowly found its way to my lips.

"I'm only concerned about one," I softly said to myself.

Chapter Thirty-Eight

A Favor

"**H**ey, man, have you seen Rachel?"

"Uh-uh," Jeff said, before he threw another dart at the wall.

I watched the dart hit a big circle, far from the bull's-eye. Then, I kept moving.

"Hey, Will, where ya goin'? I've gotta tell you something," Jeff called out, his words trailing behind me.

I ignored him. It couldn't be as important as what I had to tell Rachel.

The den led off into the living room where Jon was sitting on the couch watching the Cards' game with a couple of other guys.

"Jon, where's your fiancé?" I asked.

I watched him try to turn his head, but it looked as if his eyes wouldn't let him.

"Uh, I think she's on the front porch."

I took a quick glance at the score of the game and kept moving again. A room and a screen door later, my feet were planted on a row of old, wooden porch boards—the kind where the color of paint never changed only because you just couldn't imagine it being a different color. The fan was on high above me. I instantly felt its breeze as I turned my head and spotted Rachel.

"Rach," I said, marching forward.

Then, suddenly, I stopped when I noticed who was also sitting next to her.

"Jessica," I said, as I planted my feet.

I knew I must have sounded surprised to see her. I watched her face turn down toward the wooden floorboards before she met my eyes again.

"Hi, Will," she said.

I hadn't seen her since our night at the diner.

"I didn't realize you were here," I said.

"I came with Jeff," she said, softly, lifting her eyes only a moment before tossing them to the floorboards again.

"Oh, okay," I said, moving again.

I pulled out a chair from along the wall and fell into it.

"So, how have you been?" I asked Jessica.

"Good," she said, almost bashfully.

I smiled and caught Rachel staring at me with a strange smirk on her face. I scrunched my eyebrows together and stared back at her with a puzzled look.

"She came with Jeff," Rachel said, making sure to drag out the word *came* as if it were important or something.

My Butterfly

I slowly turned my head sideways, giving her a clue that I didn't know what the hell she was getting at. So. She was always with Jeff. I glanced over at Jessica. Was she in on this game too?

Jessica was smiling, which wasn't unusual, but there was still something different about her smile.

"I'm, uh, going to go get some more tea," Jessica said then, rising from her chair. "Rachel, you want some?"

Rachel shook her head.

"No, honey," Rachel said, laughing under her breath.

I watched Rachel's eyes follow Jessica as Jessica disappeared behind the screen door. Then, Rachel's gaze settled into mine.

"Jeff and Jessica are dating now," she rattled off.

She had said the words so quickly I almost couldn't process them all at one time.

I sat there for a second as all the gears clicked.

"So, that's what knucklehead wanted to tell me," I said out loud, but really to myself.

Rachel nodded her head in slow, exaggerated nods. She was still wearing her devilish grin—that one that Julia had always warned me about.

I sat back in my chair and let my head fall back.

"I don't know how he did it," I said again, mainly to myself.

"I know! Crazy, right?" she exclaimed. "I mean, she was crazy about you for so long."

Her eyes were wide, and she was shaking her head.

"But in the end, Jeff's really good for her," she said. "They really fit together better, you know?"

My head leveled back again, and before I knew it, I was staring at Rachel with a side-smile and narrowed eyes.

"Will, you know what I mean," she said, shoving my arm.

"You need someone with more fight," she said, as she drew her face closer to mine and used her hand to cover one side of her lips. "I mean, I love Jessica, but let's face it, that girl wasn't raised here."

I tossed my head back again and laughed.

"Jon's a lucky man, Rachel," I said, eyeing her again with a smirk still plastered on my face.

She shot me a confident look.

"He knows it," she said.

I watched Rachel toss her gaze to somewhere off into the distance. Then, I sat up straighter in my chair and cleared my throat.

"Uh, speaking of that, there's something I need you to do," I said.

My smile had faded now. A serious expression had replaced it. Rachel returned her attention to me and drew her face even closer. Curiosity surrounded her, and I was pretty sure she was wearing that devilish grin again, but I couldn't quite tell through the fog of her poker face.

"Only if it involves Julia," she said.

Her words surprised me. My eyes grew wide, and I tried to force back a guilty grin even as I pressed on.

"Do you think you can get her back to New Milford?" I asked.

"When?" she asked.

She didn't even bother to ask why, and I chuckled a little at that.

"In two weeks," I said and then lowered my eyes.

I glanced back up at her seconds later, and her eyes immediately locked onto mine. I almost felt naked, as if she could see right through me or something.

"I think I just kind of assumed that she would just be there," I went on. "But now, I'm starting to second-guess it. I mean, she just moved across the country, and she's got a new job, you know? I shouldn't have assumed she would be there."

I stopped and drew in a deep breath.

"Rach, I need her there," I continued.

Rachel's hand fell to my knee then, and my eyes quickly traveled to her hand.

"Your charity concert?" she asked.

I nodded my head and returned my eyes to hers.

"I've already got it covered," she said, winking back at me and falling back into her chair again.

I cocked my head to the side.

"What do you mean?" I asked.

"Well, the first time I told her about it, she put up a fight, as usual, and said she had to work or something crazy like that, but I called her firm last night and sweet-talked her secretary out of some information."

I felt my eyebrows coming together.

"I met her once—the secretary," she said, flipping her hand in the air. "It's okay. She's a nice girl. Anyway, evidently, Miss Lang took off that Friday for 'some charity concert up North.'"

She used her fingers to make quotation marks.

"And, honey, I don't know what changed her mind, but I do know she has a ticket," she said, mischievously smiling.

She stopped then and started waving her finger.

"You know, come to think of it actually, it just might have been a certain song that persuaded her," she said, allowing her stare to wander off into the distance again before returning to me.

My heart instantly sped up a few beats per minute.

"She heard it?" I asked.

Rachel smiled and slowly nodded her head.

"Now, we just have to pray that she gets on that plane," she said.

My lips were gradually lifting into a grin, but I knew there was still a somewhat puzzled look glued to my face.

"But how did you know?" I asked.

The sentence came out slow and broken, but I managed to get it all out, as Rachel met my stare.

"That you were still in love with her?" she asked.

I stared back at her, with my mouth cocked slightly open.

"Well, I always kind of knew," she said, shrugging her shoulders. "But then, you bought that ticket, and I knew you didn't just want to sightsee in San Diego. And then, Jessica told me about your guys' little talk that one night."

Her eyes left me and fell onto a spot off in the distance somewhere again.

"Ten years ago, I didn't so much care for Jessica," she confessed. "That was, of course, before I knew her," she said, pushing up another devious grin.

Then, I watched as her eyes returned to me.

"Thanks, Rachel," I said.

"She's your fight, Will," she said. "It's the least I can do."

My eyes fell to the floorboards at my feet, and a faint smile found its way to my lips; though, I was pretty sure it was one part hopeful and one part terrified.

"Rachel," I said, lifting my eyes to hers again.

I reached into my pocket and pulled out a small, black box. I stared at it as I turned it over in my hand. Then, I set it down onto the table's surface in front of her.

Rachel's jaw was cocked open, and her brown eyes were big when I met her gaze.

"What is that, Will?" she asked, forcing her eyes to the little box.

I couldn't help but smile.

"It's my grandmother's ring," I said.

She looked up at me again and then back at the box.

"Can I?" she asked.

I laughed.

"Yeah," I said, nodding my head.

She snatched up the little box and quickly pulled back its lid.

"Oh my gosh, Will," she exclaimed. "It's beautiful."

When she was finished examining the ring, she met my eyes.

"The concert?" she asked.

I took a deep breath in and then let it quickly escape. Then, I nodded my head.

"So, this is why we need to get her back here?" she asked.

A wide smile gradually took over my face.

Rachel carefully closed the box's lid and handed the ring back to me.

"I'll make sure she gets on the plane," she said.

"Thanks, Rachel," I said, as my eyes found a spot on the table's surface again, and then I paused.

"Rachel," I said, lifting my gaze. "I have one more favor to ask of you."

Chapter Thirty-Nine

The Find

I was nervous. I couldn't help but be. I hadn't really talked to Jules's mom in years. I tended to avoid the people that reminded me of Jules or the life I used to have with her. Her mom was one of those people.

"Rachel," I heard Mrs. Lang exclaim, as Rachel stepped into the house in front of me.

Jules's mom enveloped Rachel in a hug and planted a kiss on her cheek.

"Oh, and sweetie, Eric left some of that blackberry honey out for Jon," Mrs. Lang said. "He knows how much he likes that kind."

"Oh, thanks, Mrs. L," Rachel said, as Jules's mom released Rachel from her grip.

My Butterfly

I was now standing in the hallway behind Rachel, so when Rachel stepped out of the way, I was in plain view.

"Will," Mrs. Lang exclaimed.

I couldn't tell if she had said my name in a scolding tone or if it had come from a place of surprise.

"Mrs. Lang," I said, greeting her and tipping my cap.

She was motionless for a second, and her expression refused to waiver. But before I could think of what to do next, she threw her arms around me, just like she had done with Rachel a minute ago.

"It's so good to see you," she said, into my shoulder. "It's been so long."

She pulled away from me then but kept her hands on my shoulders, as if to get a good look at me.

"You're so grown up," she exclaimed, as her eyes turned a little sad.

"Nah," I said. "I'm not that grown up yet."

She softly smiled and then turned to Rachel.

Rachel shrugged her shoulders and squished her lips together like Rachel did when she was indifferent.

"He's really not," Rachel reassured her.

Mrs. Lang turned back to me, smiled again and squeezed my shoulders.

"Well, do you guys want some spiced honey cookies or some honey bread or tea?" she asked, as she darted into the kitchen then.

Rachel followed Mrs. L into the other room and came back out with a cup of something in her hand.

"The tea has honey in it," Rachel said, as she smiled up at me.

"Will, do you want anything?" Mrs. L asked.

"Uh, no, Mrs. Lang, I'm fine. Thanks," I said, grinning.

Jules's dad had picked up raising bees in the last couple of years. I knew that because he sold the honey and everything that went along with it at my grandpa's store.

Suddenly, Mrs. Lang appeared in the hallway again.

"Okay," she said, looking at the two of us. "Let's see what we can find."

She shuffled to the bottom of the stairs and then started her climb. Rachel followed her, and I followed Rachel.

"Oh, Will, how is the singing going?" Mrs. Lang asked.

I took another step before I answered.

"It's going all right," I said.

"It was so funny," Mrs. Lang went on. "Eric and I were up and about that morning that you were on the *Good Morning* show, you know?"

"Mm hmm," I said.

"Well, all of a sudden, we heard your voice," she continued, without missing a beat. "I knew it was your voice. And both of us just immediately stopped what we were doing. I'm not kidding. I set my cup down onto the counter—well, I guess, it more or less fell to the counter—and we both just gravitated to the television as if we were zombies. I couldn't believe my eyes."

She stopped at the top of the stairs, and Rachel slipped past her.

"I'm so proud of you, Will," she said, giving me that motherly smile that makes them look as if they want to cry too.

I smiled, and my cheeks turned hot.

"It's nothing really," I assured her.

She tilted her head slightly to the side.

My Butterfly

"And you're staying safe with the whole firefighter thing?" she asked. "No more falling from two-story buildings?"

"No, ma'am," I said, shaking my head, my eyes cast down again.

"I hope not," she said.

She rested her hand on my shoulder and lightly nudged me onward.

Rachel was already sprawled out onto the bed when I stepped into the room. I quickly glanced around and then immediately retraced my steps in my mind.

"Is this Julia's room?" I asked.

"Mm hmm," Rachel said.

"Well," Rachel continued. "It's the guest quarters now."

She had said her last words in a British accent for some reason.

"It's better than that awful lavender that Mrs. L let Julia paint it," Rachel said.

Mrs. Lang turned and smiled at Rachel.

I looked around the room. All of Jules's 4-H trophies were gone, along with all her track medals, her favorite band posters and that frightfully big, stuffed bear that always sat in the corner of the room. And while I didn't so much miss the bear, I did miss everything else—everything that made this room Jules's.

I watched Mrs. Lang pull open the closet door and tug on a beaded strand, which immediately lit the little room.

"Now, I know I saw them when I was packing away her things, so they're in here somewhere," she said, pulling down a shoe box from a shelf. "*Somewhere* is the keyword."

She smiled at us and opened the shoe box.

"Here, Mrs. L, I'll help you look," Rachel said, jumping up from the bed.

I glanced at the two of them in the closet, rooting through years of Julia's life, now in boxes.

"Let me know if I can do anything," I said to them, rocking back on my heels.

They were talking quietly to each other, so I wasn't even sure if they had heard me. I felt uncomfortable all of a sudden being in Julia's room without her being there. My eyes wandered around again, as I fell into the place on the bed that Rachel had just been. The room was painted a light greenish color now. The curtains were all white and in that material with all the holes in it. And there was a big picture of a field of flowers. The flowers were purple. Maybe they were for Jules—a lasting piece of her favorite color when everything else of hers was in boxes.

Suddenly, I heard giggling from the closet, and then I felt a soft, stuffed thing hit the side of my head.

"Remember that?" Rachel asked.

I collected myself and then spotted a small, stuffed animal that kind of resembled a cat lying on the floor. I smiled and bent over to retrieve it.

"Julia loved that thing for some reason," Rachel said.

I ran my fingers over the stuffed animal's glass eyes and sewn-on nose. *Furballs*. It was uglier than I had remembered it; though, the memory was far from ugly. I smiled to myself.

"I think I found them," Rachel screamed just then.

My eyes quickly turned up toward the closet just in time to see Rachel pull out a bouquet of butterfly weeds from a cardboard box. She smiled and held the flowers out toward me.

"Your flowers, sir," she said, with a big grin tattooed to her face.

My Butterfly

I stood up, walked over to her and took the flowers into my hands. The last time I had held them, her jeep was packed, her smile was wide, and her dreams were waiting—to escort her right out of my life.

"Now, go get your fight, Will," Rachel said, squeezing my arm.

I looked up at the two of them and smiled.

"Thank you," I said, before returning my gaze to the butterfly weeds now cradled in my hands.

Chapter Forty

The Concert

"Hey, Rach, you made it," I said.

"Of course I made it," Rachel said, shooting me a strange look.

She eyed me up and down once.

"She'll be here," she eventually said.

I shifted my weight and tried to force a smile.

"But how do you know?" I asked.

"I know Julia," she said. "She didn't have to say she'd be here for me to know she'd be here."

There were too many *heres* in her sentence, and I got lost somewhere in there, but it didn't matter. I knew the moral of her story. I just hoped it rang true.

Suddenly then, Rachel grabbed my arm and pulled me closer to her.

"Now, if you don't tell her that you love her TONIGHT," she whispered near my ear, "I'll cut your balls off and sell you for bacon."

I was tongue-tied when she finally released my arm from her death grip, but sometime during her threat, a happy grin had also managed to find its way to my face.

"Now, go break a leg," she said, shoving me hard in the bicep.

I shook my head as I watched her dance to her seat at the front of the stage. Then, I took a deep breath in and caught a glimpse of the guy I had been looking for.

"Uh, hey, Alex, got a favor for ya," I said, grabbing his attention.

Alex stopped and faced me.

"Whatcha need?" he asked.

I pulled out a photo of Julia from the inside pocket of my jacket and held it out to him. He took it in his hands and examined it.

"Pretty girl," he said and then looked back up at me.

I smiled to myself.

"You mind telling me if you see her in the crowd?" I asked him.

He slowly nodded his head.

"Sure, Will," he said.

Then, I brought my face closer to his and lowered my voice.

"Is there any way you could let me know if you happen to see her during the concert?" I asked.

He looked into my eyes and then back at the photo.

"Uh, yeah, sure," he said. "I could give you a wave or something if I see her."

"A wave," I repeated. "That sounds great."

A smile slid across my face.

"You ready, Will?" I heard Matt call out from behind us then.

I looked up at Matt and then back at Alex.

"Thanks, Alex," I said, patting him on the shoulder.

He smiled and then tucked the photo into his shirt pocket.

"Anytime, Will," he said.

I watched Alex shuffle down the steps and then off the platform before I returned my attention to Matt.

"Time to go already?" I asked.

He found my eyes and nodded his head.

"It's time," he said.

"All right," I replied, taking in a deep, anxious breath and then slowly exhaling. "Here goes everything."

The corners of Matt's mouth started to edge up his face.

"Go get her," he said, as he rested his hand on my shoulder.

I found his stare one, last time, smiled and then took my first step onto the stage.

The buzz of the crowd grew louder the closer I got to the microphone. And when I reached its stand, I paused and took a second to look out over the packed field. People wrapped around the little stage and extended back about a football field's length. I breathed in the familiar smell of aging maples and autumn air and breathed out a smile.

"How are ya doin', New Milford?" I shouted then. "Home, finally," I said, throwing my head back and extending my arms to the heavens.

The crowd cheered even louder. I took another moment to take it all in. There was nothing like coming home.

My Butterfly

Each song was a high on the outside, but on the inside, I was more anxious than I had ever been. Every moment, I craved her. I wanted so badly to know if she was in the crowd. I kept glancing up at Alex, but so far, there had been no wave.

I positioned my fingers on the strings of my guitar again and squared up to the microphone. It was the last song before the encore, and my heart had already begun to beat uncontrollably against the walls of my chest. Eventually, I heard the melody start, and as if it were pure instinct, the first words of the song fell off my tongue. Then, suddenly, I thought I saw a wave. I forced my lips to keep moving to the words, even as I made my way over to the other side of the stage to get a better look at Alex. I had to be sure.

It was only a few steps to the edge of the platform, but it had felt like a lifetime. I squinted my eyes, trying my best to block out the bright lights. Then, I saw him. And sure enough, there was his skinny, little arm waving in the air. I smiled wide, which caused the next words out of my mouth to come out labored. The jumbled words made me laugh a little and forced me to lose some of the following words too, but it didn't seem to matter. The crowd only cheered louder and even seemed to join me in my laughter. I tipped my hat to Alex, then slightly turned until I could see Matt on the keys behind me. Immediately, he caught my gaze and sent me a wide smile. I knew he could tell what was going on.

The song came to an end moments later, and suddenly, the stage grew dark—our cue to exit. I hurried off the platform and to the back of the trailer.

"Well, it all comes down to this," I heard Matt say, as he came up behind me and placed his hand on my shoulder.

I sucked in a deep breath and then quickly forced it out, as a smile found its way to my face.

"You ready?" Matt asked.

I met his stare, then slowly nodded my head.

"After you then," he said, gesturing me out onto the stage again.

I took one, last deep breath. Then, I made my way to the microphone for the last time that night. The crowd was loud. Some people were clapping; some were cheering; and every once in a while, there was a whistle or a shout.

My walk to the center of the stage was slow and calculated. I could barely see my hands through the black that filled the stage. And if it weren't for the little lights near the edge of the platform, I was pretty sure I would have fallen flat on my face.

I eventually reached the stool sitting behind the microphone stand, which was front and center on the stage. I leaned against it and propped one leg onto its rung. Then, I took the mic out of its stand and moved the stand over to my side. I heard Matt back on the piano pulling a bench closer to the keys. And the next thing I knew, he was giving a count. I closed my eyes and lowered my head. Then, the piano solo began moments later, and an instant hush crept over the crowd.

I anxiously twisted the mic in my hands, as I felt the bright lights return to my face. Then, within seconds, I lifted my head and opened my eyes. The white and yellow rays blinded me, but it didn't matter—not this time. Nothing mattered, except that she was out there. I brought the mic to my mouth, and soon, everything I had

My Butterfly

left in me—every hope, every dream, every bit of
strength—came rushing past my lips:

"The sun's a settin' on Cedar Lake
While that autumn fog settles in
The fish aren't bitin'
Crickets sing
Just me and an old friend
Remembering the good ol' days
When we were just kids
Startin' trouble, chasin' old flames
The what-ifs, the what-might-have-beens
Until slowly the conversation dies
And I know that he knows
Cause the next thing he says
Is, buddy, don't tell me lies,
How does the story really go?

Does she ever cross your mind?
Does she ever steal your nights?
Is she still a part of you?
Do you ever wish she were still by your side?
And what would you do?
If she walked up here tomorrow
And told you that she loved you?
Would you drop it all and run to her?
Would you tell her you love her too?
Or would you simply send her home?
And tell her you've moved on?
Tell me, buddy, what would you do?

Then I looked at him with two, sad eyes
And I said,
More than every once in a while,

More than most dreams,
More than just my heart,
More than anything,
More than you know,
And more than I can say,
I've loved her more
Every passing day

And every time I close my eyes,
She's here with me
Her soft, green eyes,
Her hand in mine
It's her I see
And I tell him,
I wish your dreams kept you close
Or that one led you back to me
And that I'd trade it all
For the day he didn't have to ask me,
Tell me, buddy, what would you do?

Now, I'm tellin' you,
Julia, My Butterfly,
More than every once in a while,
More than most dreams,
More than just my heart,
More than anything,
More than you know,
And more than I can say,
I've loved you more
Every passing day
Julia, I've loved you more
Every passing day."

My Butterfly

I sang the last line and then let my eyes fall to the wood under my feet. The piano grew silent soon after, and the lights faded again. I listened through the quiet for a moment. Then, suddenly, the crowd's cheers returned, and they were the loudest they had been all night.

After several moments, I lifted my head, and out of the corner of my eye, I spotted Alex near the back of the crowd, waving his skinny, little arm again. I narrowed my eyes. There were spots still floating around everywhere. But I could see him just enough to notice that he was dramatically lifting and lowering his arm, and he was pointing. I stood up. It looked as if he was pointing toward the parking lot.

"Jules," I whispered to myself.

In no more than a second, I was off the stool and darting toward the side of the stage.

"Will, where are you going?" Matt asked, grabbing my arm and stopping me fast.

"She's leaving," I said.

He loosened his grip on my arm, and I took off again.

"I'll be back," I shouted over my shoulder.

I made it to Lou behind the stage, jumped behind the wheel and turned the key. There was a second way out of the field. It was the same way we had gotten the trailer in. I flipped on my brights and stepped on the gas.

After a rough and fast hundred yards, my wheels hit the blacktop, just as a car was pulling out of the parking lot. I sped and caught up to it. Its license plates were from Tennessee. So, unless someone else had come across the state boarder to see this concert, it was a rental, and it was her. I quit tailing her and fell back. There were two places she could be going. She was either on her way back to her new job and her new life in South Carolina or she was going home—either way, I'd follow her.

The sedan slowed when it reached a highway that led out of town. I tapped my brakes and watched as the car turned and hit the blacktop. Then, I knew for sure; it was Jules, and she was going home.

I slowed up and fell farther behind her. I didn't want to scare her. And through bends and turns in the path, I stayed just close enough that I could see her as she made her way down the highway and then onto the winding gravel road.

Eventually, she made the last turn before her parents' house. I watched the sedan kick up a dust trail as it neared the white-graveled drive, and I waited for it to slow down and turn, but it never did. Instead, the car stayed on a straight path.

My foot slowly fell off the gas pedal and hit the brake, causing Lou to come to a stop. Then, I sat back in my seat and let my head fall against the headrest. Moments later, a big smile edged its way across my face, and I glanced out the window and up into the heavens.

"Gonna see some stars tonight, Jules?" I asked out loud.

Then, I set my eyes onto the gravel road again and stepped on the gas.

"It's a good night for it," I said to myself, smiling a wide, happy grin.

Chapter Forty-One

The Chase

I made my way across the creek slab and pulled off to the side of the road. There was a black sedan already waiting there. I smiled, reached into my backseat and then climbed out of the truck.

It was dark, but there was still a piece of the moon in the sky, so I could make out her silhouette on the hood of the sedan. She was sitting up, and her face was turned back toward me.

"Hi, Jules," I said.

She seemed to hesitate before she spoke.

"Hi," she eventually said.

Her voice was cheerful. She didn't seem surprised. It made me smile wider, as I walked toward her.

"Mind if I take a seat?" I asked, when I reached the car.

"Not at all; it's a rental," she said, patting a spot next to her on the hood.

I nodded my head and chuckled to myself.

"Aah," I said.

My eyes traveled from her hand to the color in her eyes. Then, I cautiously climbed onto the car's hood, leaned my back against the windshield and made myself comfortable, all the while, trying my best to conceal the object in my hand.

"Did you know I was here?" she asked.

There was a suspicious air attached to her question. I was quiet for a second but then turned my face toward hers.

"Of course. Where else would you be?" I asked.

I watched her pause in what looked as if it was a thought.

"But how? I never…," she started.

"Oh, you want to know how I knew you came at all?" I asked.

"That would be a start," she said, shooting me a coy smile.

"You promised," I said.

"Wait, you remembered that?" she asked.

"Of course, and from the looks of it, you did too," I said, gently elbowing her arm.

"A promise is a promise," she said so softly I almost didn't hear it.

There was silence for a second then—that perfect kind of silence, when it almost had a hum of its own.

"But seriously, how could you have known?" she asked.

My Butterfly

I paused and met her eyes again. She looked puzzled. I missed that puzzled face of hers. I missed all of her faces.

"Did you see the camera guy scanning the crowd?" I asked.

"Umm...yeah, I guess I might have noticed him," she said, slowing shaking her head.

"Before the show, I gave him a photo and asked him to look for you," I said.

"You didn't?" she demanded.

"I did," I said. "And turns out, he's got a good eye."

I gave her a wink, shrugged my shoulders and then sent a wide grin up into the heavens.

I felt her eyes linger on me before, eventually, her head fell softly back onto the windshield.

"You never cease to amaze me, Will Stephens," she said, laughing softly to herself.

I listened to her soft laughter until it faded. Then, there was silence again—well, except for the crickets and the tree frogs. It had its place, but I wasn't much for the quiet in this stage of the game.

"Did you hear the last song?" I asked.

She took a moment before she spoke.

"I did," she eventually whispered.

"I meant every word of it," I said.

"It's a beautiful song, Will," she said, slowly nodding her head as she spoke. "And how does 'the one' feel about this song?"

My head shifted to the side, and my eyes darted to her eyes. She looked serious. But it was too late to stop the smile already squeezing past my lips.

"I don't know, Jules, how do you feel?" I asked, chuckling to myself.

I watched her let out a slow, uneasy breath before she locked her stare onto the moon again.

"You're the one, Jules, and I should have told you years ago, but I knew it wasn't the right time. I knew that you weren't ready yet."

Her eyes quickly darted toward mine again.

"Ready?" she asked. "Will, what…"

She let her words trail off.

"Jules, you've always been the only one for me," I confessed.

I stopped then. I knew I had to tell her everything now, but I had to start from the beginning. I sucked in a breath and swallowed hard.

"Jules, I know I let life get in the way of us, and I'm sorry," I said. "I'm so sorry. But I didn't take the record deal in search of some kind of fame or elusive fortune or anything like that. I didn't take it for me, Jules. It's been great. You were right; it's all been great. But you know that I would have been just as happy to spend the rest of my days playing my guitar for my number-one fan."

I turned onto my side and faced her. Her eyes were still on me.

"But when I realized that I might not even get that dream—my dream of playing for you for the rest of my life—I remembered a promise you had made to me," I said.

I paused and watched as a word formed on her soft lips.

"Why did you wait so long to tell me this?" she asked. "I had thought that you had moved on. I moved on. I almost got married. You know that."

Her voice was stern, but I felt the corner of my mouth slowly lifting into a boyish grin despite it.

"Yeah, seeing the ring hurt just a little," I said.

My Butterfly

Her expression didn't change, and then I knew she wasn't in the mood for any of my stupid jokes. I lowered my eyes and then took a deep breath and slowly forced it out.

"You know, Jules, I wish I could say that I knew all along that you wouldn't go through with it—that you wouldn't marry him—but I didn't know for sure," I confessed. "I just prayed like hell that you would realize he wasn't the one for you."

I watched a smile fight its way to her pretty face. It was playful but also laced with sarcasm.

"Thanks, Will," she said. "I'm glad I had your best wishes."

My eyes fell to a spot on the sedan's hood before they returned to her.

"I'm so sorry, Jules," I said. "I hadn't really realized how fast everything had gone until it was too late. I was so busy trying to find a way to get you back—listening to every piece of advice from every person who would give it—that I kind of got lost along the way."

I stopped to take a breath.

"And Jules, I knew you had wings—wings like no one I have ever met," I went on. "You had your dreams, and they were bigger than this town, and they were bigger than me. I knew that, and I knew you. I would have loved to follow you and to be with you when you graduated college or got into law school or passed the bar. I would have loved to be there with you living your dreams. It kills me that I wasn't."

My smile faded then, and my eyelids fell over my eyes, as her soft voice hit my ears again.

"Will," she said, "when it was all said and done, it hurt, and I was hurting. I just needed time to figure things out, but that day—that day we broke up—it was like you had already given up on us."

I forced my eyes open.

"Jules, I was foolish," I pleaded. "I shouldn't have let you walk out of my life. I should have protested. I should have fought for you, but I was young, and I thought you would change your mind in a short while and come back to me. And more than that, I was selfish. I wanted all of you, and I wanted you to want me too. And, believe me, I wanted to tell you. God knows I wanted to tell you so many times, but you see, I had to wait. I loved you too much to lose you twice."

There was silence again as my last few words fell off my lips and hit the empty space between us.

"Will, I loved you," she eventually said.

Her words were gentle, but they still managed to sting.

"We were going to get married and grow wrinkly together," she continued. "But you made me a different person, Will. I was fighting for survival in the last days we were together. You made me never want to hurt like that again."

I watched her chest rise and then fall. Then, her eyes seemed to get caught on a spot somewhere up in that big sky.

"Jules, I'm so sorry," I pleaded. "But you've got to know that the longer I waited, the more my heart broke."

She turned to me again, and I caught her stare.

"My ship sank, Jules, and my plan failed, and before I knew it, I was lost without you," I continued. "Even though I could no longer wrap you up into my arms or kiss your pretty forehead, I still saw you."

I paused for a moment and swallowed hard before I continued. I could feel the lump forming in my throat.

"You haunted my nights and then even my days," I said. "I lived for sleep at times when you would come to me, and it would be just like you had never left. Dreams would always end with you, and then mornings would steal you away with a cruelty that haunted my days. The start of each new morning, Jules, pained me as I opened my eyes only to face my merciless reality. No matter how hard I tried to push you to the back of my mind, you always found a way back to the forefront. You always won," I added, gently nudging her arm.

She lowered her head and smiled, as my eyes found the tops of my boots and locked onto them.

"I eventually learned to live as normally as possible again," I went on. "I learned to get out of bed and to put on a smile everyday, though even in my laughter, my heart ached. And I learned to hide my hurt when someone asked about you or mentioned your name, which they often did and still do. I mean, Jules, even hearing your name in the grocery store would send me into a crazy, downward spiral that usually ended with Jeff acting as my badly equipped therapist."

She cocked her head to the side and caught my eyes, but I only nodded my head and sucked in another deep breath, as I tried to smile.

"But I slowly learned to live a quiet existence without you by my side, carrying the heavy burden that was my secret," I said.

I stopped then for a moment before I continued.

"Then one day, I received an answer to my prayers—in the form of a business card," I said, starting to laugh. "It sounds crazy, I know, but it was almost as if fate had conspired for us, Jules. It took me a little while to realize it, but once I had, I was on a mission. Jules, I took the offer for you. All of this—the performing, the tours, the songs—is for you. I did it all to bring you back to me."

"What?" I heard her softly ask. "How could you have done this all…?"

I listened to her words trail off.

"I had just finished recording your song, and I knew that it would only be a matter of time before you'd come back," I said. "After all, you promised."

A happy smile finally broke free from my face.

"Jules, I've already waited too long to tell you this…," I said and then stopped.

I reached behind me, grabbed the butterfly weed and placed it in between us.

"Julia, when I said that I would love you until the last petal falls, I meant it," I said. "You're the answer to my every prayer."

She took the stem into her hands and gently caressed its silk flowers.

"Will, where did you find these?" she asked.

I smiled wider.

"Under that raggedy, old teddy bear of yours and some track medals," I said. "I had some help."

I watched her lips turn up into a smile, as she stared into the flowers for a long moment.

"Will," she eventually said. "I'm not the same person I was when we were in high school."

Her confession took me aback.

"Well, Jules, if you haven't noticed, I'm not exactly the same person that I was ten years ago either," I said, with a half-smile. "I'm here fighting for you, aren't I?"

A coy expression shot to her face.

"I'm just trying to tell you that you might not be saying all these things if you really knew me now," she said. "You might not even want a girl like me anymore."

She peeked at me from behind her big eyelashes.

"Hmm," I said, nodding my head in a pretend, reflective thought. "Then, just who is the new Miss Julia Lang?"

I watched her eyes quickly travel back to mine. She looked a little surprised.

"Well, okay," she eventually said.

She took a second, and I watched as she inhaled a healthy dose of the night's cool air before letting the breath pass through her lips again.

"Well," she said, meeting my eyes, "for starters, I make a living arguing. Not many people understand why I do it, and it's tough sometimes, but I love it."

I kept wearing my smile as she continued.

"And I don't wish on stars anymore or entertain fairy tales, and I can't remember the last time that I climbed out of a window in the middle of the night," she said. "Oh, and I'm a vegetarian now."

She lowered her eyes.

"And I don't believe that there is a perfect someone for anyone," she softly said.

I sat back against the windshield again and let my eyes stare off into the black distance. She had changed a little, that's for sure. No meat? No meat at all? No cheeseburgers?

"A vegetarian? Really?" I asked.

Her eyes searched mine. I could tell that she was trying to judge my reaction.

"That is a big change all right—but I'm afraid that you're going to have to do a little better than that if you want to scare me off, Miss Lang," I said.

Her eyes smiled then, even though her lips refused to waver.

"Look, Jules, it really is simple," I said. "See, I'm in love with the person you can never outrun. I'm in love with you, Julia."

She was quiet for a good minute, and I watched as her eyes searched my own. Somehow, I just knew that she wasn't buying my confession.

"Will," she said, finally, taking a deep breath, "I just think...I think that it has been a long time. We're two, different people now, despite what you might think. We're not two sixteen-year-olds. It's been ten, long years, Will. And you have your life here, and I have mine in Charleston. You fight fires and have an amazing singing career. And I have a great job doing something I love also."

She paused and bit her bottom lip and then returned it to its natural place again. I barely noticed that she had stopped. Something was telling me that I didn't want to hear the rest of her story.

"You see," she continued, despite my silent protests, "no matter how you look at it, our lives just don't match up anymore. I mean, there was a time that I really wanted them to—to match up—but that was some time ago."

Somewhere in her last, few words, my eyes had fallen to a dark place on the car's hood.

"I just don't think it would ever work, Will," she said. "We're living our realities now. Besides, it just makes sense that we couldn't have possibly known what was best for us at sixteen."

She was quiet then for a moment, but I couldn't find any words.

"But I promise you that you'll be with me in my dreams," she eventually went on. "When I rest my head on my pillow each night, when time is all my own to escape the world and dream, I'll meet you there. We'll

My Butterfly

both be sixteen, and we'll be happy, and we'll do all the things we used to do. We'll climb out windows, and we'll wish on stars, and we'll watch old movies and make fun of Jeff."

She stopped again, and I met her eyes.

"What we had belongs in dreams and meeting there each night seems to work well anyway," she said, with a soft smile. "But, Will, as for us in this lifetime, we've just changed too much, become two, different people and followed two, different paths. It's life, Will, not a fairy tale."

I swallowed hard.

"Why did you come back, Jules?"

"I made a promise," she said, in almost a whisper.

"But why now?" I asked.

"It's a good cause, Will," she said.

I sat there frozen for a moment. Did she really believe what she was saying? Or was what she had said only what she had told herself to believe?

I let out a heavy sigh.

Either way, it seems as though it ends the same.

Eventually, I turned toward her and took her hand in mine and gently kissed the back of it. She looked a little thrown off, but she let me hold her hand all the same.

"Julia," I said, meeting her eyes again, "you have been my world since I first laid eyes on you, and you may not realize it, but I have taken you with me every day in the last decade. Please know that there is not one moment that I stopped loving you. You are the reason for my smiles and my songs. You are my hope and my inspiration. My heart has only beaten for you. I do admit that I had my doubts, none of which involved my love for you. I did worry that you had forgotten me and that you had forgotten what we had, but just being here with you now, it's proof. It proves to me that you haven't. I see no change in your eyes, and it's the most comforting feeling I've ever known. Jules, please know that I will love you unceasingly for many lifetimes to come."

I took a shallow breath and then let it quickly escape before I continued.

"Jules, but no matter what big dreams you're living or what lucky guy you end up marrying…"

My voice cracked, and I tried hard to swallow the growing lump in my throat.

"Please know that I love you," I continued. "Even if I have to do it in secret—or in dreams—I'll love you forever."

Then, I set her hand gently back down onto her bended knee and slowly slid down the hood of her rented sedan. And when my feet hit the ground, I turned around one, last time.

"I guess I'll be seeing you in my dreams," I said.

I tipped my baseball cap toward her. Then, I started to turn but then stopped.

"And, Jules," I said.

Her eyes darted to mine.

"I believe that there is a perfect someone for everyone, and I know that you still believe that too," I said. "There is a perfect someone, even if the road to that someone isn't all that perfect."

I felt the warm liquid behind my eyes again. It was an all-too-familiar part of our story in the last ten years or so.

Then, I slowly turned and made my way back to my truck. And when I reached its door, I stopped, thought about turning back but didn't. Instead, I opened the door and slid behind the wheel.

I sat there for a moment, staring into the dashboard, still trying to figure out if my dreams had just slipped away right there on the hood of her car in the middle of this black night. I sat there trying to find the words to say that I hadn't already said that would make her say that she loved me too. I searched through every moment that I had kept locked away in my chest for the last decade. I searched every piece of us, but I couldn't seem to find another way to say: *Stay with me, Julia. Love me like I love you. Be my world again. Love me.*

The turn of the key in the ignition was my head telling my heart it might be over. I couldn't look at her. I couldn't say goodbye. If I was going to leave, if I had to leave, at least I was leaving with one, last tiny hope that this wasn't goodbye.

I slid Lou into gear, made a u-turn over the uneven ground and then felt the tires hit the loose gravel once again.

Chapter Forty-Two

Radio

I pulled back into the makeshift parking lot behind the stage and killed the engine. Then, I forced out a heavy sigh and lowered my head onto the steering wheel and let it rest there.

"Will," I heard a voice shout out a second later.

I lifted my head to Chris staring at me from the other side of my window.

"They're lookin' for you for the radio," he said.

I took a moment and then nodded my head.

"Okay," I said.

I sighed and then slowly pulled on the door handle and stepped out onto the soft soil again.

"They're around the side," I heard Chris say.

I looked up at him and nodded my head again. Then, I shuffled around the corner of the stage and stopped. In front of me was a van with a radio station logo painted across its body. Its back doors were open, and there was a guy standing right beside one of the doors talking into a tiny mic that was attached to a big set of headphones. He noticed me and waved me over.

I hesitated, then took a deep breath in and then slowly forced it out. And before I knew it, I was being escorted to the van and fit with my own tiny mic and set of big headphones.

"This is *98.7 Wolf Country*, and this is Jason David standing here with local heartthrob Will Stephens," the host said. "Will, tell us what it felt like to sing for the first time in front of your hometown."

I didn't say anything at first. Instead, I looked up and caught Matt standing a few yards away twirling his finger in a sideways, circular motion at me. My gaze froze on his moving finger for a second. Then, I quickly forced my attention back to Jason David and cleared my throat.

"Well, it was a pleasure," I said.

As soon as I had gotten the words out, my eyes lowered and caught the outline of a small box inside my jeans pocket. I took another deep breath and then cleared my throat again and tried my best to force out more words.

"I had my mom and dad and my grandma in the first row," I said and then stopped.

I looked up and caught Matt's stare again. Now, he seemed to be nodding me onward.

"And," I continued, "I looked down one time, and even through the lights, I could see my grandma bustin' some moves."

I tried to make the words that came out of my mouth sound happy, though I knew they were soft and unsure as to what *happy* actually was without her.

"So, that was Grandma down there?" Jason asked. "I thought that was your sister."

I laughed, and it took me by surprise. I wasn't sure I would be able to laugh again.

"No, seriously," I said and then stopped.

My voice was still quiet. I concentrated hard on making it more audible.

"It was great, a real treat for me to be here and to play for all of the people who have supported me to this point," I said.

"Now, Will, let us not forget what this whole concert is about," he said. "It's about raising some support for those victims of the recent floods, right? Tell us a little about that."

"Yeah, uh, this whole night was for those who have been affected by the flooding," I said and then took a second before I continued.

"My heart goes out to all those who have lost homes or livelihoods, and I'm just asking everyone, even after tonight, to continue to give to local efforts to support victims and to remember to keep them in their prayers," I said.

"Well, thanks so much, Will, for coming out and speaking with us tonight," Jason said. "It's definitely a great cause to support."

There was a short pause then, and Jason's eyes quickly darted toward mine. It caught me off guard.

"I just have one more question," he said. "You didn't think you'd get out of this interview without me asking it, did you?"

I nervously chuckled, secretly dreading his question.

My Butterfly

"No, I suppose not. Fire away," I said, eventually.

"Well," he said, "Will, we've never heard that last song, and it was pretty obvious to me that it was about a special girl in your life. Care to tell us about that?"

I sat there, frozen and speechless, while the moments of my life with Julia—both the ones I kept close and the ones I still dreamed of—were awakened again inside my chest and now threatened to erupt. I desperately tried to swallow them back down.

"Well, it was for a special girl," I finally said. "She was my high school sweetheart."

"Was she here tonight?" I barely heard him ask.

All of sudden, it felt as if I were in a small tunnel with all my memories buzzing past me instead of in the open, empty field.

"Uh, yes, she was here tonight," I said.

"Well, where is she now?" he asked.

I let silent moments pass. Honestly, I hoped she was still here, that she had changed her mind, that she had stayed. But what is hope if it's not fleeting?

"Well, I recon she's on her way back to South Carolina," I said.

I knew there was a sadness tightly wrapped around my voice now, and out of the corner of my eye, I saw Matt's head slowly lower.

"South Carolina, huh?" Jason asked. "So, does this mean you're still on the market, for all those ladies listening tonight?"

A smile somehow squeezed past my lips.

"I'm pretty sure there wouldn't be any of those ladies here," I reassured him. "See, they all knew me in junior high."

Jason threw his head back and laughed.

"But no, sir, to answer your question," I continued. "I'm taken, and I have been since I was sixteen or six. It's all the same," I confessed into the little mic.

I watched him nod his head.

"Well, all right, if she's listening now, is there something you'd like to say to her?" he asked.

"I...," I started and then stopped.

I was fighting back a stampede of emotions. My eyes were locked on my pocket and on the small box holding the life I thought I would have with her.

"I just want her to know that she's still the same beautiful, after all these years, and that I'm here—always."

Chapter Forty-Three

One Knee

I thanked Jason and pulled the headset from my ears and set it down.

"I'm sorry, man," Matt said, as he walked over to me and patted my shoulder.

I glanced up at him but then quickly lowered my eyes.

"I just need a minute, Matt," I said, starting to walk away.

"Sure, buddy," he said.

I took off for the fence line and made my own path alongside it. It was dark, and there were trees grown up around me, so I felt hidden from the world. I walked until the posts and the wire ran out and the trees stopped.

Then, I planted my feet and took a deep breath, breathing in the familiar smell of tall grasses and dirt. I let it fill my lungs, and then I sent it back out into the cool air again.

What was I supposed to do without her?

The sound of metal hitting metal forced my attention back to the stage behind me. I turned but couldn't see anything from where I stood. I figured they must have started cleaning up.

I sighed and then started my slow hike back to the stage. But this time, I followed the line of grass that had been pressed down by tires. I knew the line led to the makeshift parking lot, so I didn't even bother to look up as I set one foot in front of the other and tried to think about my last conversation with Jules. I tried really hard to replay it in my head, but somehow, I just couldn't. Then, I tried to think of what day it was, but I couldn't think of that either. *God, would I even be able to think without her?*

I heard something else slam hard against what sounded like a bed of a truck. The loud noise forced my eyes upward again. Then, suddenly, I stopped.

"Julia."

She turned in the plastic chair and then quickly stood up.

"Wha...," I started to say.

I swallowed hard and tried again.

"Did you forget something?" I asked.

I wasn't sure if I had spoken loud enough for her to have heard me or even if I had spoken at all.

She was quiet for a moment, and she didn't move. Then, I watched as her eyes fell into mine and stayed there.

"Yes," she said, finally.

My breaths became short, and I tried to swallow again.

"I forgot how much I love you," she said.

I watched the sides of her lips anxiously turn up. Then, suddenly, I noticed that I couldn't move, and my heart began a violent pounding against the inside of my chest.

"Could you use a hand?" she asked, taking a quick glance around at the field of plastic chairs before settling her gaze on me again.

I couldn't take my eyes off her. And I couldn't move, and I couldn't speak. This went on for seconds, maybe even minutes. Then, finally, the words came.

"You're beautiful," I said.

A faint smile found my broken lips.

"You're even more beautiful than in dreams," I said, feeling my smile widen. "Though, I'm still prayin' like crazy this isn't one."

Her pretty stare was still on me when I finished. She was smiling, but her eyes were pleading with me to do something. I remembered those eyes.

I forced my legs to come alive again, and I took a couple of steps in her direction, keeping my gaze locked in hers for my journey to her place in the field. And eventually, I planted my feet directly in front of her. But instead of taking her into my arms and squeezing her close—like I wanted so much to do—I stopped. I had one more thing to do that just couldn't wait.

I felt my lips start to turn up as I bent down and touched one knee to the soil and the grass. Then, I reached into my jeans pocket, felt for a small box and pulled it out. I turned the box over in my hand, feeling its soft velvet against my fingertips. There was still a part of me trying to figure out if this were all real. But after a moment, I brought the velvet box to view in between us and lifted it toward her. And with my other hand, I took the lid and slowly pulled it back.

"Julia Austin Lang," I began, "I love you more than anything in this world, and I could never imagine spending a second more of my life without you. And I've more than learned life's lesson. I'm not gonna let you get away again."

I paused to let my smile grow wider.

"Jules, will you marry me—some day very soon?"

I watched as her lips fell open and her hand rushed to cover them. Her green eyes were big and bright, but she made no sound.

I kept my eyes in hers, feeling every, exaggerated heartbeat in my chest.

Then, eventually, I spotted a smile behind her delicate fingers. And soon after, a nod followed.

I lowered my eyelids and then my head.

"Thank you, God," I whispered to myself.

Then, I lifted my eyes to hers again. I was pretty sure a smile was permanently tattooed to my face as I rose to my feet. And once I was standing, I gently took her hand from her lips and slipped the ring onto her pretty ring finger. Then, I brought my forehead to hers and breathed in her perfume and her smile and this moment. And when I couldn't take not holding her for one more second, I scooped her up into my arms.

She squealed her little, high-pitched squeal and wrapped her arms around my neck, as I put my lips to her ears.

"Thank you for coming back to me, Jules," I whispered.

A moment went by. Then, I felt her breaths near my ear.

My Butterfly

"I told you I'd come back," she whispered, as she rested her head gently against my shoulder. "I'm sorry I took so long."

"You ready?" I asked her.

She flashed me a wide smile.

"Okay, no turning back now," I playfully warned her.

She shook her head back and forth and laughed that pretty laugh of hers.

"Everyone," I announced, "this is my wife-to-be."

I held Jules's hand tightly in mine.

The heads in the tiny bar, which was more crowded than usual, all spun in our direction. I found Jules's pretty eyes and waited for her to find mine. She did seconds later. I smiled at her with a smile that could only be for her. And as she held her gaze in mine, the corners of her lips started to rise again. And right then, I saw in her every moment that made her, her and every moment that made us, us. I saw her blond hair bathed in the sun's rays as she sat atop a set of monkey bars, laughing and calling out my name. I saw the fire's flames dancing on the gold in her eyes the night I knew she had found it in her heart to see me differently than her monkey-bar days. On her sweet lips, I saw the words she had wanted to say in the years we had been apart but just somehow couldn't because it wasn't the right time. And I saw all our goodbyes and our hurts written on her face, but now, they were also intertwined with our hopes and our dreams and the moments that now bind us together. And I couldn't help but think right then: *I love this girl.*

"To Will and Julia," I suddenly heard Jeff shout from the back of the bar.

"To Will and Julia," the people echoed.

And then, as if it were fate itself smiling down on us—or maybe just Jeff, now standing at the juke box—a song came pouring through the walls. And it was a song about us.

"Our last, first dance?" I asked, extending my hand toward Jules.

She smiled at me again and then touched her hand to mine.

I took her hand and led her to the tiny dance floor. Then, I wrapped my other arm around the small of her back and pulled her close.

"Tell me this is real," I said.

I could hear her softly laughing.

"I believe this is real," she said.

"Jules," I said then.

I pulled back and found her eyes.

"I'll quit the firefighting gig," I said.

She sent a puzzled look up to my face.

"No," she said, shaking her head. "Why would you do that?"

"I know about your dad," I whispered near her ear.

Her eyes started to gloss over.

"I mean, I didn't know until just recently," I said.

"No," she said, stopping me and pressing her head against my chest. "I want you just the way you are."

I paused then and let a slow and steady breath escape past my lips. Then, I pulled her closer, closed my eyes and let my head come to rest on the top of hers as I breathed in the smell of her hair and breathed out a smile.

Chapter Forty-Four

I Do

"Will, you ready?" Jeff asked.

I found his goofy stare and then lowered my head and smiled.

"Right," he said. "Ten years."

I met his gaze again. He was smiling too.

"Let's go," I said, standing up and readjusting my collar.

As I walked past him, he put his hand on my shoulder and followed me out. We made our way across the street and through a grassy knoll. Then, I stopped when I saw the people. They were our family and close friends, and they were sitting around the gazebo that sat at the edge of the levee. I took a deep breath and then felt a smile start to edge up my face. A moment passed as I reflected back on the journey to this very place. Every grand adventure has its own missteps, right? Luckily, mine didn't do me in.

"You have the rings, right?" I asked, eventually turning to Jeff.

I watched as he reached his hand into the pocket of his slacks, and suddenly, his face went blank.

My heart sped up, and my eyes widened.

"Jeff," I said, dramatically drawing out the letters in his name.

We stood there staring at each other for several seconds—neither one of our expressions changing; his was blank and mine was setting into panic—before the left side of Jeff's mouth started to lift into a grin.

"I'm just pullin' your leg, buddy," he said, snickering to himself.

Speechless, I watched as he pulled out a small, black box, held it out and then quickly shoved it back into his pocket.

I closed my eyes and took in a deep, slow breath.

"But I do have a piece of advice for ya, buddy," he said, patting my shoulder.

I found his eyes again.

"You sure?" I asked him.

He flashed me a puzzled look. Then, he seemed to catch on.

"No, no," he said. "I think this is pretty good advice for once. It's actually from my dad."

"Well, in that case," I said, starting to smile again.

"All right," he said. "My dad always told me that there are two sides to every argument."

I kept one eye narrowed on him.

"Okay," I said, slowly starting to nod my head.

My Butterfly

"Well," he continued. "You find out which side is hers, and you jump on it. Then, you both win."

I closed my eyes, lowered my head and laughed.

"Thanks, Jeff," I said, patting him on the shoulder. "That's probably pretty good advice."

He smiled his proud, goofy grin.

"But now, I have some advice of my own for ya," Jeff said. "And it's not like all the other advice."

"Oh, yeah?" I asked. "What is it?"

"You love her?" he asked.

I met his stare. His face was straight and serious.

"Of course," I said, as my lips edged up a little higher at the thought.

"And you've loved her ever since you could spell your own name—well, the short version anyway?" he asked.

"Yes," I said, nodding my head.

"And you lost her once?" he asked.

My smile faded, and I lowered my eyes and nodded my head.

"Yeah," I said, eventually.

"Then, Will," he said and then stopped.

I lifted my eyes again.

"Don't ever let her get away again," he said.

I felt a grin fighting its way to my face.

"I won't," I said, shaking my head.

"All righty," he said, pushing me forward. "Now, let's go get you two high school lovebirds hitched. It's about damn time."

I smiled wider and then took the last few steps to the gazebo and planted my feet in front of it. The air was warm—almost hot in my suit. I adjusted my jacket and then spotted my mom and dad in the front row. They both smiled that proud smile that parents get sometimes.

Then, my gaze caught a piece of the river behind the levee and fell onto the butterfly weeds that danced along its edges. I gently smiled as my eyes lingered on the flowers for a few more seconds and my grandmother's words replayed in my head: *They bring the butterflies back.*

Yes, they do, Grandma. Yes, they do.

The song of a violin suddenly forced my attention back to the aisle runner, and what I saw there made my heart skip a beat. There, standing at its end, was a pretty girl—my butterfly.

She was beautiful. The sun's rays were cast against her silhouette, and her hair was down. And there was a veil over her face, but I could still see her pretty, green eyes and her pretty, soft lips. And I watched her lips now as they turned up into a soft smile.

I smiled too and memorized the way she took her slow, perfect steps, each one bringing her closer to me.

Her dress was simple but perfect. I noticed it now. It looked as though it was made for her. It was the kind that didn't have any straps and that showed off her sun-kissed shoulders and arms—the kind that made me long to touch the places it didn't. And in her hands were little, orange flowers—butterfly weeds. My smile beamed across my face, as my eyes made their way back to the green in hers.

Finally, she got close enough that I could touch her, and I reached for her hand. She planted her eyes in mine and gave me that playful, happy look that always drove me crazy. Then, she handed her flowers to Rachel and placed her hand in mine. There was a second where my eyes were locked in hers, and I couldn't move. I could barely breathe. Then, I felt something soft nudging against the palm of my hand. My gaze darted to our hands and then back up into her eyes. She was still smiling, but that didn't keep my heart from starting to race. I didn't need any more surprises today. I just needed her to say *I do* and then to love me for the rest of my life.

My gaze found our hands again. Then, I took the object and turned it over. It was a napkin, and there was writing on it—a couple of lines. I breathed in another slow, deep breath and then allowed my eyes to carefully follow over each word: *Since my wish has come true, I guess I can tell you now. It was for you—for always. Love, Jules.*

When I finished reading the words on the napkin, I reached for her other hand. My mind was already rushing back to the hood of my old truck and a warm, starry night when I brought my lips close to her ear.

"Thanks for marrying a country boy, pretty girl," I whispered.

I watched as her lips started to part and then form a soft smile.

"I love you," I whispered near her ear again.

Her eyes found and searched mine for a second. Then, her lips fell open.

"I've always loved you," she whispered. "I've always loved you, country boy."

Epilogue

I've only got one story—the only story I live to tell. It's about a girl. She was my first love, and she was my last love. And she was every love in between. Julia Lang stole my heart probably from the moment that I first laid eyes on her. Yes, that moment when she was in pigtails wanting to ride the big tractor at my grandpa's store— that same moment I chased her off—I loved her then too. But, as life would have it, it would take me a few more years to figure out what it was that I felt for her then—what this love stuff was all about. Yet, even in her pigtail days, I always knew there was something in those moments—in those little moments when she waited with me, her hand on my knee, calming my fears or when she

My Butterfly

smiled and made me believe I was the only one in the world worth smiling for. In those little moments, she made me want to know her more. And like I have said, she was my first love, and little did I know at seven or at seventeen that I would spend the rest of my life chasing after that pretty girl—to college, across the country, across town to that dusty, gravel road where we spent a lot of our days and a lot of our nights too and even across the lawn when we played tag with the children we would raise together. I didn't know then where life would lead us, but I didn't have to know either. Love has a funny way of hiding the past and the future, so that the only moment that matters is right in front of you.

But I did make some mistakes in my life—lost some years I shouldn't have, but then, I guess, that's life. And that's youth, I guess, too—always being wasted on the young. But in the end, I'm pretty sure that life is all about finding your way through it, around it, over it, any way it takes to get to the one you love.

Jules, I'm sorry I didn't find my way to you faster.

My eyes follow over the words again I have written to the love of my life, knowing she'll come across them one night as she sits next to an empty chair. The words in the letter aren't anything I haven't already said, but my hope is that they will remind her of some things after the good Lord takes me home.

A deep breath fills my lungs, and then I feel it escape past my lips in my next exhale. I just want her to know that I love her and that I'll be waiting for her. And I want to remind her to live, to live each day just like she always has—full.

I reread the last piece of the letter:

Now, you and I both know that I'll wait a lifetime for you—

remember, Butterfly Weeds never give up. So take your time down there. And tonight, as you watch that big, orange sun disappear into the earth and your world gradually grow dark, I'll help God turn on the stars, and I'll wait for my dawn—when you return to me, Julia Stephens.

I love you, My Butterfly. You'll always be my endless song.

I know I'll be there with her, just like every night before, as she writes her life's story in her journal and we watch the sun escape back into the lake. The only difference then will be that I won't be right beside her. Instead, I'll be watching her from above.

"Daddy," I hear my oldest say as she enters my room. "How are you doing?"

My thoughts are put on hold, as I quickly turn over and lay into my lap the letter to her mom.

My little girl, who's not so little anymore, makes her way over to me and kisses the bald spot on my head. She has a worried look on her face, but I know she doesn't think I can tell. She tries to wear her pain on the inside. She always has. It's the trademark of the oldest sibling, I think. She smiles and speaks in this calm and upbeat kind of way. But I'm her father. I recognize the hurt in her eyes. I only wish I could make it disappear.

It's hard when your children get older and a simple hug or reassuring word can't make the monsters or the fear of the dark simply disappear. Somewhere in the course of life, children struggles morph into adult ones, and the pain becomes too deeply rooted for a hug or a word to cure anymore. But it's life, I remind myself again. And we must go through all of it—the good and the not-so-good—to be with the ones we love—even if it is on the other side.

My Butterfly

"I'm as good as I've ever been, my dear, now that you're here," I say to my daughter's brave expression.

I smile and stretch out my arms to hug her, forever hoping that a hug can still heal even a small piece of her heart today.

"Mom said you haven't been feeling well today," she says and takes a seat in the chair beside my bed.

Her expression hasn't changed. It's calm and soft.

"Oh, your mom worries about me too much," I say, with a gentle smile.

I watch her lips slowly rise at their corners.

"But dear," I say and rest my creased palm on her own, delicate hand.

Her eyes meet mine.

"Your mom's a strong woman," I say and then pause.

I see her eyes turning sad as her poker face slightly falters.

"After all, she put up with me for fifty years," I say.

Her eyes turn down as she laughs to herself. I secretly wish I could see her laugh more—see all my children laugh more. My children know my time here is coming to a close. They're wrestling with the one certainty of life we all must face at some point. It's not easy, I know. I wish I could heal them and erase their fears, but again, I know I can't. But that's why God made grandchildren, I guess. Aah, the blessing of grandchildren. They know not of life's trials or its most hated foe. My grandchildren are wonderfully oblivious, and they still laugh. And I love their laughter. If it weren't for them, I fear that there would be very little laughter in my last days.

"But take care of her—your mom—will you, dear?" I ask her when our eyes meet again. "Just come visit her when you can and bring your two, little ones, and tell Jackson and Abigail to do the same."

She lets out a sad sigh and pushes her lips together. Then, a renegade tear escapes from her eye, and I reach up to wipe it away.

"I love you, Austin," I say. "You've always been so strong, like your mom."

She squeezes my hand and holds it tightly.

"I love you too, Daddy, and I will," she says, slowly nodding her head.

Then, we hear a "mommy" echoing through the hallway. It's one of her little ones. The voice sounds shaken but not life-threatened. It's probably nothing a kiss and a Band-Aid can't heal.

Austin rises from her chair, still holding my hand. Then, she kisses my head and rests my hand back onto the bed before turning to tend to her child. I watch her hurry to the doorway, but before she disappears into the hallway, I remember something.

"Austin," I say, regaining her attention.

"Yes, Daddy?" she asks, as she turns around.

I gather the letter from my lap, carefully fold it twice and hold it out toward her.

"Will you put this in your mother's journal?" I ask.

She hesitates, her eyes locked on the cream stationery.

"Sure, Daddy," she says, walking back toward me.

I release the letter into her keeping and softly smile. She forces a smile too. It's a knowing smile. It understands. I'm thankful and also saddened—only because I can't make her hurt go away. It's all a part of life, I tell myself. And I would tell her the same, except that she already knows.

"Mommy."

My Butterfly

We both hear the little voice calling from the hallway again.

"Go," I say, smiling wider and nodding in her direction.

She glances at the letter pressed in between her soft fingers, and then she looks back up at me. I watch her take a deep breath, and I can tell she's fighting back tears.

"Go, go," I say, chuckling and shooing her out the door. "And bring him in here once you've made him all better."

She smiles one, last time and then turns and exits the room, with the letter in her hand.

I rest my head back against the headboard behind me after she's gone. I'm well aware that my time here is short, and there are no late check-outs when the Big Man calls you home. I know that, and anyway, I'm not looking for any. I've said my peace, and I've lived a good life—a full life, with my butterfly at my side. That's all I ever wanted. And now, I have a new mission—to spend forever with her. *Get to forever. Get to forever. Meet her at the gates of forever—do what I've got to do to meet her there, so she has someone there waiting for her, so she's not alone.*

I turn and reach inside the nightstand drawer next to the bed and pull out her photo.

"My Jules," I whisper, as I clutch the old photo in both hands.

And suddenly, a silhouette appears in the doorway. I look up and then quickly shove the photo under my leg and fight back my tears. I can't explain the tears. I'm at peace, but I guess it's still hard knowing I have to leave her for a little while.

"I brought you some tea, dear," she says, shuffling into the room.

I watch her make her way toward me, set the tea tray down onto the nightstand and then fall slowly into the chair beside the bed.

"Thank you, sweetie," I say, meeting her eyes and gently smiling.

Her eyes are the same—the same eyes I remember from her pigtail days and her cut-off-jeans days and her eight-months-pregnant days. They're soft and sexy and beautiful. I smile again at the thought. The only thing I didn't see back then was just how loving they really are.

"Here," she softly says, bringing the cup to my hands.

I notice her eyes lock onto the photo. A piece of it is sticking out, revealing the side of her young face. She acts as if she doesn't see it, and she meets my eyes again and smiles.

"I love you, Will Stephens," she says.

I take the tea cup in one hand and squeeze her soft, creased hand with the other. I look deep into her eyes then. I'm remembering all the moments that we loved and we cried and we loved so much that it made us cry. And I'm remembering all the hell we put ourselves through just to realize we should have been together from that very first moment. I love those moments, though. I love every one of them now. They're our story now. Every mistake, every hurt, every joy, every longing—it's ours, only ours.

"Jules," I start to say, and for some reason, I just can't get the words out.

I'm fighting back the tears in my eyes, and I'm remembering a lifetime of memories, and I just can't get the words out to let her know how much love I have for her. I feel my lips quivering, and I quickly press them tightly together.

My Butterfly

"I know," she says softly. "I know."

I search her eyes and let the air escape my lungs, as she buries her face into my hand near the mattress. I set the cup onto the nightstand's surface and then place my other hand near hers. I can't see her face, but I feel her tears falling wet onto my hand.

"I know," she says again.

She buries her face deeper into both of my hands now and slides something hard in between my fingers. Then, she lifts her head and releases my hand, and my eyes fall onto a small, metal object.

"She kept you safe all these years," she says, in almost a whisper. "I can't come with you now…"

Her words trail off as I meet her gaze again. Pieces of her soft, gray hair have fallen near her face, and there are tears in her eyes. They make my heart break for her.

I squeeze the guardian angel, and then I rest my hand on top of hers again.

"Don't be sad, sweetheart," I say.

A forced smile is edging up my face.

"Will," she says then, so softly I almost don't hear her.

"Yes, sweetheart?" I say.

"Sometimes, I feel like we're just kids," she says and then pauses.

I follow the path her eyes make to the open window.

"And I think I hear rocks hitting the window, and I get the urge to climb out in the middle of the night and fall into your arms," she says, returning her gaze to mine again and smiling through her tears.

"And sometimes," she continues, "I just want to go to the end of a gravel road and stare up at the stars from the hood of your truck or climb that big bluff downtown and watch the fireworks dance to the sky—just one more time."

She stops and smiles wider.

"And there are actually times when I just want to fight, about nothing—because that's what you do when you're young and in love," she says, as a tear escapes from her face and lands gently on my hand.

"Will," she continues.

I gaze deeper into her tear-filled eyes. There's a sincere, yet longing smile on my lips now.

"I loved being young and in love with you," she says.

I take a shallow breath and then let it escape my lungs.

"Me too," I say, squeezing her hand tighter.

"And I know we missed some of those years," she goes on. "But from those years we missed, I can only remember you in them now."

She takes a moment before she continues.

"I remember your face when you first looked up and saw me in the doorway that New Year's Eve so long ago," she says. "You looked so happy, and for a second, you made me forget that we were ever apart. And I remember that night in the hospital. I never told you, but I woke up early that next morning and told myself that I should leave. But I took one look at your handsome, sleeping face and snuggled back into your arms. Those are the parts, along with all the other wonderful parts before them and after them, that I remember. Those are the parts I hold onto.

And Will, I love being not-so-young and in love with you too. Because whatever the moment, I love us."

I watch her bury her face into my hands at my side again, and I let my head fall back as I squeeze my eyelids shut and fight back my own tears. Then, suddenly, I feel her lift her head again, and my eyes open and fall into hers.

"Sometimes, I'm scared I won't remember who I am without you," she says.

There's a longing and an anxiousness in her eyes now. This part makes my heart ache, and finally, a tear wins the battle and escapes down my cheek.

"But then I remember that I'll never truly be without you," she continues, as a smile finds her face again. "Even in those years that you weren't by my side, I was never without you, Will. I carried you with me everywhere I went. I carried you to the mountains and to the deserts and to the sand of San Diego. And I carried you to the live oaks and to the rivers and to the beaches in Charleston too. Because in the end, our story is one full of stumbles and tears and smiles and holding on and refusing to let go. It's the best kind of fairy tale, Will," she says, with a happy smile. "And I couldn't imagine living any of it without you. I love you, sweetheart. I love you a million times a million."

Her face falls to my hands again.

"And to the moon and back," I manage to say.

I wipe the tear from my face and then rest my hand on hers.

"Jules," I say.

She gradually finds my eyes.

"You'll meet me there, won't you, My Butterfly?" I ask.

I watch her smile her perfect smile, and I know that she knows what I mean.

"I promise," she says, slowly nodding her head.

Then, I rest the guardian angel on my chest near my heart and take hold of Jules's hands with both of my hands again. I want to tell her she's my everything, but I can't say the words and still be brave. There are more tears in her eyes. I fight back my own tears and force a smile to my lips.

"I'll save a spot for you on the hood of my truck," I whisper.

I watch her beautiful lips lift into a smile right before she lowers her face and softly kisses the top of my hand.

Then, I take a deep, labored breath and rest my head against the headboard. There are butterfly weeds lying on a chest in the corner of the room. They still have all their petals. I smile, knowing they always will, as my eyelids fall over my eyes and my mind replays the song of our life:

Little girl, little boy
If love has a way
Fill their fields with laughter
And scatter the sun on their day
And if it should happen to rain
Make their raindrops kisses
Straight from heaven above
That touch their hands and faces
And that fill them with love
And make the moon reflect their smiles
And their stars plenty
And, above all, keep them together
And hold them as you may
Forever and ever
Until their last day.

The End

ACKNOWLEDGMENTS

First, I would like to thank God for giving me the opportunity to do what I love to do every day. It's a blessing, and I am so thankful for it.

Thank you to my amazing editors and sources for all your time and contributions. Thank you especially to Donna, Calvin, Kathy, April, Sharon, Jenny, Kyle, Dominick and Jon. I am truly grateful for your patience and support and for all the time you put into making this novel what it is today.

I would also like to thank those wonderful readers and those amazing bloggers who are also readers for their enthusiasm and loyal support of my first novel, *Butterfly Weeds*. Through your love for Will and Julia's story, you made it what it is today, and further, you single-handedly inspired the creation of this novel. I will be forever grateful for your continued support and your wonderful fervor for fairy tales. Thank you for welcoming Will and Julia and their little story into your hearts!

And I would like to thank my family, who continues to be my biggest fans and greatest supporters. And thank you also to my friends and mentors, who are ever inspiring me—whether they realize it or not.

And finally, I would like to thank my husband, Neville, for being exactly what I need when I need it—whether it's an editor, a personal assistant, a public relations specialist or just a shoulder to lean on. And thank you, most of all, for your constant encouragement from the very beginning of this whole, grand adventure. Honey, I love you—a million times a million and to the moon and back.

OTHER BOOKS BY LAURA MILLER
Butterfly Weeds
For All You Have Left

★★★★★
~Back Porch Romance Book Reviews on *Butterfly Weeds*

"A MUST-READ!"
~Nancy's Romance Reads on *For All You Have Left*

★★★★★
"This is certainly one of my favorite love stories ever."
~A Novel Review Blog on *For All You Have Left*

"One of the most beautiful love stories I have ever read."
~Jelena's Book Blog on *Butterfly Weeds*

A LOOK AT *FOR ALL YOU HAVE LEFT*!

Logan Cross met her first love on the playground when she was nine. She married him at eighteen. But life had different plans for Logan. And now at twenty-two, she is in the midst of starting over when Jorgen Ryker moves in next door. Jorgen suspects that Logan might be hiding a few secrets, but neither he nor Logan is ready when she reveals her biggest secret from her past—a secret that neither of them realizes they share.

Please turn this page for a preview of

For All You Have Left

Prologue

Only two things about that afternoon stick out to me—two things that I don't think I'll ever forget. One of those things is the smell the tires made after they had laid a jagged line of black rubber across the faded highway and into the ditch. There were tall wild flowers growing up every which way around me, but all I could think about was that bitter smell of burnt rubber. I remember a breath and then a moment where I think my mind was trying to catch up with my body. Then, there were muffled sounds and blurry images and panicked movements. But that smell was so distinct. Even now, just the thought of rubber pressed deep into a surface makes my stomach turn.

That's one thing I remember about my last ride—about the day that changed my story forever. It's the dark thing—the memory I wish I had lost, along with most of the others.

The other thing I remember, though, is my light—my little piece of hope when all hope seemed lost. I remember the way it felt in my hand. It was hard, and its edges were just sharp enough that I could almost feel pain again when I squeezed my fingers around it. I wanted that so badly—pain. I wanted to feel pain on my skin and in my bones, anywhere that wasn't my heart. I was starting to feel numb, and it was almost more terrifying than the thought of a tomorrow—a new day where I would be living someone else's life.

No one had told me at the time, but I already knew. I already knew my life was going to be different. I knew my life had changed. I remember squeezing my bloody fingers around the metal edges of that shiny figure, pressing the sharpest edge into my thumb—until I felt something. I knew I was leaving my life out there along that quiet highway, among the swaying wild flowers and that bitter smell of burnt rubber. And as the doors shut and the ambulance pulled away, my eyes fell heavy on the hope in my hand. And I remember thinking: *If I could still feel, maybe I wouldn't just wither away—maybe there was still hope for me.*

Photo by Marc Mayes

LAURA MILLER is the national bestselling author of the novels, *Butterfly Weeds, My Butterfly* and *For All You Have Left*. She grew up in eastern Missouri, graduated from the University of Missouri-Columbia and spent some time as a newspaper government reporter prior to writing fiction. Laura currently lives in the Midwest with her husband. Visit her and learn more about her books at LauraMillerBooks.com.

Made in the USA
Middletown, DE
09 February 2017